THE HOMECOMING

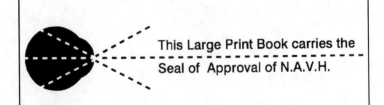

This Large Print Book carries the
Seal of Approval of N.A.V.H.

THE HOMECOMING

ROBYN CARR

WHEELER PUBLISHING
A part of Gale, Cengage Learning

GALE
CENGAGE Learning·

Farmington Hills, Mich • San Francisco • New York • Waterville, Maine
Meriden, Conn • Mason, Ohio • Chicago

GALE
CENGAGE Learning®

LIBRARY OF CONGRESS CATALOGING-IN-PUBLICATION DATA

Carr, Robyn.
    The Homecoming / by Robyn Carr.
      pages cm. — (A Thunder Point novel) (Wheeler Publishing Large Print Hardcover)
      ISBN 978-1-4104-7145-1 (hardcover) — ISBN 1-4104-7145-4 (hardcover)
      1. Life change events—Fiction. 2. Homecoming—Fiction. 3. Self-actualization (Psychology)—Fiction. 4. Love stories. 5. Large type books.
    I. Title.
    PS3553.A76334H66 2014
    813'.54—dc23   2014028319

Published in 2014 by arrangement with Harlequin Books S.A.

Printed in Mexico
4 5 6 7 18 17 16 15

The Homecoming

ONE

When Seth Sileski was a kid, Thunder Point was his playground. Even as a freckle-faced, towheaded little kid he'd held this town in the palm of his hand. He could run the fastest, hit the hardest, throw the farthest and charm the most cantankerous teachers. His two older brothers, Nick and Norm Junior — affectionately known as Boomer — had also had great childhoods, but they never matched Seth's notoriety. He went from beautiful kid to adored adolescent to most popular and accomplished teenager — great grades, superb athlete, handsome, a good and loyal friend. He'd had it all. And then, at the age of twenty, his life took a dramatic turn and all that great luck and good fortune seemed to blow away.

Or, if you listened to his father, Norm Sileski, Seth *threw* it away.

So now he was back in Thunder Point, a little scarred and damaged but whole. And definitely humbled. He'd traveled a long way since leaving town at the age of eighteen and if you'd told him five or ten years ago that he'd return home he'd have called you a lunatic. Yet here he was, and by choice. This time he was wearing a deputy's uniform. He was thirty-four years old, and his battle to regain a sense of pride and accomplishment had been mighty and difficult. Seth was taking over the Sheriff's Department Thunder Point substation from Mac McCain. He'd be the officer in charge while Mac moved to a lieutenant's position at the headquarters in Coquille.

Seth had been back to town fairly often over the past sixteen years. He visited his mother and tried to check in with his father. Every time he drove into this small coastal town he was surprised by how little the place had changed. People changed, the economy changed, the world changed, and yet Thunder Point, Oregon, always seemed to remain the same. The linoleum in the diner had been old and cracked when he was a boy, all the same fast-food establishments were present, Waylan's Bar was still the only real dive in town and it looked frozen in time. In fact, Waylan still propped the door open with a paint can, as if he intended to paint the place. It hadn't happened yet.

It was the second week in September and school had resumed just a couple of weeks ago, so there was still a lot of optimism and excitement winding up the students. Those on bikes weren't staying out of the middle of the road very well, but a little *whoop-whoop* from the police SUV moved 'em over quick, followed by yelps of laughter and shenanigans.

Seth caught sight of Iris McKinley, his next-door neighbor and childhood friend when he was growing up. She was still riding her bike to school, but now she wore a skirt and carried a briefcase in the basket. When the wind caught her skirt it revealed tight, black bike shorts underneath. The kids raced her. The school buses passed her, honked their horns and kids leaned out their windows to wave. Iris jingled the bell mounted on her handlebars and waved in response. She threw back her head and laughed as a bus driver laid on the horn for a long blast. She still had that wild, unrestrained laughter he remembered. Before she noticed him, he turned off the main street, heading back to the substation to park.

The Sheriff's Department substation was one sign that some changes had taken place in Thunder Point. The department had always had a strong presence in the town as there was no local law enforcement, but the substation office was only about ten years old. The clinic next door was quite new so Seth made that his first stop. He walked into the clinic to face a beautiful woman standing in the reception area. She could be mistaken for Catherine Zeta-Jones with her dark straight hair and brown eyes.

"Hi," he said, smiling, putting out his hand. "I'm Seth Sileski and I'll be your new neighbor. Mac starts working in Coquille in about a week."

"Well, it's a pleasure," she said. "Peyton Lacoumette, physician's assistant. And this is Devon Lawson, our office manager. Scott?" she yelled. "Do you have a minute?"

The doctor came to the front of the clinic wearing the native dress — blue jeans and denim shirt. "Hi, I'm Scott Grant. So, you're the new guy," he said with a smile.

Seth laughed and stuck out his hand. "Seth Sileski. I'm not exactly new. I grew up here. Norm is my dad."

"No kidding. Which one are you? He said he had three sons and none of them lived in town."

"I'm the youngest. I've only been back to visit since leaving for college."

"Then welcome back," Scott said. "We'll be glad to have you. And we're darn proud of Mac — moving up in the world."

"Those are going to be hard shoes to fill," Seth said.

"Did you know Mac before now?" Peyton asked.

"Sure, from the department. I think I've known him eight years or so, though we worked in different parts of the county. He has a very good reputation. Before it's down to me — are there any needs you have or issues you're concerned about? Anything you want me to know?" He grinned. "As your neighbor and your cop?"

Scott chuckled. "Trash pickup is Wednesday in the alley behind the stores. I'll have to think about anything else."

"Trash," Seth said. "Good to know. Let me ask you this — how do you get along with the youth in town? Any problems I should be aware of?"

Scott shook his head. "I had to stitch up some wild ones in the E.R. in North Bend — a fight at an unsupervised party. I haven't dealt with any injuries caused by bad behavior around Thunder Point in the past year. Mac had some bullying issues before I opened up the clinic, but I'm not sure of the details. I've just had the usual stuff and the kids around here are better than most."

"Strict parents, for the most part," Seth said. "And a nosy town in general."

"Do you have teenagers, Deputy?" Peyton asked.

He shook his head. "I'm not married and don't have kids, ma'am. Asking about the teenagers is just something I do when trying to get a profile on a new place. The town isn't new to me but the people are — the faces have changed after sixteen years. Right now I'm in orientation with Mac as my supervisor and part of the process is to introduce myself to the businesses. The stores haven't changed much but the owners, managers and employees have." He looked over his shoulder at the diner. "We used to go there after school and I hear Stu is still the owner and cook but now Gina is the head waitress. Gina's mom was the waitress in charge when I was a kid."

"And now Carrie has the deli next door and some of the best sandwiches and take-out dinners you'll find around here," Peyton said. "I haven't cooked in a long time."

"I'll stop in and say hello to both of them."

"What about Cliffhanger's?" Peyton asked. "Was Cliff the owner when you were growing up?"

Seth shook his head. "His dad built that

place about twenty-five years ago. I'm not sure when Cliff took over. Sometime after I left. Cliff's family owns a lot of property around the marina. My dad used to say that place would never work here — too fancy for this town."

"It's full almost every night," Scott said. "It's where people around here go when they want a tablecloth."

"I've been in there once or twice," Seth said. "Good food, nice atmosphere. Listen, it's nice meeting all of you." He pulled out a business card. "I'm going to continue my rounds, but here's the office number and my personal cell. Feel free to use it."

Peyton laughed and took the card. "It really kills me the way everyone gives out their cell numbers! Everyone knows Scott's and Mac's and now yours. I'm used to the city where you never do that."

The doctor put his arm around the P.A.'s shoulders and gave a squeeze. "I have her cell number and with the right incentive, I can be talked into giving it to you. Until then, just call me if you need me. And I'll call you."

"Hey, if this is my town, I *want* to be called if there's a problem. There are three ways to reach me — the office, the cell or 911 in emergencies. If you call 911 you'll

13

never get voice mail and whatever deputy is on duty will respond immediately. Don't hesitate." He smiled and gave them a little salute. "See you later."

Seth made his way to the diner to say hello to Gina. They'd known each other growing up, but they hadn't been in the same class or part of the same crowd. It was safe to say that he knew Carrie better. Carrie and his mother, Gwen, had been friends for years.

After a quick visit with Gina he went into Waylan's. Damn if it didn't look like the same crowd of old boys who had been in there the last time he'd stopped by at least ten years ago.

He headed for the flower shop, which still bore the same name although the owner was relatively new. Pretty Petals had been owned by his next-door neighbor when he was growing up, a single mother and Gwen's good friend, Rose McKinley. Rose's only child, Iris, had been Seth's best friend when they were kids. Iris had sold the shop a few years ago after her mother had a stroke. Then Rose had passed away after a couple of years of infirmity.

Seth talked to his mother at least once a week, usually more often, and she kept him current on the happenings in town. Rose's death had taken a toll on Gwen — they'd been close to the same age. Rose had died too young and it left Gwen feeling as if she was living on borrowed time. Gwen was now sixty-five.

Norm was seventy-two and just as cranky and unforgiving as ever. He might've sold the service station he'd owned for decades, but he wouldn't retire. He still worked for the new owner. Gwen wanted to spend some of their money and retirement doing fun things, traveling, maybe taking a cruise or two, but Norm wasn't at all interested. Why Gwen wanted to spend leisure time with the old coot was beyond Seth, but he felt sorry for her, sitting out her last years in the same small town, not having much fun except for church, cards and bingo, missing her best friend, Rose.

He walked into Pretty Petals and took off his hat. He said hello to Grace Dillon, the new owner. His mother had mentioned her several times. She was an attractive young woman about thirty years old or even younger, living the dream. She'd bought the flower shop from Iris and was thrilled to own her own business. Looking around, he saw that it had been updated since the old days.

"Well, Seth, are you back to stay?" she asked.

"I am for now. Just introducing myself to the folks in town, or reintroducing, as the case may be. How are things in the flower business?"

"Very pretty," she said.

"Anything you'd like me to be aware of now? I'm prepared to take over Mac's post in less than a week."

She shook her head. "No flower thefts that I'm aware of. Do you have any plans to move to town, now that you'll be here all the time?"

"Not at the moment." He laughed a little. "My mother offered me my old room, but I think . . ." He ended by just shaking his head and Grace laughed with him. "It might not feel like a bachelor pad, living with Mom and Dad." Not to mention, Dad hadn't offered, he reminded himself. "But there's no question, I'd eat well!"

"Maybe you can just swing by Mom's at the end of your workday for a little something to eat before heading home to the bachelor pad."

"There's an idea. In fact, I should swing by there now. . . . How about a nice arrangement to take along? That always makes her so happy with me."

Grace turned and pulled a centerpiece out of the cooler. "Do you like this fall arrange-

16

ment? I can give it to you cheap — I worked it up a couple of days ago and it hasn't sold yet."

"I'm all over discounts," he said, fishing out his wallet. "Have you seen Iris lately?" he asked without looking up.

"I see Iris every week. At least once, usually more. She likes fresh flowers in the house — it's a hard habit to break. Sometimes she comes in and makes her own arrangement. I can't tell you how often I wish she worked here — she's got a gift. That'll be ten dollars, even."

"Ten? Wow, you're sucking up to the law!"

"I hope I never have to use my brownie points," she said. "Welcome back, Seth. It's nice to know you'll be taking care of us."

"I'll do my best. Be sure to let me know if I can help in any way. It won't be flower arranging, I know that." He gave her his business card with all the numbers on it. Then he gave her a second one. "One for the shop, one for home," he said, though he secretly hoped that second card might make its way into Iris's hands.

He wished he could reconnect with Iris. When they were kids, they'd been inseparable, playing kickball, softball, fishing, hanging out on the beach or sitting at one of their houses playing video games for

17

hours. In junior high and high school they had taken different paths — he was on all the sports teams, and she was doing girl things, plus helping her mother in the flower shop. But she'd always been his closest friend even if he didn't admit that in mixed company. He could tell Iris anything. *Anything.* If he had trouble in school, frustrations with football, couldn't get his homework right or even if he liked some girl and she wasn't liking him back. They talked on their porches, on the phone, anywhere they met around town. If their second-story bedroom windows had faced each other's, they'd have been hanging out of them, talking.

Then there was some misunderstanding their senior year. Something to do with prom, but he didn't remember all the details. She'd been angry that he wasn't taking her to the prom, but he was going steady with someone and was planning to take his girlfriend. He and the steady girlfriend had a blowup, a messy breakup and Seth had been bummed. He had a few beers, and as usual leaned on Iris to talk about his girl problems. It was senior year, he'd had a spectacular year, was going to the University of Oregon on a full football scholarship in the fall and how dare that girl dump him right before senior prom. He could only vaguely remember, but knew he had uttered some lame thing to Iris like, *I wish I was taking you, anyway.* And then he got back together with the girlfriend the very next day. He thought Iris would be happy for him. He had expected her to understand — it had been a stupid spat and he and his girlfriend were all made up.

But Iris did not understand. He obviously didn't remember the details the way she did because that was the end of their friendship. There was something mysterious about girls and proms because he couldn't remember Iris ever being so angry. She'd beat him up a few times when they were little kids but even then she hadn't been so mad. He apologized about a hundred times, but she was through. She wasn't going to help him with his homework, listen to him moan and groan about his love life, cheer him on through all his big-headed accomplishments and then just sit home with her mother on prom night. Over. Done. Find yourself another sap to be your pal.

From that day on, they were only cordial. When he'd been in the car accident at age twenty, she'd sent a card to the hospital. When her mother died, Seth came back to take his mother to the funeral. He also bought the biggest bouquet he could afford. They'd run into each other a few times over the years. They exchanged news, said nice things to each other, then . . . nothing.

He'd reached out to her. "Iris, are we ever going to be friends again?"

"We are friends," she had replied.

"I mean real friends. Like we used to be."

She wouldn't even consider it. "No. I'm afraid not."

"Why?"

She'd sighed deeply. "Because you could always count on me and it turned out I couldn't count on you. I don't do friend-ships like that anymore."

Now he was back. Policing this town was going to be a big job. Mac had told him to be prepared to be on duty all the time whether he was on duty or not. There might be four deputies on the clock in town as well as the whole Sheriff's Department not all that far away, but as the supervisor he could be called upon whenever a supervisor was needed. Seth understood; he knew that when he'd signed on.

Along with a commitment like that, he had two other impossibly big projects ahead. He had to somehow make amends with his father. And he had to get Iris back. He was going to find a way to show them

20

both he might have been a shiftless, inconsiderate kind of teenager, but he was not that kind of man.

Iris popped into the diner on Saturday at around one. She was wearing running tights and shoes, a fleece vest and a long-sleeved T-shirt. Her thick chestnut hair was pulled into a ponytail and poked through the back of her cap. She sat up at the counter.

"Out for a run?" Gina asked.

"Sort of. I told Spencer I wanted to bump into him this weekend and he said he'd be around all day today. So I thought a jog out across the beach was a good idea. That made me hungry and I'm thinking BLT, fries and a chocolate shake. I know, I should be looking for cottage cheese and fruit but Stu might burn it."

"Stu makes a great BLT and fries." Gina slapped the ticket on Stu's counter. "You work closely with Spencer?"

"It's only his second season, but if he sees me as a friend rather than administrator or counselor, we can keep the whole football team playing. If I know where those guys stand on schoolwork I can line up tutors before anyone goes delinquent because of grades."

"Do you get tutors from the high school?"

"Some. And some from town. Scott will take at least one science or math student, I can take a couple, Laine Carrington can tutor in a number of areas including Spanish. Lou McCain teaches middle-school English so she can handle high-school English tutorial — she's willing to help with a couple. Then there are teachers. Some of them get a little pissy about the attention the athletes get, but that's in their minds — I'm paying attention to every student. Tutors are everywhere I look, including some students. I'd ask you, but I figured with a new husband and four kids . . ." She laughed. "And of course I have the usual number of requests from football players for pretty girls. I'm afraid they're going to be disappointed."

"Are they basically in good shape with grades?" Gina asked.

"They are, but it only takes one tough class to sideline a player. And if there's one thing I've learned about high school boys, they'll die before they ask for help. That's why we watch the grades so closely. And the football players, in danger of being suspended from the team for failing grades, are a lot more visible."

"Iris, what made you decide to be a high school counselor?" Gina asked.

"I thought the fact that I didn't have it

that easy in high school gave me something to offer. Especially to the girls."

"Grades?"

"Oh, hell, no," she said with a laugh. "Other vitally important things — like hair." She sighed. "I was awkward, not very popular, lonely . . . like a lot of girls. Boys, too. Even football players."

"You're so smart to make a career out of something that also gives something back. Or pays something forward."

"Smart was never my problem. Like I said, it was fitting in, having good self-esteem, identity — like about ninety percent of the girls I know. The job is very fulfilling."

The bell dinged and Gina turned to pick up Iris's BLT. "Speaking of football players, an old football star is back in town. Seth Sileski."

"Hmm," Iris said, chewing her first bite. "I heard. Then I ran into him — we were both getting gas."

"Didn't you date him in high school?"

"Me?" Iris asked. "Oh, God, no! He was the most popular kid in school! The homecoming king and star football player. He dated the pretty girls." She took another bite.

Gina laughed. "Excuse me, Iris, but you're

23

beautiful."

"Don't be ridiculous. I've grown into my looks a little bit, but back then? Ugh. Seth and I grew up next door to each other and we were friends. In fact, I helped him with English and biology. *And* I helped him prepare for SATs, which he could've cared less about since he was banking his entire future on football."

"How'd you do on the SAT?"

Iris grinned. "I killed it."

"Good for you! Big dumb jocks. Hey, what happened to his amazing football career? It seemed like it was here and gone awful fast."

"Car accident," Iris said, chewing. "He had a good year with the Ducks, then dropped out of college to take a contract with the Seahawks and played one season, or mostly watched one season with the pro team and then had a car accident. He was injured pretty badly. That was the end of his pro football career." She took another bite, washed it down with chocolate shake. "We try to impress upon these young men that education really does come in handy. Football careers are fragile. Unpredictable."

"Ah, I heard something about that, but no details."

"As far as I know it was an accident. An unfortunate accident."

"That's where the limp and the scar came from?" Gina asked.

Iris nodded. She looked down at her plate and picked at a couple of fries. "It's not that much of a limp," she finally said. "He never told me exactly what happened."

But Gwen Sileski had. Gwen told Rose and Iris everything about Seth. He'd fractured bones in his right leg and required rods, plates and screws just to hold him together. He'd had a lot of other injuries and was lucky to be alive. He'd had several surgeries to save the leg. The injury and the repair had left his right leg a little shorter and he wore a lift in his shoe. His mother said he wasn't in pain, but it had taken a lot of therapy and training to get to that point. Iris couldn't imagine how hard the police physical exam must have been.

"The accident. A leg injury," Iris said. "But that scar . . . it almost does something for his looks, don't you think?"

Gina smiled. "It would take a lot more than that to make Seth Sileski hard to look at." She drew an invisible line across her cheek with her index finger.

"I know," Iris said, patting her mouth with the napkin. "Do you remember him in high school? What a lady-killer."

"I dropped out at fifteen because of a

25

lady-killer," Gina reminded Iris. "At that time in my life, they were everywhere. But I admit, I wasn't paying too much attention to your slightly younger crowd. I remember Seth better from the past ten or twelve years, the times he came through town and sometimes stopped here for a burger or cup of coffee. Gwen must be so thrilled to have her son back in town."

"I think so," Iris said. "Listen, can I have the rest to go? I don't think I'll get through the whole plate."

"Sure. I can't put the shake in the carton for you."

"I'll work on that a little more. So, while I do that, tell me about married life and your new family."

"Very complicated," Gina said. "We have two college freshmen, my daughter and Mac's daughter, still living at home and each working part-time, applying to universities to attend next fall. Mac's schedule is going to be different — he'll work nights for at least a year. Then there's an eleven- and thirteen-year-old committed to lots of teams, clubs and lessons — that means driving. My college girls help a lot but their time is at a premium because of studies and jobs. But life as Mrs. Mac?" She shot Iris a very large smile. "I didn't know I could be this happy."

Iris sucked the last of her shake through the straw, making it gurgle. "You took your sweet time finding the right guy."

"I know. Or he took his sweet time moving to town. Who cares? He was worth waiting for. Are you seeing anyone, Iris?"

"Nah. Not at the moment. There have been a few I thought had potential, but in the end I preferred my own company." She stood and fished into her pocket while Gina transferred the rest of her BLT and fries into a carton.

"And the company of high school students," Gina teased.

"They keep me on my toes. But I have my eyes open for an older, more settled model — say thirty-five, single, sexy and really into me. . . ."

The diner door opened and Seth Sileski walked in, as if made to order. Beautiful Seth. High cheekbones, chiseled chin, moody eyes, white teeth, thin scar slanted across his cheek. Iris's mouth fell open and Gina just laughed.

"Well, hello, ladies," he said, taking off his deputy's hat. "Iris, what are the chances you'll let me buy you a cup of coffee?"

"Unfortunately, I'm on the run. I have

plans that won't wait. In fact, I could already be late." She grabbed her to-go carton. "Thanks, Gina. See you around."

"Why do you always seem to be rushing off the second I show up?" Seth asked.

"I'm sure it's just a coincidence. Next time, Seth. I'd better go." She gave him an accommodating smile and headed out the door. She took off at a gentle jog down the street and up the hill toward home.

Why? she asked herself. *Why the hell does he have to be here? Is this just some vindictive angel's idea of a slow and miserable death for me? What did I ever do to deserve this? He could be here for a long time! How am I going to avoid him? Especially if he's the person I have to work with if I have teenagers in trouble?*

Really, hadn't she been through enough in high school?

Two

Iris had loved Seth since she was about four years old. He kissed her when they were six and she beat him up and that's when she knew she'd probably love him forever. When kids teased her because she was named after a flower, he stood up for her. He punched Robbie Delaney for saying she looked like a scarecrow. Of course, she had punched Robbie other times, but it was still nice when Seth avenged her. When her curly hair was flat on one side and springy on the other, Seth laughed but then he said sorry. Then he laughed again and said sorry again. They used to play house, until his older brothers caught him and teased him — then he said it was rocket men and aliens or nothing.

When they were older, but not that much older, they each helped out with their parents' businesses — Seth at the gas station and Iris in the flower shop. Because it was just Iris and Rose running the little flower shop, Seth would sometimes help with the heavy chores, if he could get away from the Sileski gas station where Norm's boys all had chores. Seth knew, from paying attention to adult conversation at the dinner table, that Rose didn't pull much income out of that little shop so he refused pay from her. He'd haul trash, and there was a ton of trash every day. He'd sweep, mop, clean shelves, deliver flowers on his bike and sometimes he even helped Iris make arrangements, but he made sure he was out of sight. He always claimed he was helping Iris get through her chores so they could play *Doom* or *Super Mario Bros.*

In high school when he helped out he used the excuse that he wanted to free Iris up so she could help him with homework. She was always a little ahead of him in school. When she was a sophomore, she didn't make cheerleading, was devastated and he even let her cry all over him. In fact, it shook him up — Iris hardly ever cried. Even when she took a softball in the face!

The Sileski family did well financially. Flower shops in small towns are not the hottest ticket. Gas was a necessity, flowers were a luxury. Plus, there were no men in the McKinley family . . . except Seth. He cut their grass and was the guy they called if something heavy had to be moved or lifted. Since Iris's mom and Seth's mom were best friends, this pleased them both.

And Iris was the one Seth talked to. His brothers didn't have a lot of time for their baby brother, except to burst their buttons proudly when he played some amazing football. Seth and Iris never walked to school together — they stuck with their friends of the same gender during school hours. They were only friends. Good friends and neighbors. But away from school, dates — which Seth had a lot of — and practices, they spent hours together. Iris had more girlfriends than usual her junior and senior years because Seth lived right next door and all the girls were hot for him. Seth had his buddies, but when it came down to confidential stuff, important stuff, they had each other. Of course, by high school Seth was confiding in Iris about girls he crushed on. He asked her advice all the time. Sometimes he fixed her up so they could double date, a special kind of torture.

Then in the spring of their senior year, when homecoming king Seth was planning to take homecoming queen Sassy to the prom, there was a little crisis. Sue Marie Sontag, known to everyone as Sassy because she was, cheated on Seth. She snuck out with Robbie Delaney and let him touch her boobs. Seth and Sassy had a big fight and they broke up.

Seth, destroyed by hurt and betrayal, went to an unsupervised party and downed a bunch of beer, something he was *not* known for. By some miraculous twist of fate, Iris had been at the party. She was hardly ever invited to cool parties. She didn't drink, not because she wasn't any fun but because she was a little nervous about what the cool kids might do to her if she got drunk. She'd heard tales. And since she had no experience with alcohol, she was afraid to sip a beer because they might strip her and nail her to the door.

But there was Seth, stumbling, falling down, blabbing his head off about Sassy cheating and dumping him, and good old Iris grabbed him. "Jesus, you're disgusting," she said. "Come on, let's get you out of here. You're trashed."

She put him in the flower shop van. "I can't go home yet. I'll get in trouble," he mumbled.

"Yeah, because you're wasted," she said. "Smart."

And then he poured his heart out. He couldn't believe Sassy did that, went out with another guy and let him feel her up and everything. And the guy was someone Seth thought was a friend!

Iris couldn't believe Seth hadn't known that Sassy had the most handled boobs in the senior class. And Seth went on and on and on, as though Iris enjoyed these conversations about other girls. He actually nodded off now and then in the middle of his tirade.

He was completely toasted and she saved his ass, as usual. She drove out to a popular make-out spot, a lookout just off Highway 101, and parked the van that said Pretty Petals all over it. She listened to him moan and groan about his lousy luck with girls.

Then there was a twist.

"Why am I not with you, Iris? Why isn't it you and me? We'd never do that to each other. You're the only girl I ever loved anyway. You're at least the only girl I ever believed in. Or trusted. You've been my best friend forever. I'm taking you to the prom, that's what I'm going to do. It's what we should do anyway."

He started snuggling and nuzzling her. It occurred to her to push him away, but it was the first time he'd made sense as far as she was concerned. They *had* been best friends forever. They always got along better with each other than anyone else. And he was right — they'd never cheat on each other. If they went to the prom together, he wouldn't have to worry that she'd flirt with other guys or pout or sulk. She'd have fun every second and make him laugh all night long. Of course, she wasn't sure she could afford a prom dress, but she could work that out later. She had the love of her life telling her he'd finally seen the light and knew she was the right girl for him. At last.

He was kissing her. Not just nuzzling but full-on kissing, pulling her closer. Iris's insides went all squishy. He was literally climbing on her, but there was a steering wheel in the way.

"Come on," he said, pulling her out of the driver's seat and onto the passenger seat on the other side of the console. He made room so she would be under him. He reached down to recline the seat as much as he could, hovering over her, resuming the hot, wet, fabulous kissing, his hands running all over her. He was pushing his pelvis against her and it felt so good she pushed back. She instinctively assumed a kind of pelvic circular, rhythmic motion.

She considered stopping him. She knew she could tell him he was just drunk. But that squishy feeling inside traveled through her whole body and she was overwhelmed with yearning.

"You're the one for me," he said, kissing her neck, her shoulder, pulling her blouse apart so he could kiss the top of her breast. The next thing she knew he was licking her nipple. Then he had it in his mouth and she went crazy. She had absolutely no idea breasts were magic. It was as if there was a silk cord that attached her nipple to her girl parts and pulled tight. It was fantastic!

Iris had never been so far with a boy. She knew she was behind all the other girls, but she hadn't dated that much and she sure hadn't dated anyone who could compare to Seth. She would never forget the night the boy she'd loved for years finally realized they were meant for each other.

He fussed with her shorts, trying to open them. She honestly wasn't sure what he was thinking, planning. She thought he might want to slide his hand in there, but frankly she'd rather they just resume that lovely grinding thing they were doing. "Come on, honey," he said, kissing her. "I need you."

Well, she'd always been there for him. Through thick and thin. If he needed her, she was there. She kissed him back and felt her shorts slide down. Her panties went with them. Then he was probing against her, pushing into her, groaning and saying things like *ah, God* and *holy God* and *oh-oh-oh, God.* . . . Then he trembled, panted and went a little limp.

It took him a long moment to recover but when he did he put a big hand against her cheek, gave her a sweet, gentle kiss on the lips, eased his weight off her and rose up. With a knee braced on the seat beside her, he pulled up and closed his pants. He helped her slide back into her shorts and made room for her to move back to her assigned seat. Once she had shifted across the console, she began adjusting her clothing. She had babbled. "Wow, I can't believe we did that. And with no rubber or anything. I never expected anything like that. I don't even know what to say. . . ." But as she babbled what she'd been thinking was how happy she was to know that Seth felt the same way about her that she felt about him. And that she'd like a little more of that kissing, touching and grinding.

She got her shorts in place and fastened her blouse. Then she looked at Seth. He was asleep.

Iris wanted to get her head out of the past, get her mind off Seth. She called Grace. "Want to go up to North Bend? Maybe go dancing?"

"First of all, I couldn't dance if you had me on puppet poles — I was on my feet all day and took flowers to Bandon for two weddings. Second, two women out at a bar on Saturday night are either looking for a pickup or want to be mistaken for a couple."

"I haven't completely ruled out a pickup," Iris said.

"I have," Grace said. "Little antsy tonight?"

"I'd just like something to do, that's all. You used to be more fun."

"I'm not sure about that. I think maybe you were slightly less fun."

Grace had turned the flower shop around. She had done things Rose had never thought of. She reached out to neighboring towns with coupons and internet ads. She hired a PR firm from North Bend, had a great portfolio from the florist she had worked for in Portland and, after hiring a couple of local housewives part-time and training them, she was capable of flowering big events. Iris was glad it was Grace and not her working the flower business. But success could be draining.

"Tell you what I'll consider," Grace said. "I'll go out to Cooper's with you for a drink and a sunset. We're not going to have too many more late sunsets. . . ."

"It's only September!" Iris said.

"And I'm getting out the fall arrangements and putting together a Christmas catalog. Before you know it, sunset is at four-thirty and I'll still be working. I'll even stop at Cliff's for clam chowder on the way home if you want, but please don't make me dance."

"You're a wuss," Iris said. "I ran today and everything."

"It sounds like you didn't run enough. . . ."

So they went out to Cooper's. Iris thought it was probably better anyway — it was casual and laid-back. Troy Headly, fellow high school teacher whom she'd dated briefly, was behind the bar. He worked part-time for Cooper. He explained that Cooper was gone because the Oregon Ducks played California today and Cooper and Sarah had driven to Eugene for the game. The place was full but not busy — it was pretty quiet for a Saturday night. Iris and Grace sat at the bar and kept an eye on the deck, ready to pounce on a table out there when one became available. After getting a glass of wine each, Grace poked her and they dodged for an empty table and settled in.

Iris put her feet up on the porch rail and

smiled. "I wonder what the poor people are doing."

Grace laughed. "They're having a glass of wine at Cooper's."

Grace was young to own her own successful business. She'd been working for a popular florist when she got a settlement or inheritance of some kind and went looking for a shop for sale. It was an ambitious venture for such a young woman, committing all her capital like that. But she knew what she was doing; she had been a shop manager before, kept the books, bought the stock, supervised the event contracts. She stretched her money further by renovating the space above the shop into a small apartment. And Iris was so glad Grace had been the one to buy the shop because they became good friends almost instantly. They had a lot in common — both very serious about their work, didn't date much, both alone and without family.

Thunder Point was Iris's family; the kids she was responsible for were her family.

Iris enjoyed having a friend she could actually be quiet with — Grace was almost like a sister. They spoke little as the sun was making its downward path. Just a remark here and there about the week, the special challenges. And how nice Sunday was going to feel. They watched the red-orange collage of sun, ocean and haystack rocks before them. And then the sky began to darken.

"How are you feeling about dinner?" Grace asked.

"Not that hungry," Iris said. "A bowl of soup at Cliff's will do it for me."

"How about another glass of wine and one of Carrie's deli pizzas? Cooper's got a bunch of them in the cooler and Troy will put a couple in the oven."

"I could do that," she said.

"I'm going to go get us some tortilla chips and salsa and another wine. Hey, is that our new guy?" Grace asked.

Down on the beach, running at the water's edge, it was him. Seth. What was he doing? He didn't live here. But it was obviously him. She could tell by his light hair, his slight list to the right because of his limp. He was wearing fitted running pants and a sleeveless T-shirt, a jacket tied around his waist. "Yeah, I think that's him," she said to Grace.

"I'll be right back," Grace said.

So, he's out for a run, Iris thought. What incredible dedication that must take, to keep up all his physical fitness even though he had issues with his leg. But then, that's why he did it. He was a cop. He couldn't be the slow one or the weak one if he came up against a bad situation. And by the look of his arms and shoulders, he didn't end his workout with a run. He was so beautiful.

He must not have a good place to run near his residence, which she had heard was near Bandon. He got to the dock in front of Cooper's and she expected him to turn and jog back to town. But, no. Hands on his hips, he walked in circles, slowing down, cooling off. Then he looked up to the deck. And smiled.

Crap! she thought. *Is there no God? What the hell?*

He walked around a little more, then wiped his face with the towel that hung around his neck. He climbed the stairs. Just as he hit the deck and headed for Iris's table, Grace came out of the bar holding a glass of wine for Iris and a basket of corn chips.

"Hey, Seth," Grace said in greeting.

"Hey, yourself. Is this chair taken?" he asked, indicating one at their table.

"No, please join us. Can I get you anything while I'm up?"

"Water would be good. Thanks."

Grace disappeared again. Iris frowned. And what really pissed her off was Seth smiling. In fact it was a smile she remembered. It was the "gotcha" smile.

Grace was back with the water, adding salsa to the table, then disappearing again. Seth put on his jacket and zipped it up. "I don't think this is going to work out for you, Iris," he said.

"What?"

"Dodging me all the time. Avoiding me. Pretending you have important business elsewhere or appointments you're late for. All your excuses. Sooner or later you'll have to actually talk to me."

"Oh, didn't anyone mention? I'm *moving.*"

A laugh burst out of him. He opened his water bottle and chugged down half of the liquid in a couple of gulps. "No one mentioned," he said.

"Are you everywhere?" she asked in a lowered voice. "You don't live here! What are you doing here on a Saturday night? Running on the beach."

"I had some paperwork to finish up today and I brought my running clothes. I wanted to see what's happening on the beach tonight — Saturday night."

"The kids usually hit the beach after games," she informed him as though he wouldn't remember.

"I know. I was watching last night from

Cooper's parking lot. It looked pretty familiar. And pretty tame. If memory serves, every night they're not busy is party night."

"And you decided to spy on them?"

"Well, I thought I'd have a look. And let them look at me — not far away in case anyone needs anything. Iris, we have to talk out this little grudge you've been nurturing for over fifteen years."

She leaned toward him. "Two things, Deputy. One — we have talked. Several times. And two — I haven't been nurturing anything. I'm merely minding my own business." She grabbed a chip from the bowl and crunched down on it. Hard.

"Bullshit. You forget I know you. It takes a lot to piss you off and you've been stroking this one since our senior prom. I said I was sorry a hundred times. I was a dumb and insensitive teenage boy and I really regret hurting your feelings. I had no idea what it was going to cost me. Or you, for that matter." He drank the rest of his water.

Iris looked over her shoulder and saw that Grace, in the bar, was up on a bar stool, laughing with Troy about something. She was probably giving Iris time to work things out with Seth while waiting for their pizzas. Grace knew about the prom thing, knew Iris was pissed. She didn't know everything,

43

however.

"I don't know what it is about girls and proms," he said. "You were absolutely crazed. And I never knew you to be that kind of girl, crying and carrying on. You used to beat me up, for God's sake!"

"Apparently, I fell down on the job," she muttered, lifting her wine.

He smirked. "I am an officer of the law, ma'am. Watch your threats."

"Why aren't you out with some skinny blonde tonight? Like usual?"

"I don't think I know any around here. Is Sassy still around town?"

"She is, indeed. Need me to hook you up?"

"No, thanks," he said. "She never left town? That's a surprise. She was ready to move on. How's she getting along?" he asked.

Iris took another sip of wine. "It appears she's gained a couple of pounds."

"That must thrill you."

"And she lost a tooth," she added. She pointed to a very obvious incisor. In front. "Here."

He threw his head back and laughed so loudly that people actually turned and looked at him.

"Stop it!" Iris hissed. "You're making a

fool of yourself!"

"So you still hate her, huh? I'm honored." He pushed back his chair and stood. "I think I'll get a beer and order one of those little pizzas."

"Don't you have to go home?" she asked.

He leaned his face toward her. He shook his head and grinned. "Nope."

He went inside to place his order and grab a beer and was back altogether too quickly. He sat down and got comfortable. "I'd like us to talk about some things," he said. "You're obviously not quite ready to give up your anger, but there are other things. First — you've been really good to my mom. A good neighbor and friend. Losing Rose was probably as hard on my mom as it was on you. She's so grateful to have you in her life and I'm grateful, too. At least your anger didn't extend to her. Thanks for that."

"Your mom is wonderful," she said. "And I love her."

"That's very kind, Iris," he said. "And I'd also like to talk about how we can work together on special programs for the high school. I have some ideas."

"I just expect you to let me know if trouble comes to my school and I'll do the same. We don't do those horrific movies of horrible car accidents right before prom and graduation anymore. You know those awful things, trying to scare the lives out of the kids before they drink and drive or something. . . ."

"That wasn't what I had in mind, but if you like I can make an appointment."

"What did you have in mind?"

"Maybe a few true stories on how to be successful in life. How not to be dead or maimed before the age of twenty-one." He raised his brows. "How to have fun every day for life? Become millionaires in three easy steps? If I can figure out how to get their attention, I think I can hold it."

She relaxed back into her chair. "I think I'd like to see your proposal, Deputy."

"Sure," he said. "And I'd like to try to make it up to you."

"Not necessary."

"I'd like to try," he said. "What's it going to take, Iris?"

"A miracle," she said.

He lifted half of his mouth in a sly smile. "I'll get right to work on that."

Grace returned, followed by Troy bearing two individual pizzas. "Yours will be out in just a minute, Seth," he said.

It was the three of them at the table and the conversation turned to general subjects. Troy brought a pizza for Seth and a beer

46

that he claimed for himself. As a foursome, they told stories about the town, the people, old times and recent times. Troy thoroughly enjoyed hearing funny stories about Iris as a kid because, as Iris well knew, Troy had a crush on her. Before ten minutes had passed they were all laughing as though they'd been best friends forever. Laughing almost wildly.

Later that night, at home in the house she'd grown up in, alone in her bed, for the first time in a very, very long time, Iris cried. Cried for all she had missed, all she'd lost, all she felt was forever out of her reach.

She had missed Seth so much.

That pivotal Friday night so long ago, Iris woke Seth and took him home a little after midnight. He disappeared into his house after thanking her for the ride. She had expected a little more with the good-night than that, but she let it go. He was impaired, after all. But she did wake her mother and, sitting on her bed, told her that Seth had broken up with his girlfriend and asked her to go to the prom.

"As friends?" Rose had asked.

When your mother and your boyfriend's mother were best friends, when you lived next door to each other, Iris knew she had to be very careful. "Maybe more," she said, looking down shyly. *Shy* was never a word people used to describe Iris, because she had learned to compensate in high school. She could fake confidence she didn't really have.

Iris knew even buying a prom dress would be tough for Rose. Prom wasn't far off and Pretty Petals was only closed on Sundays so they went right away. They were just going to look around, decide if they should drive farther than North Bend, see what was out there. But they found a dress right away and fell completely in love. Iris didn't think she'd ever stumble on a dress that she didn't feel fat or pale or stupid in, but she did. It was dark purple and sleek, making her height feel like an asset. It took every ounce of her willpower to keep from running next door to tell Seth about it.

At school on Monday morning she could hardly stop beaming. Books clutched against her chest, she went straight to his locker. "Hey," she said.

"Iris! You'll never believe it. I made up with Sassy! We had a long talk and decided we both deserved another chance. So — we're going to the prom."

Iris couldn't move. Her mouth stood open, her eyes watered and she felt all color drain from her face.

"What?" Seth said. "I mean, she's got the dress and everything. And she really wants another chance."

"Don't you remember?" she asked in a whisper before she could stop herself. "You don't!"

"What?" he asked again.

"You said you wanted to go with me. You said we'd have more fun anyway," she said quietly.

He rubbed his hand around the back of his neck and shook his head uncomfortably. "I sort of remember. I was just really mad. And I was kind of drunk. . . ."

"Kind of?"

"Okay, I was drunk. I probably said a lot of things I shouldn't have. But you understand, right? God, Iris, good thing you got me out of there before something worse happened."

And then, like magic, Sassy was standing with them. Pretty, slim, sexy Sassy, threading her arm through Seth's, smiling beautifully, her large blue eyes twinkling.

"Hey, see you later, Iris," he said. "I gotta get to class, but I'll catch ya later, right?"

She didn't respond. She just stood there. Seth put a hand on Sassy's shoulder and steered her down the hall. The warning bell rang — one minute to class. Just enough time for Seth to get Sassy to her class and then take off at a dead run for his own.

Iris didn't go to class. She went to the girl's restroom, to a stall in the back. She stayed while the final bell rang. *He sort of remembered?* Obviously, he didn't remember much of anything. He didn't remember that he needed her, that they did it, that he helped himself to her virginity. He sort of remembered talking about prom, but he'd been trashed, blabbering, was somewhere between furious and whiny and obviously not sober enough to be serious. Iris hated him. But at the moment, she hated herself more. Why hadn't she realized he was sleepwalking through a haze of beer? Or something?

Maybe he wasn't sure it was her. Maybe he not only couldn't remember what he said but who he was with. There were a lot of kids at school who drank at every party, but Seth wasn't one of them.

She spent about half an hour in the bathroom. Then she went to her locker, got her books and walked home. He'd come around later. That's how it was with them — if he didn't come looking for her, she'd go looking for him. But she made a pledge to herself — she was done talking. No one would ever know. Oh, she could get mad, fight with him about it, but if she did that, she would only end up humiliated. If anyone found out they'd only say, "You hear about Iris? Thinking Seth would take her to the prom instead of that hot Sassy?"

No, that wasn't happening. She'd tell him he was an ass, accept his apology and then never talk to him again. She'd always thought Seth was special. Different. But he was just a dick.

THREE

Seth's days were long, but that was by choice. Thunder Point was his town and he had a terrible fear of missing something important. He didn't have hard days, just long ones. He was scheduled to work five days a week from nine to five, but he started much earlier. He was usually in his office by six in the morning, while the next deputy didn't come on duty until eight. And he didn't leave Thunder Point before six or seven each evening. Until he got the lay of the land and figured out when the town was busiest, when there was potential for problems, he was there. Not always in uniform, but always ready. The office was closed Saturday and Sunday with a deputy or two on duty or on call in the evenings. Being on call on a quiet evening was the prime job in a quiet little town — you could go to a movie with your family and chances were good you wouldn't be called out and you were still getting paid.

Seth was usually in town on the weekend, as well, for a couple of hours, maybe more. Not only was he trying to learn the town, he was trying to become the familiar face. To that end, he hung out a lot. He did about five hours a day of management, which included paperwork. He spent the rest of the time driving around, having coffee, grabbing a meal, talking to people on the street. He ran into folks at Cooper's on the beach, Waylan's, Cliffhanger's, Carrie's, the diner and the service station.

The service station was now called Lucky's and the new owner, Eric Gentry, was a heck of a good guy and he'd turned that old wart of a gas station into a show-place. It was completely remodeled down to new pumps, and in addition to the extended maintenance shop he had added a classic car restoration garage including a paint bay. And the place was as clean as his mother's kitchen. Eric's equipment was new. It was no longer the greasy, run-down old shop of Seth's youth.

"Every time I come to this place I wonder what happened. It's nothing like the garage I spent half my life in. We all worked for my dad growing up. Forget labor laws, he had a broom in my hand when I was ten." Seth laughed at the memory. "He said if he didn't pay me it wasn't against the law and he wasn't a man to break laws."

"That sounds like Norm," Eric said. "He must be glad to have you back in town."

Seth raised one eyebrow. "Does he seem happy?"

Eric laughed. "Well, no. But he must be. . . ."

"Yeah, I don't think so. My dad and I have what you'd call a prickly relationship."

"I have to admit, he's good with the customers," Eric said. "How is he with your brothers?"

"He's easier on them. But I was a big disappointment to Norm. I was supposed to have a big pro-football career, make lots of money . . ."

"Norm had his eye on your money?" Eric asked, sounding surprised.

"Nah, he has money. No one on earth knows how much, but he's always been a miser, and he was real proud of the fact that this station was paid off when he put it up for sale."

"And he asked a high price, too," Eric said. "The station needed a lot of love, but the land it sits on is prime land. It was covered with junk, but it's a good plot. It allowed me to expand. So if it wasn't money?"

"I think it was bragging rights," Seth said. "I was all-conference in high school, went to the U of Oregon on scholarship, was on the shortlist for the Heisman, took a pro contract with the Seahawks, played about an hour the first season and then, *bam.* Car accident. Football over forever."

"How can a guy be mad about a car accident? Was it your fault or something?"

Seth shook his head. "Miraculously, it was not my fault, but I was speeding. I was cited for speeding, but the other guy blew a stop sign. Thing is, we might not have been so badly injured if I hadn't been going too fast, so even though he caused the accident, I still feel responsible. Wrong place, wrong time, young guy who felt bulletproof in his fancy little car. That was me. If I'd been going slower, I might've been able to avoid impact. Or maybe we wouldn't have been seriously injured. We'll never know."

Eric shook his head sadly. "Norm should be happy you're alive."

"Somewhere under that crusty exterior, maybe he is."

"I know how you feel, buddy. I disappointed my parents, too. That might be the definition of youth."

"How'd you do it?" Seth asked.

Eric looked surprised. "You mean you don't know? Even Mac didn't tell you?"

"Tell me what?"

"I guess I should feel relieved — at least I'm not a legend around here." He clapped a hand on Seth's shoulder. "Brother, I went to jail. I served some hard time."

"No kidding?" Seth asked, completely shocked.

Eric nodded and for a moment his green-eyed gaze was hard. "With a couple of buddies who decided to boost some beer while I waited in the car. One of them poked a finger into the pocket of his hoodie and said, 'Gimme your money,' which elevated it to armed robbery even though there wasn't a weapon between us. We were pulled over ten minutes later, taken into custody and the two lunkheads I was with either got better lawyers or lazier judges. I didn't have a clue what was happening until my public defender explained it to me. He wasn't very good, it turns out. I did five."

"No shit?" Seth said.

"Stupidity can be so expensive. And time-consuming."

"I guess you turned yourself around. . . ."

"Prison made me very smart. This is my second garage. I sold a profitable body shop in Eugene and invested in this place and it's going well. Some of my old classic customers have followed me, we're doing more maintenance work and staying open longer."

"Are your folks still disappointed?"

"I think there are some years they wish I could erase. But I have a good woman in my life — Laine. Just having her with me has smoothed things over. I'm sure they can't believe it — she's smart and beautiful and a former FBI agent. My dad came around faster than my mom, but if I'm honest, my mom has always had a hard time being happy with me. How about Norm?" Eric asked.

"Oh, Norm has always been a little bit on the irascible side, but when I blew a pro football career, he got downright grumpy."

"What are you gonna do about that?" Eric asked.

Seth smiled. "I'm gonna wear him down."

Seth thought adding a good woman to the mix wouldn't hurt his reputation, but the only one he could think of was still pissed about the senior prom, even though she was thirty-four years old.

It was weird, his feelings about Iris. They had developed over years and largely in absentia. He'd always known Iris was his best friend, even if he was loath to admit that to the guys when he was young. He and Iris always seemed to understand each other and met on equal ground. Since they'd never crossed that line into a romantic relationship, he'd dated other girls. Iris had dated other guys . . . hadn't she? He'd always thought she was pretty. It was all irrelevant because they'd had a misunderstanding, the friendship was lost and Seth went away to college where the girls were plentiful and eager. He had fun for a while, no denying that, but there was always something missing for him. They didn't understand him, for one thing. Iris had always understood him, even when he'd rather she not.

In the years that followed, after his recovery from the accident, there had been women now and then. Much to his surprise, they hadn't seemed to be repulsed by his scarred face or his unsteady gait. There were a few he'd felt comfortable with for a time, some he had satisfying sex with, some who shared his interests, others who had been interested in building a future with him. But there'd never been one who could take Iris's place. And it made no sense to him at all.

He thought by coming back to Thunder Point he'd figure it out. If he could just restore his friendship with Iris to what it had once been, he'd see their relationship in proper perspective, the way he had growing up. They were good friends, and that was enough. He'd marry someone someday and maybe have a couple of kids. Iris would do likewise. Partnered with other people, they'd be couple friends. Their kids would play together. Life would be fulfilling and logical once again.

Of course, it was all complicated by one small thing. He sometimes had dreams of making love to Iris. Okay, two small things — Iris had always been pretty but over the past dozen years she'd grown truly beautiful. It was obvious to him that she didn't realize it, but there was no question about it — she was a knockout. Maybe it was as simple as fixing her hair or realizing her confidence, but the reason hardly mattered. The same girl he'd taken for granted when they were kids, the childhood friend who could kick a soccer ball as far, hit a baseball farther, was now the most beautiful woman in town.

And those dreams. They embarrassed him, and he'd had dozens over the past fifteen years. Why Iris? The only girl in school he *hadn't* tried to seduce. Truth was, he would have been scared to death to try — she'd probably coldcock him! He'd tested her out several times by carefully explaining his lust for other girls, and right after telling him he was a pig she'd give him pointers on how to talk to a girl, where to take her on a date, what to do to get her attention. If Iris had any interest, she wouldn't have done that. But still — he dreamed of her. He had to figure out how to make that go away.

At the end of business, he changed into his running clothes and took off across the beach. It always made him feel better about his new position. Then he grabbed his duffel and dropped in on his mother, who let him use the shower. Normally, he'd just head home in his running gear but tonight he had a date. Sort of. Mac was off duty. His wife was busy with their girls so Mac had suggested they get together for a beer and some crab cakes and talk over how things were going for Seth in the new job.

Seth walked into Cliffhanger's. He liked this place — the bar was upscale and the dining room was kind of fancy. A person could take a woman to dinner here and feel downright adequate. In fact he saw the back of an attractive blonde standing at the bar having a glass of wine — pretty hair, even though it was pink on the ends. Nice body. She might turn around and have the face of a horse, but from the back . . .

"Seth?" the woman said. She turned toward him. A better detective than he was, she'd seen his face in the mirror. "Is it really you?"

He smiled at her. "Sassy?"

"Please, I'm Sue. I left that horrible nickname behind."

"Sue," he said, his grin widening. Fat? Missing a front tooth? Iris had been baiting him. It made him feel loved. He wasn't sure why. "How have you been?"

"What are you doing here?" she asked.

"I'm your new town deputy. Mac was promoted and is working out of Coquille now."

"Really? That's fantastic! We'll have to get together!"

Seriously? he thought. *Never gonna happen.* "You're married, right?"

"Not anymore. But if you are I can get a date and you and your wife . . ."

Seth instantly saw nightmares. But then, even though Sassy hadn't gained weight and wasn't missing an incisor, of all the women he could think of, Sassy was the last one he'd like to spend an evening with. "I'm not married, but my work schedule is terrible," he said.

"What are you doing here at Cliff's?" she asked.

Seth, bedeviled, started to laugh. He couldn't help picturing Sassy as overweight and missing a tooth. He tried like hell to stop, but he couldn't seem to suppress his laughter. That damn Iris! She was a trouble-maker.

"What's so funny?" Sassy asked. She frowned as she sipped her wine.

"I'm sorry," he said, his thumb and fore-finger rubbing his eyes while he tried to get control of himself. She had pink hair! And he couldn't remember her boobs being that big, but then, she was older. Did boobs grow? "I'm meeting Mac," he said, still laughing. "It's kind of a business meeting, since I'm taking over his post."

"Sue," someone said. "That's fish and chips, coleslaw, garlic toast." Cliff put an enormous brown bag on the bar.

She passed him a credit card but glared at Seth. "Are you laughing at me? At my *hair*?"

He sobered instantly, though the laughter stayed right there, right behind his lips. He sought an excuse. "Your hair? No, of course not. I was just thinking, remember when we were about sixteen? Remember when you were cheering a hockey game? Out on the ice? And you were skating backward and got rammed by Robbie Delaney? And he sent you flying across the ice at about fifty miles an hour?" He didn't add, *The same guy you cheated on me with.*

"It wasn't that funny," she said. She leaned on the bar to sign the charge slip.

"Sorry," he said. "I'm sure if you're the one getting hit, it's not. Sorry."

"I had problems with my tailbone for years. . . ."

"Ah, there's Mac!" he said. "You know Mac, right?"

"I don't spend a lot of time with the law," she said stiffly.

Still struggling not to laugh, Seth stuck out his hand. "Hey, Mac. You know Sassy . . . I mean, Sue Marie Sontag, right?"

"Delaney," she corrected. She shook Mac's hand but gave him a tight smile.

"You *married* Robbie Delaney?" Seth asked. "Wow."

"I'd better get this home to the kids." She lifted her wineglass and gulped down what was left.

"Kids?" Seth echoed. And then in spite of himself he started to laugh again, picturing her with a hockey-player's smile. He was going to kill Iris.

"Three," she said, greatly irritated with him. "See you around."

When she'd cleared the door, Seth sat at the bar and started to laugh again. He put his elbow on the bar, his head resting on his hand and just shook his head.

"That must have been some joke," Mac said.

"That damn Iris," Seth said.

"Iris is here?"

"No. No, she's not," Seth said. "Iris and Sassy — I mean Sue Marie — were kind of competitive in high school. It's a long and complicated story, but I accidentally asked Sue and Iris both to the prom, but I went with Sue. And I had a horrible time, but I never did have good instincts about stuff like that. Iris apparently still hates her. I was surprised to hear Sue was still around Thunder Point and Iris told me . . ." He stopped to laugh a little more. "She told me Sue had gotten fat and was missing a tooth right in front. She didn't mention the pink hair."

"Cliff, two beers, whatever is on tap," Mac said. Then he turned to Seth. "You're an idiot."

"I know," he said.

He remembered the last time he and Iris had had that problem — out-of-control laughter. They'd been seventeen and in English class. They sat at the same table for two. Their teacher, the dowdy and homely Ms. Freund, had noticed Mr. Gaither, the new, slightly younger and handsome advanced algebra teacher in the classroom next door. Ms. Freund had been seen staring and nearly swooning. He and Iris had been joking about how easily Ms. Freund could be had if Mr. Gaither played his cards right. And then she came to school with her hair streaked and, boy, was it streaked, nearly *striped* in yellow, and in some bizarre updraft style that looked lacquered together. Her eyelids were blue and she damn near killed herself in her spike heels. She wore a new outfit — a skirt so tight she could hardly move and a fitted sweater with a low neckline so she had some pathetic cleavage. In fact, they thought it looked like there might be cotton peeking out. And before class was over, after all that action at the blackboard, Ms. Freund's left boob slid to her rib cage. Iris and Seth lost it. They started to laugh so hard they almost had to be physically removed from the classroom. They could not get things under control in the principal's office. They had been completely consumed by the stupids and couldn't even talk about it weeks later without losing control. Every hour of detention was worth it.

Damn, he had missed her.

■ ■ ■ ■

Since John Garvey, the senior guidance counselor, had taken his retirement from the school district, Iris was left in charge of the counseling office in the high school. Garvey said it was an early retirement but if you asked most of the teachers, and Iris for that matter, it wasn't quite early enough. Garvey had an antiquated notion of what high school students needed and often he did more harm than good. He was quite famous for telling young girls they "weren't college material." As if these girls didn't have self-esteem problems enough!

It did leave Iris with an awful lot on her plate. A new counselor was being sought to work with her and, in the meantime, she was promised an intern from the college. It was going to take time to find another counselor — the requirements were steep and the pay wasn't great. Iris needed that intern yesterday — it was testing time in the high school and she was setting up SAT and ACT test schedules. Doing this without help left precious little time for actual counseling. And everywhere she looked, she saw the need. She was on the lookout for behavioral problems, academic struggles, self-esteem issues that led to things like an-orexia and bulimia, bullying — and that wasn't just students bullying each other. Sometimes teachers were far too corporal or verbally abusive and sometimes they suffered the same from students. She kept vigilant for signs of depression, anxiety, drug and alcohol issues, unstable home lives. Her days were long and she worked at home on evenings and weekends — no spare brain cell was unused.

And she *loved* it.

Iris hadn't known when she was in high school that this was the perfect direction for her, but then her counselor was John Garvey, who had not done one thing to help her discover her aptitude. At the time, neither Iris nor her mother had any idea what Garvey should have been doing with her — a student who'd not only graduated with honors but had done some serious damage to an SAT. Fortunately, Iris had had better guidance at the university and really took to social work. So began her driving need to get her master's degree and return to her high school as a guidance counselor and do for the kids and teachers what John Garvey had not. Since she'd been at Thunder Point High they'd instituted a no-tolerance drug-and-alcohol program and a zero-tolerance-for-bullying program. And while it hadn't exactly been an issue, there was also a no-tolerance-for-cheating program in place now. Three absolutely necessary and useful programs that Garvey had neglected if not ignored.

Her desk was awash in paper she'd been struggling to control for hours when Troy Headly gave a light tap on her open door and stuck his head in. "Hey," he said. "Got a minute?"

She put her pen down and smiled at him. "Are you here on business?"

He didn't smile, which was very unusual for Troy. Often his visits to her office had more to do with flirting, since they'd been a couple for a while last spring and she'd broken it off, to his extreme displeasure. Troy was a great guy, a lovely man, but it just wasn't working for her. Troy had been looking for another try ever since. He fully expected her to come around and admit they were right for each other.

"Can I close the door?" he asked.

"Business, then," she said.

He sat in the chair that faced her desk. "How well do you know Rachel Delaney?"

She shrugged. "I know her a little. She's never been referred to me. I went to school with her mother." She grinned. "Back in the day they called her mother Sassy. She was the most popular girl in the senior class."

"I guess the apple doesn't fall far from the tree," Troy said.

"Sassy was kind of mean."

"Rachel seems to be enjoying similar popular status, though she's a junior this year. Beautiful girl and I've never seen her be mean. She's very sweet. Know anything about her family? Home life?"

Iris folded her hands on top of her pile of papers. "Where's this going?"

"Maybe nowhere. Just that I have this hunch . . . it's possible she's being abused."

"In what way? What gave you your hunch?"

"Either she's one of the klutziest girls in her class or someone's knocking her around. A few weeks ago, I noticed some bruising on her neck and shoulder and asked her what happened. She said she got tackled playing football on the weekend. A few weeks later she claimed to have taken a volleyball in the face, causing her black eye. Since then she's wearing lots of sweaters and high necks."

"It's getting cold," Iris said.

"Yeah, I know. I touched her arm yesterday to stop her from leaving class so I could

69

give her back her paper, which was very well done and I wanted to praise her. But she winced and jerked away. I asked her if anything was wrong and she said she was sore from a big workout. She was very nervous and not too convincing."

"Do you have any experience with this sort of thing?" Iris asked.

"I have some experience at how people cover it up. When I was growing up our neighbor was physically abusive to his family. He was such a smooth-talking bastard, all smiles, always had the best of everything. Except his wife and kids had no freedom of movement and everything had to be perfect. The wife and mom — she couldn't even visit at our house for a cup of coffee. My mother kept saying it was all wrong, my dad kept saying she had a wild imagination and should mind her own business. Then one day the police came. The oldest girl was taken away in the ambulance, the rest of them were bruised and shaken up and he was arrested. It had been going on a long time, we learned. My mother could tell. My father wanted her to leave it alone. That's it," he said. "That's all I've got. Could be she's really clumsy or maybe her father is hitting her."

"Actually, her father isn't in the picture

just now. She, her mom and two younger brothers are living with her mom's sister and brother-in-law and their kids. It's very crowded and it's not a big house. I suppose that could be an issue, but Sassy and her sister were always close. And if you knew Sassy — she wasn't one to take any crap. From anyone."

"Is there anything you can do about this?"

"Uh-huh. There's lots I can do. I can give the PE teacher a heads-up to let me know if Rachel has signs of problems that include injuries. I can talk to her teachers from last year and ask if they had concerns about her. I can check for absences or illnesses, look over her grades, watch her movements around campus. If someone is hitting her or otherwise hurting her, there will be other signs. And then, of course, I can talk to her."

"She's a good student," Troy said. "And she's not isolated. Batterers usually isolate their punching bags. Rachel is popular and has quite a posse."

Iris grinned at him. "Why don't you get your master's and work with me? You have such good instincts about this sort of thing."

"Why would I want to go back to school when I can surf and ski and dive on my time off?"

That was Troy, Iris thought. The fun guy.

Active, busy, always on the move, dive trips to faraway waters, ski trips to exotic runs, very athletic and every sport was extreme and on the edge. It was one of the things she had enjoyed about him even if she didn't share his kind of fun — he was untamed. Adventurous. He was a little younger than Iris — just turned thirty. And he was an exceptional history teacher.

"You can leave this in my hands," she assured him. "If you think of anything more, let me know."

FOUR

Seth hadn't expected his return to Thunder Point to mean he'd spend so much time with his mother, but he visited her several times a week. He had planned to spend more time with *both* parents, gradually wearing down Norm's orneriness. Every week or ten days he'd wrangle an invitation to dinner. "Don't mention to Pop that I'm coming or he'll find a reason he's needed at the station," he told his mother.

"Oh, I think I know your father by now," she said. And Seth could see by the look on Norm's face that he was always surprised to see his youngest son present.

While Seth wasn't making much progress with his father, something he hadn't intended at all was showing on his mother. She was growing stronger, more confident and happier because he came around so much. He brought flowers or sweets sometimes. He happily ate her leftovers for his lunch — pot roast and potatoes, chicken, stuffing and gravy, meat loaf, lasagna — all the calorie-rich meals he grew up on. He worked out a lot so he needed those calories. Norm was cursed to be skinny but strong as an ox while Gwen grew ever rounder and softer, her exercise coming from housework and cooking. But her cheeks were definitely rosier, her eyes sparkled again.

The sparkle had left Gwen's eyes for the first time when he'd been in that accident and lay in a hospital in Seattle, fighting for life, fighting for his leg. And then again some years later when her next-door neighbor and best friend, Rose, died. Gwen was strong — she had carried on. But it was apparent that having Seth home, obviously trying to reconnect with the father who had once been so proud of him, was filling her well.

While he was there for lunch she chattered about her mah-jongg group, shopping, his brothers, Nick and Boomer, and the grandkids. She asked about his business in town — she wanted to know all about the problems he encountered from warning drivers to slow down to the occasional arrest. She scurried, making him comfortable and feeding him. When she finally sat with him she didn't eat; she just gazed at him and listened to every word he could get in between swallows.

"Do you see Iris?" she asked.

He nodded and wolfed down more of his meat loaf sandwich. "I run into her sometimes. You probably see her more than I do."

"During school she seems to be busy all the time."

"That's understandable," he said.

"I could have her to dinner! You could come!"

He put down his sandwich. "Let's not do that, Mom."

"But Seth, have you spent any time with Iris?"

"Sure. A couple of weeks ago I wrapped up my run at Cooper's place and had a beer and pizza with Iris and Grace. We caught up on a lot of old stories. But if it's all the same to you, I don't want you to set me up."

"But Seth, you and Iris were always so close and I —"

"Mom, no matter who the girl is, if I'm going to date someone I don't want to be hooked up by my mother!" He narrowed his eyes a little bit. "Do you understand this?"

"Well, of course!"

"And you swear — no funny business?"

"Humph. I suppose."

"Behave or I'll stop buying you flowers."

"Seth . . ."

He took another bite of his sandwich. "I have wondered — who's cutting her grass? I've been away a long time," he said.

"This or that high school boy sometimes, but mostly she takes care of her yard herself. You should see that house, Seth. All she's done inside since Rose passed — she turned it into a showplace. It was always a nice house, but Iris really made it modern and beautiful." Then, with a hand cupping her mouth, she continued as if imparting a secret. "I think selling the flower shop gave her a little nest egg."

Seth laughed at his mother. It was Thunder Point at its best — everyone knew everything about everyone, right down to who they were dating and how much there might be in their nest egg. Plus, his mother really wanted him to see the inside of that house.

There were high school football games every Tuesday and Friday night and when they were home games, like tonight, Seth was absolutely certain to be there. Since he was still fairly new on the job, he wore his uniform. There were two deputies on duty plus school security, but being uniformed was all part of the town recognizing him as the law. A few more weeks and he'd be at the high-profile sporting events in civilian clothes, just as Mac had done the past few years. And with a gun on his ankle and a cell phone in his pocket, he'd be as much at the call of his staff in need of a supervisor as any other time.

Seth didn't wander around in the stands but stayed at the end of the bleachers, on the track. From that position he had a view of the stands, the field, the parking lot, the concession area. Football was one of the town's priorities and most of the town was there. As people passed him they said, "Hey, Seth." Some stopped to talk a minute, shaking his hand. He saw some familiar faces — Mac, Gina and Mac's younger kids gave him a wave; the coach's wife, Devon, and their kids, Austin and Mercy, were right behind them. Predictably, there were a few guys he'd played ball with in high school, but it wasn't the first time he'd seen them — the ice had been broken before he took over the substation.

He saw Iris climbing up a bleacher aisle to a higher perch. She was followed by Troy and Grace. She looked over her shoulder and laughed at something and it made him smile. That might be the thing he missed most — her wit, her unrestrained laugh. When she forgot she was mad at him, she laughed like old times, like that night they had pizza on Cooper's deck.

"Hi," a voice said.

He turned and, standing right there, a few inches shorter than him, smiling kind of wistfully, was Sassy. Um, Sue Marie. He smiled at her. He forced himself *not* to think about a gaping hole in her mouth from a missing tooth.

"I have a feeling we got off on the wrong foot," she said.

"You still come to all these games?" he asked, because surely she wouldn't know that he'd be here. He didn't even live around here.

"I didn't for years, but my daughter is cheering." She pointed over to the line of varsity cheerleaders in their short skirts. "Rachel, third from the end."

Whew, Seth thought. *Little glass of wine before the game, Sassy?* Her breath smelled like a winery.

"She looks just like you," he said. "Hard to believe you have a daughter that old. You still look sixteen."

"Aw. You're just flattering me. That's what I remember best about you — you've always been such a gentleman. Why don't we try this again, Seth. Let's get together for a drink or something. Have a few laughs. We can talk about old times."

He gave her a very patient smile. "Tell you what, Sassy. I think we'd be better leaving the past where it is."

"Come on," she said. "We had a few problems. We were kids. . . ."

He shook his head. "We've moved on from high school and I won't hold a grudge if you won't. But if we talk about old times, we won't be laughing. I'm sure I'll see you around town."

"That's a no, then?"

"Not that I don't appreciate the invitation," he said.

"I guess you're seeing someone," she said.

"Well, not exactly, Sassy, but I —"

"Sue Marie!"

"Sorry," he said with a chuckle. "You were pretty sassy back then. No, I'm not involved with anyone at the moment. We've already tried this and it didn't work then. I doubt it will work out now."

"Did it ever occur to you that I might want to make amends?"

He looked at her with patience. Or maybe it was tolerance. "I believe we've already done that, too."

"Oh! I take back what I said about you being a gentleman!"

They weren't going to talk about the elephant standing right between them, he thought. They dated, she cheated, they made up, dated some more, she cheated some more. And she had married one of the guys she'd cheated with — Robbie Delaney. Robbie, who had once been Seth's close friend and teammate, though they'd been competitive. He hadn't known, until coming home, that Robbie had won.

And Seth had dodged a bullet.

"I apologize if I was rude in any way, Sue. Thank you for the invitation. I'm afraid I have to decline the offer. I do wish you the best in everything. Really."

Against all good sense, she reached out and gave his biceps a gentle stroke. "I guess I'll have to be patient. It will take time for you to realize I'm just not the same girl."

He stopped himself from saying, *I think we've done that before, too.* Instead he said, "I guess none of us are the same. A lot of stuff happened between then and now."

She flashed him a brilliant smile and then turned away. Those jeans of hers couldn't possibly have gotten any tighter. And he wondered if she found boots with platform soles and four-inch spike heels inconvenient on the dirt track or in the bleachers, but so far she was maneuvering very well.

He turned to look up at where he'd last seen Iris and met her eyes instantly. She'd been watching. She didn't look very happy. And he smiled.

This was the problem with never getting over what you were determined to get over. Iris saw Sassy approach Seth and her brain went into rewind, remembering every detail of her senior year. Sassy in her short skirt with her pom-poms, her blond hair flouncing, her blue eyes shining at every male within a twenty-mile radius, her big straddle jumps that showed off her itty-bitty panties. Sassy had been a cheerleader since about the sixth grade while Iris couldn't even dance, much less leap into the air. She'd probably kill herself trying.

"God, are you into him?" Troy asked.

"What?" she replied, turning to look at Troy.

"The new deputy. He seems to have your complete attention. Crush time?"

"No! I grew up next door to him, you know that. I've known him all my life! We're barely even friends now — just acquaintances. We've hardly seen each other in years. But that woman is Rachel's mother."

81

Troy squinted toward the track where Seth stood and watched as Sue departed. "Looks like she could be Rachel's sister."

"She's our age. Up close you can tell she's not a teenager. Even if she dresses like one. Apparently *she's* into him — Seth."

"You were watching her?" Troy asked.

"Shh," she warned. "Let's not talk about this in a public place."

Of course she'd been watching Seth, but Iris had managed to remain circumspect until she'd seen Sassy saunter over to him. And even though they were quite far away, it looked as if she'd stared up at him with adoring eyes as he'd looked down at her with a sweet smile. And then she'd affectionately rubbed his muscled arm. *I've been here before,* she thought dismally. And she wasn't entirely surprised to note that it bothered her just as much.

It was another win for Thunder Point and when the game was over, Iris, Troy and Grace headed out of the stands. "Let's get something to eat," Troy said.

"You had two hot dogs!" Iris reminded him.

"I'm a growing boy and you girls are starving, I can tell."

"I'm getting out of here," Grace informed them. "Saturday is a work day for me. I have a wedding tomorrow — I'll be up to my eyeballs in flowers by nine and the wedding is in Coos Bay. See you later."

Grace bolted for the parking lot but Iris and Troy were sidetracked by students and teachers who stopped to say hello and talk about the game a little. Out of her peripheral vision, she saw Seth walking away from the field and noted that he didn't have much of a limp. She frowned. Maybe he wore that lift in regular shoes but not in his running shoes? Then he keyed his radio and jogged away toward the parking lot.

"Come on, Iris, let's get something to eat. How about pizza?" Troy said.

"Do you know what that place is going to be like after the game? It'll be all night before we get one."

"I'll take you to Cliff's. We'll get something light — oysters or crab cakes or something. Come on."

She stopped dead in her tracks. Seth and one of the other deputies had a trio of boys with their hands braced against the police SUV. Seth was on his phone while the deputy was patting them down. "Are those our boys?" she asked.

Troy squinted toward them. "I don't recognize anyone. Maybe there was some trouble from the other school."

Iris strode purposefully toward the scene and when she got closer she nearly bumped into the assistant principal, also checking this out. "What's going on, Phil?"

"Just a little scuffle," he said. "Except two of those boys are from Canton and one of them is ours. Looks like two on one."

"What's going to happen to them?"

"Seth is taking the two Canton boys to his office, Charlie will bring in our boy. They'll sort it out from there."

"But if our boy wasn't doing anything wrong . . ."

"If he wasn't, and I think he wasn't, then he'll make out fine." He nodded. "I'm sure Seth and Charlie know what they're doing."

"I'm sure," she said. But she watched while the boys were loaded into two different Sheriff's Department SUVs. She had great math skills — that would leave only the high school security guard at the stadium while it was being emptied of football players, cheerleaders, band members and fans, and one on-duty deputy to keep an eye on the town tonight. But then, Seth wouldn't leave Thunder Point until he was comfortable that everything was under control.

She turned and bumped right into Troy. "Oops, sorry. I think maybe you're right —

we should get a pizza."

"We could be standing around for a long time," he said. "Unless you want to drive over to Bandon . . ."

"No, I thought maybe it would be a good idea to hang around Thunder Point tonight in case there are other kids from Canton who aren't happy about the results of the game."

He smiled, shook his head and chuckled. "What are you going to do, Iris? Bust up fights?"

"Hey, you've never seen my right hook."

"A testament to my good manners. I'll meet you over there."

There had been no trouble in town after the game, but hanging around the pizza place made for a late night. Troy was a very popular history teacher — and surfer, skier, scuba diver, white-water kayaker — a young legend with some of the students with similar interests. He tended to draw teenagers like a magnet. Iris was popular in her own right. Though her title was guidance counselor, she liked to think of herself as a social worker assigned to a high school. The result of Troy and Iris hanging out in town after a big game was typical — they were surrounded by a crowd. Everyone wanted to know who was being taken away in the police cars, or wanted to talk about the game, or wanted to gossip about teachers, students, townsfolk. And of course the girls always questioned Iris. "Are you *dating* Mr. Headly? He's so *hot*."

The evening even ended in a fairly typical way, with Troy following her home and jumping out of his car to catch her before she got inside her house. He grabbed her hand and pulled her close. "The whole high school wants us to be dating again."

"They don't know we were dating before," she reminded him. They had mutually decided it wasn't a good policy unless they were serious. If they turned serious the staff at least deserved full disclosure.

Troy had been serious. Iris had decided, after giving it a great deal of thought, that they weren't really right for each other. Not that there was a single thing wrong with Troy. For her, there just weren't any bells.

"Kiss me good-night and see if you suddenly change your mind," he begged.

She laughed and touched his lips with a finger. "You're just about my favorite teacher in the world. There's not another at the high school I have more respect for. And you're fun! I want to hang out, do fun stuff, be your friend, but that's all I've got. Troy, if you don't hear me on this, then we can't even be friends."

"I think you could be making a big mistake here, Iris," he said. "You could be giving up the best thing that ever happened to you!"

"Oh, you could be right. But I have to go with my instincts here. Are we on the same page or do I have to stop walking to class with you?"

"Whatever," he said, backing off. "Really, I think I'd rather you hate me than find me so appealing in all areas but one."

"There's no but," she said. "I think you're wonderful in all areas. But I don't think we have a future together because I'm not in love with you. I think you'll eventually find someone more suited to you and agree. Someone who makes your whistles go off in a huge way. But not if you keep looking at me and neglect keeping your eyes open for the one who's really right for you."

"You're just about out of time," he warned. "Pretty soon I'm going to get sick of trying."

She gave him a brief, sisterly kiss on his cheek. "I love you in every way except the right one. The one you're looking for. Besides, if I took you as my chosen one, it would break the hearts of countless high school girls."

"And of course I take great consolation in *that*!" he said with heavy sarcasm. "You're going to regret letting me get away."

In fact, she knew she might. It kept her awake very late into the night. They'd known each other for about a year when he'd asked her to go mountain hiking in late spring. They'd gone river kayaking in the summer. They'd also taken in movies, eaten pizza and popcorn, sat on the beach for quite a few sunsets. And they'd made love. Yes, they'd tumbled into bed after the third or fourth date and it was good. Very satisfying and completely five-star. But it hadn't done to her heart what she'd been looking for, what she'd been needing. She'd had several long talks with herself about being ridiculous — there was nothing about being with Troy that put her off or sent up a red flag. But there was also nothing that made her chest expand and brain completely lose focus. She didn't think about him constantly, didn't want to phone him at three in the morning, didn't miss him horribly when he went on his rafting or scuba trips. She could marry him and probably be 75 percent content.

But if she could see a life as 75 percent happy with a man before she even met him at the altar, what were the odds of them having a successful family life together? Shouldn't she be at least 100 percent first? Then maybe after marriage and all its familiarity and struggle and predictable disharmony from time to time, 75 percent would look pretty good. . . .

She came to a sudden realization. *Oh, God, that's probably what Seth thinks about me! He likes me a lot. He misses me and wants me back, but as his buddy, his pal, not as the love of his life! He's been trying to explain that to me for twenty years at least and I just won't get it! Troy isn't right for me in all ways just like I'm not right for Seth in all ways!*

It took such a long time to fall asleep and then, just because sometimes she was the most unlucky person alive, Norm Sileski decided it was the perfect Saturday morning to cut his grass. She rolled to her side and put the pillow over her head. During the week she had to be up early, perky and ready to face three hundred and fifty high school students with a positive attitude and creative problem-solving skills. On the weekend she liked to sleep in.

The pillow wouldn't make Norm's mower go away and she rolled over with a growl. She looked at the clock — it was nine o'clock. When she had finally nodded off at three she'd had a mental plan to wake up at about eleven and have lunch for breakfast. He'd robbed her of at least two hours!

Then she heard the mower ram into the side of her house under her bedroom window and she sat up with a start. What was he doing in her yard?

She grabbed a flannel shirt hanging on the peg in her closet and put it on over her skimpy pajama tank top. Barefoot in the cold October morning, she stormed outside to tell him to stop, to go worry about his own grass, hers was only going to need one more mowing before winter anyway. But when she got to the backyard she was nearly run over by Seth. He stopped the mower, put it on idle so it only hummed and grinned. "Morning."

"What are you doing?"

"I'm giving your grass a mow. I'm being a good neighbor."

"A good neighbor would let me sleep!"

"Out late last night, Iris?" he asked.

"Sort of. Then I had trouble falling asleep and Saturday is my sleep-in day. Now put your mother's lawn mower away and go home."

"Come on, Iris. I'm just being helpful. Now you don't have to pay a kid to do it and you don't have to do it yourself. You can go fishing or something instead."

"I just want to sleep for two more hours!"

He laughed. "Jesus, are you ever grumpy in the morning. I'll be done here in a flash. . . ."

"Just quit. I'll finish it. Go away. I'm sleeping!"

"That's obvious," he said, making a motion with his hand over the left side of his head, indicating a protruding, springy mound.

She hadn't looked in the mirror. Her hair tended to go a little berserk at night, especially if it was a tossing-and-turning night. She glared at him. "I. Said. Go."

"Come on, Iris," he cajoled. "Go make some coffee. You'll feel better in a few minutes and by then I'll be done here."

She took a couple of steps toward him. "What the hell are you doing to me?"

He smiled pleasantly. "I'm wooing you. I'm wearing you down. I want you back."

"You're full of shit," she said. She turned to walk away.

"Come on, Iris. I need you."

She wasn't thinking. She really had been asleep and she was really tired. And he really had pissed her off before he said the thing that brought a curtain of red over her eyes, like a fountain of blood. She whirled and slugged him in the jaw as hard as she could before stomping off.

Just like when they were eight years old.

Seth's heel caught on the wheel of the lawn mower and he tripped backward, landing on his ass. It ran through his mind that if he'd seen that coming he wouldn't have let her get away with it, then just as quickly he reminded himself she already had. So he grabbed his left knee and began to moan and groan very loudly. "Ohhh. God, Ohhh. Ah! Jesus! Ohhh."

Through the slits of his eyes he saw her turn and cast a stricken look his way, her mouth open in a nice, shocked O.

"Seth," she said, rushing to him. "Oh, God, did you hurt your bad leg? I'm so sorry. I don't know what —"

Then she squealed as he grabbed her, pulled her down and rolled until she was under him. He pressed her down and his eyes glittered as he flashed an evil smile. "My bad leg is the right one. But you hit a police officer. That's assault. It might be a felony. Depends on the extenuating circumstances."

"Like you're just a bastard?" she asked, struggling to push him off.

He held her down effortlessly. "Like temporary insanity. On your part."

"Get off me, you brute. Or I'll scream so loud your mother will bring the cleaver."

"You already screamed. The mower is still humming. Why'd you hit me? I was trying to be nice."

"No, you weren't! You were being your usual manipulative self!"

Offended, he grabbed her arms. "When was I manipulative? I'm never manipulative! Unless it's work oriented! I'm trained to manipulate criminals!"

"Oh-ho, is that right? The last time you said you *needed* me, you helped yourself to my virginity and took someone else to the prom! Now let me *go*!"

He was stunned. He went perfectly still. And he was much heavier because he wasn't holding his weight off her. Iris was gasping for breath and pushing with all her might. He outweighed her by a good fifty pounds. He lifted up, but just enough so she could breathe. He obviously wasn't letting her get away until he had answers. "What?" he said.

She took a deep breath. Tears came to her eyes. "You heard me. That night. When you broke up with Sassy, got drunk and I took you out of that party before you got in real trouble. I took you to the lookout to sober up a little. You said, 'Come on, Iris, I need you.' Then you got me out of my shorts

93

and . . ."

"No," he said.

"I know. You don't remember, right? After it was over I could figure out — you probably didn't even realize it was me! Jackass!"

"No," he said again. "Why didn't you say anything?"

She laughed. "So everyone in school, in town, could say mean things like, 'Who is Iris kidding? Why would he hook up with her?' Don't you think it hurt enough without that?"

"God," he said, shock still paralyzing him. "Iris . . ."

"Oh, shut up and get *off* me!"

He rolled off her and sat on the grass. He pulled his knees up and leaned his arms on them. "Jesus, what an asshole I must've been."

Iris sat up. "Yes to that."

"Iris, seriously, I'm sorry. I took advantage of you. Did I hurt you?"

She shook her head and a couple of tears slipped out of her eyes. She brushed them away impatiently. In the moment, it had been like a dream come true! "Not physically. I think you were just moving on instinct and I didn't stop you. I didn't realize you didn't know what you were doing. Or who you were doing it with," she added with a bit of a choked voice. She looked away.

"Oh, I didn't know what I was doing, but I must've known who I was with." He shook his head. "I guess that explains the weird dreams."

"What dreams?"

"Dreams about . . . Let's save that discussion. It's pretty embarrassing. Are you sure I didn't force myself on you? Like a drunk seventeen-year-old moron?"

"No," she said weakly. "I must admit I had stupidly been waiting forever for you to discover all those skinny, acrobatic cheerleaders weren't right for you and you belonged with me, so . . ." She shrugged. "Thus, my broken heart. Then my anger. Maybe we can get over this now that you know. And you can leave me alone."

"You're sure I didn't hurt you?"

She just shook her head.

He looked down at his knees. "It must have been thrilling for you," he said sarcastically. "A teenage drunk climbing all over you."

"Yeah, well . . . I'd always heard the first time is awful."

"Jesus, Iris. I don't know how I'm going to make this up to you. Sometimes it feels like every time I turn around I have one more stupid move to make amends for. This one is really going to take some thought."

"Yeah? Well, listen, Seth. Let me make it easy for you because I *have* thought about it. It would be best if you just let it go, get on with your life and stop expecting me to be that girl again. I'm not, okay? I'm not your best friend anymore. I'm not going to be the one to pull your fat out of the fire every time you're in trouble. You're on your own. Just leave me alone." She pulled herself to her feet.

"I don't blame you for being angry," he said.

"It wasn't just the prom, you stupid shithead," she said quietly, looking down at him. "It was everything. You used me as your tutor, your counselor so you could talk about your problems with all the pretty, popular girls, your playmate if you were bored. That night you said I was the only girl you'd ever really loved and then you just used me and tossed me out the next day."

"Iris —"

"I'm over it, Seth. I'm over you. If you think I'm ever going to risk that kind of hurt again, you've lost your mind."

Then she walked away and didn't look back.

FIVE

Iris wiped her eyes and blew her nose. She looked out her kitchen window and there he sat on the ground beside the lawn mower like the big dumb ox he was. Well, she was glad it was out. Now Seth knew everything that had pissed her off. Now he could go away because she was over it. Over him.

She made sure her doors were locked, then she threw herself facedown on her bed and smothered her cries in the pillow. She let all of the emotion out.

Before too long she heard the mower start up again. It ran for about ten minutes, then stopped and she was enveloped in silence. But the noise inside her head was deafening.

This was good, right? Getting it all out, all of it. Venting all the hurt and anger and feelings of betrayal. Because he hurt me so much. He's been such an ignorant fool!

He'd been seventeen and stupid. *And you*

were seventeen and not much smarter, her thirty-four-year-old self added.

Well, of course that internal argument was going to happen — she was a social worker, a counselor to young people. Young people who made mistakes every day, some that were hard to recover from, very hard to move on from.

Iris didn't turn on the TV or her stereo. She cleaned house, literally. She cleaned out cupboards, closets, washed clothes, scoured the bathroom and the kitchen, threw away stuff in the refrigerator, filled bags and boxes with things she'd been meaning to get rid of for a long time. Clothes for donation were bagged, kitchen items that had been around since she was a teenager were boxed up — some to donate and some to pitch. She folded her underwear into little squares, rolled her towels and put them in an attractive wicker basket, changed the sheets, washed the rugs that fit into the washing machine. When the sun came out and the afternoon grew warm, she opened the windows to air out the house.

On Saturday night she had a glass of wine with her light dinner and put on an old movie — one of her favorite old chick flicks that always made her cry. She'd learned a long time ago that if there was a good cry growing in your chest and throat, a nice tearjerker could get it out of you without forcing you to dwell on the real issues.

What if she'd gotten pregnant from that spontaneous drunk coupling? she wondered. What would they have done? Would they have talked about it? Gotten married or something? Gotten married and given up their educations? Gotten married and maybe missed that fast car that had ended a prestigious football career? Gotten married because they had to and divorced later because Seth hadn't been ready to be a husband and father, only a famous football player?

As it had happened, her period had started right away and she'd devoted herself to avoiding Seth. About a week after his reconciliation with Sassy, Seth had approached her. "You have any plans to go to the prom?" he'd asked.

She'd looked at him in horror. "You know I don't, you imbecile. You said you wanted to take me, then you said you couldn't because you made up with Sassy."

"Hey, I would've taken you, Iris! I'm sorry, but I didn't know you'd take that so seriously. I was just pissed."

"Good for you," she had said. "And now

I'm just pissed. I hope you have an awful time!"

"What do you want me to do, Iris? Tell Sassy I can't take her and take you instead?"

"I wouldn't go with you if you were dying and it was part of your Make-a-Wish list!"

That was so vulgar of her, she thought. She'd been that outraged. It wasn't like Iris to make cruel remarks like that. Although they hadn't talked about it, she'd heard he had a miserable time at prom and the homecoming couple broke up again. That made her perversely happy.

Iris didn't talk to anyone all weekend. She didn't leave her now sparkling house until three o'clock on Sunday afternoon when she drove to a donation bin and unloaded her stuffed car into it. Then she filled the Dumpster behind the flower shop with all the trash she'd cleaned out of her little house.

That night she had a long soak in the tub. She lit candles in the bathroom. She put on soft, clean pajamas, curled up on the couch and got out one of her favorite books of inspirational quotes — something to buoy her spirits and put her back on track. After an hour of skimming she found one that spoke to her. *Resentment is like drinking poison and then hoping it will kill your enemies*

100

— Nelson Mandela.

"Enough," she said aloud. "That's enough. Moving on now!"

She closed the book and went to bed. She slept soundly for ten hours.

Seth wasn't nearly busy enough all week to distract him from thinking about Saturday in Iris's backyard. There was no way he was ever going to remember the events she described, but he couldn't help but wonder how closely her description fit some of his dreams. He had dreamed of making love to her in the flower van. It had been clumsy and embarrassing in his dream. From what he gathered, it had been so in reality, as well.

There had been other dreams about her, but they'd been fantasy dreams that took place in ideal settings — rooms with satin sheets, forest glens covered in silky grass, even on the hoods of sports cars. He had enjoyed those. There might've been a dozen starring Iris in as many years but since he'd had lots of dreams about lots of women, he hadn't thought the ones with Iris had any real significance. In the past seventeen years he'd only had a couple of serious relationships. They hadn't lasted too long nor had they been very fulfilling. He'd had plenty of dates but the right woman had always eluded him. Probably because she was back in Thunder Point, mad as hell at him.

He saw Iris twice that week. Once, he'd seen her riding her bike to school on a sunny morning, waving and laughing with the kids. The other time he'd seen her from his office as she went into the diner. He had lacked the courage to follow her in there and try to talk to her. No, he wasn't going near that until he knew what he was doing. And he didn't. Not yet.

The following weekend it was time for him to head to Seattle to visit his friend Oscar Spellman. He was driving up on Friday afternoon, would spend Saturday with Oscar and return to his home in Bandon on Sunday, ready to take on Thunder Point on Monday morning. The timing for a long drive alone in the car couldn't be better.

Friday night was clear and the weekend was sunny, not so unusual on the coast of Oregon in October but in Washington it was a treat. All the way up the freeway he'd been thinking. Remorse is a lot of hard work and boy, had he done a lot of hard work.

He'd been drafted by the Seahawks when he was in his first year of college. He heard they'd been surprised to find him available, but they wanted him before he got hurt because he was fast and strong and there was a very good chance he'd make them money. He got himself an agent to negotiate a good deal. His first pro year, during which he'd played a little bit, he made four hundred thousand dollars, all of which he spent on taxes and a late-model Ferrari sports car. Considering he'd never driven anything but his dad's old clunker truck, he really thought he was somebody. And one night, right before training camp for the Seahawks started, he took his new car out for a long drive along some Washington back roads. A miserable old Chevy sedan blew through a stoplight in front of Seth and Seth couldn't stop. He tried to avoid a collision but his car basically T-boned that old Chevy.

That was Oscar.

It was determined that Oscar had fallen asleep at the wheel after working a double shift at a manufacturing plant near Seattle. He was a forty-five-year-old machinist with a wife, Flora, and two kids. There had been two witnesses stopped at the same crossroad who could validate it. Oscar had been responsible for the accident. But Seth had been going eighty in a fifty-five zone. Ironically, he had just slowed down around the curve. He'd probably been doing ninety, maybe more. He was cited for speeding.

Both drivers were rushed to the hospital after being cut out of their cars. Seth hit Oscar's car on the driver's side. Seth and Oscar were both gravely injured, but Seth recovered. It took a long time, several surgeries and a lot of determination, but Seth pounded his way through the worst of it. Oscar's spinal cord was severed.

About a year after the accident lawyers for Oscar Spellman filed a civil suit alleging that the injuries to Oscar would not have been as catastrophic if Seth had been traveling at the speed limit, if he had exercised caution while entering the intersection. All Seth had left was his signing bonus, but it was huge to a kid from Thunder Point . . . or a crippled black man and his family from Seattle. Seth's league insurance had paid for his hospitalization and rehab, but Oscar, a husband and father, was going to spend the rest of his life in a wheelchair, unable to work, without the use of his limbs, without income. And all for the thrill of seeing how fast that little silver car could go.

"Don't worry. We can win this," Seth's lawyer had said.

But that wasn't a concern for Seth. "I don't want to win it."

He'd lost his education, his career, his savings, his potential to play sports all in one split second. All for a stupid mistake.

He'd visited Oscar for the first time about a year after the lawsuit. Seth was still walking with a cane, the scar on his face still bright pink. The first half-dozen visits had been really short and awkward, but then Oscar started to just sigh deeply whenever Seth appeared. "What the hell you doin' back here, boy? Like I ain't got enough trouble in my life?" he'd say.

Over time, Oscar regained the use of his left arm and hand. It was clumsy and not very strong or reliable, but he could feed himself and he could play checkers. He was a smart man and Seth taught him to play chess. Oscar had more time to learn about the game and practice than Seth did so the challenges became pretty one-sided with Oscar on the winning side.

"At least you have your mind," Seth said. "Ever think of being grateful for that?"

"Ever think it might be a curse?" Oscar replied.

For the past dozen years Seth had been dropping in on Oscar and Flora every other month or so. He went to the graduations of Oscar's kids and held a new grandchild. Seth always called ahead to make sure they weren't having friends or family in. He didn't want to be in the way. Oscar was sixty now and his health was rocky; just being confined to a wheelchair meant all kinds of medical problems chased him. He occupied the same motorized wheelchair with a neck brace that he'd been riding around in for years, but his kids and his church had fixed him up with some computer equipment so he could study, read, learn everything under the sun he wanted to know. With the fingers of his one good limb he could write and he had developed a whole network of friends outside the walls of his home.

Flora opened the door to Seth on Saturday morning. She'd mellowed a little over time and she'd grown beautiful in her maturity. She had help tending to Oscar from her son and daughter, and a nurse's aide visited regularly to bathe him and exercise his limbs. Flora's life was challenging but it wasn't a torture of hard labor. It was safe to leave Oscar for a few hours at a time and she could take him places sometimes. When she saw Seth she smiled at him and he admired her handsome face. She was also sixty, but her face was smooth and un-wrinkled. She kept her hair very short and black; she was trim and muscular, a vision both admirable and unfortunate to him. She had to work hard every day of her life.

She hugged him. "How you doin', son?"

she asked, her arms holding him sweetly.

"I'm getting by fine, Flora," he lied. "You have somewhere to go? I can sit with the old boy for a few hours if you need a break."

"Who you callin' old?" Oscar called out. The whir of the wheelchair accompanied his voice and he was instantly a presence in the room.

"I got nothing pressing," she said with a laugh. "But I think I'll give you boys some lunch and leave just because I can. Can you stay awhile?"

"All day," Seth said. "You just tell me if there are any chores I can help with while you're gone."

"I got no chores, Seth. Except keeping Oscar entertained and that's a chore in itself."

They ate grilled cheese and chips. Flora was an outstanding cook and over the years he'd had some great dishes, traditional Southern and otherwise. Occasionally Oscar would insist Flora warm up something for Seth so he could rave. But Oscar always had a sandwich, something he could grip and wouldn't spill. Seth knew when they were alone, just Oscar and Flora, and he was bibbed to his chin, they had soups and greens and beans with ham and some of her other slippery but delicious items. But

Oscar found it damned humiliating to be covered with food at the end of a meal when he had company.

Seth washed up their plates and got out the chess board. Seth and Oscar had this in common — Seth hadn't grown up with a chess board in the house, either. He had learned during his long rehab. Usually it was Oscar whose moves were slow and thoughtful, not to mention the fact that his one working limb was weak and shaky at best. But today it was Seth who was taking a long time with each move.

"One a' these days, you gonna get whatever it is outta your gut?" Oscar asked.

Seth took a breath, met those rheumy chocolate eyes and told Oscar about Iris. All about her. All about *it*. Everything.

"*Shew,*" Oscar finally said. "I guess you're feelin' real bad about that."

"Real bad," Seth admitted.

"You sure she wasn't just trying to make you feel better 'bout yourself, saying she never tried to stop you?"

Seth laughed. "No, Oscar. Iris is a lot of things, but not a liar. Not a woman who plays up to a man. Plus, she had no interest in making me feel better about anything! She clocked me, f'chrissake!"

Oscar laughed. "Gotta admit, I like a

108

woman won't take no stuff off a man. You see Flora? She's the sweetest thing ever come at me, but she has a limit. She understands when I get to feeling sorry for myself and she's kind, but I get a little ungrateful or maybe too ornery and she puts me right in my place. She's got no problem livin' with a cripple but she won't take no attitude. That's a real woman."

"Flora is one helluva woman," Seth said.

"She's that," Oscar said. "More woman than I deserve. You got some regrets, son?"

"Oh, boy," he said, with a hollow laugh. "Sometimes I feel like I've got nothing but regrets. Doesn't just about everyone?"

"I expect so. You think I don't wish I hadn't worked that second shift? But it was overtime and we always had more month left at the end of the paycheck. I'd done it a hundred times. I never really thought about what it could cost. How about you?"

He sighed. "Well, of course I regret speeding, even though I've made peace with the changes it brought my life. But it kills me to think I lost Iris before I ever knew how much I needed her. I took her for granted, and I'm not just talking about that night. I think I took her for granted her whole life. No wonder she hates me."

"She don't hate you, son. Likely she

109

grieves you. When she told you the truth about what you done, did she get upset? Cry a little?"

"Oscar, she decked me. Then she cried a little, yelled a little, stormed away and told me to never bother her again."

Oscar laughed. "You just another idiot man. A woman doesn't hurt over someone she doesn't care about! You were the love of her life and you weren't smart enough to run with that. You wish you'd been otherwise, just like I wish't I wasn't just a workin' man looking at some overtime. But here's where we are. Now, we can either work with those regrets and let 'em prove something or we can live in the past and be sorry souls."

"And how do you suppose we work with our regrets?"

"Well, I don't know what you're gonna do, but I ain't that man anymore, son. I'm gentler now. I used to be ornery and tired all the time. Used to have myself a temper. I can't run or play or work second shifts so I talk to my wife and my kids. We have the best talks. My grandkids like me, strange as you think that is. Bradley is only ten and he already plays some mean chess. I taught him. And you sure as hell ain't no tight end anymore. 'Bout time you let that girl know who you are now. I'm not sayin' that'll be easy. She might knock you flat again. But you're smarter and better now. She should know before she gives you up altogether. Show her you're not that stupid seventeen-year-old boy anymore. That'll be hard for you since you like feelin' sorry for yourself."

"How do you suggest I do that? Show her I've changed?"

He gave a slight one-sided shrug. "I don't know. Lucky you ain't dead yet. You still have time."

Seth loved that man. There he sat, a brace holding up his head, gesturing with one hand, immobile and in relatively poor health, yet he'd turned his infirmity into his opportunity. He'd grown closer to his wife and his kids, developed close relationships with his grandkids. If he could do that with a body that didn't function anymore, how could Seth admit defeat?

"When did you get so smart? So wise?" Seth asked him.

"What the hell else you think I got to do with my time?" Oscar said. Then he smiled.

Iris didn't see Seth all week and it was a good thing for her psyche. She'd spent years nurturing the anger she'd felt toward him and the one thing she hadn't expected was that he would be devastated by the truth. There was no denying it. He was shattered to think what he'd done to her. For some reason she had expected him to blow it off, the way he'd blown off the prom incident when they were seventeen.

The other thing she'd expected was that he'd get in touch with her and try a new approach to his apology, but that didn't happen, either. It took great strength of will to keep from looking for him. She knew he stayed at the office every day until five or later and there were lots of places she could run into him. Though she didn't want to, she kept her eyes open for his car at his mother's house, but it wasn't there. The weekend was especially hard because she wasn't busy at school. The only thing that kept her from reaching out was that she wasn't quite sure what to say. *Never mind, it's okay? I'm over it, we were young and dumb? Let's pretend we've never met before and see if we're friends now?*

She had no idea what followed confrontation. Hang on to the rage? Let it go and never speak of it again? Apologize for the honesty?

When she got home from school on Monday afternoon there was a basket of the biggest, most beautiful apples she'd ever seen on the porch in front of her door. There was a bow on top but no note. The next day there was a wreath for her front door made out of fall leaves, pine cones, dried flowers and wheat stalks. On Wednesday there was a box holding a beautiful white knit scarf. Thursday brought a tin of cookies in the shape of fall leaves, iced in yellow, orange, red and brown. On Friday came a horn of plenty filled with gourds, oranges, grapes and nuts. This time there was a note. She opened the small envelope and read the neatly printed card. "Dinner tonight at Cliffhanger's at seven. My treat."

She had begun to suspect but now she was sure. Seth was trying to make amends. He might even be trying to court her. *But, no,* she thought. *He just feels guilty and wants his shame to go away. At any cost.*

She was terrified of her feelings.

Iris had plenty of friends but few confidants. The only person who came to mind was Grace, so she drove to the flower shop.

When she walked in, Grace poked her head out of the back room. She grinned, happy to see Iris. In her hands she held a clipper and green molding tape. She wore her green utility apron and her fingers were dirty. There was no way to work with flowers and plants without getting dirty and

113

wearing gloves just wasn't tactile enough. Flowers were hard, messy work. "Well, you're the last person I expected. How are you?"

Iris shook her head. "I have a problem. I really need a friend at the moment."

"You've always got a friend here, you know that. Come on back."

The shop was empty. Only Grace was working. None of her part-timers were in. The bulk of the design work was done by Grace herself. And she got right back to it, indicating a stool at the worktable for Iris. It appeared Grace was designing a romantic arrangement, perhaps for a wedding or anniversary — white with green-and-red accents. Lilies, roses, baby's breath, fluffy white hydrangea in a large glass vase.

"You look very serious," Grace said. "What's going on?"

"It's about Seth," she said. "We had it out. Cards on the table. I didn't plan it but launched a full frontal attack, a confrontation. I really let him have it."

"Well, Iris, I suppose you should've done that a long time ago. This has been eating at you for years and if you'll forgive me saying so, it seems you were a little over-the-top about the prom thing."

"There was a lot more to it than the

114

prom," Iris said. "It's between you and me, right?"

"Right, of course. But what more?" she asked, as she kept clipping and slipping stems into her arrangement.

"Well, remember how I told you I rescued him from that party when he was drunk?"

"Yes. And he was mad at his girlfriend and asked you to the prom and then unasked you when he made up with her and then —"

"We had sex," Iris said.

Grace stopped arranging. She looked at Iris over the hydrangea. *"Sex?"*

Iris nodded. "He got all sentimental and touchy, told me I was the only girl he loved, started kissing me and it just went where that sort of thing usually goes. We got naked. In the flower van. Except he was drunk and I was a young girl who had lived for him to notice me as a female and not a buddy. I couldn't see that it was one of those stupid, groping, meaningless —"

The bell on the front door of the shop jingled. Grace's mouth was hanging open. Her eyes were fixated on Iris. "I will kill whoever that is. Don't lose your place." She dashed out of the workroom.

Damn the luck, Grace thought as she saw her customer. It was old Barney Wilcox. He

115

came by every week or so, poked around at the flowers, made conversation, left after spending a couple of bucks on a single flower for his wife of fifty-two years. He was there as much out of boredom as affection for his bride.

Grace took the bull by the horns. "Barney, so nice to see you. Listen, I'm rushing to meet a deadline and don't have much time. Can I fix you up with a beautiful hydrangea stem in a vase for about three dollars?"

"That would be nice, I suppose," he said. "But I —"

Grace dashed to the back room, plucked a stem out of her arrangement, plopped it in a slim vase, tied a length of white ribbon around it and sped out to her customer.

"Think that will make Mrs. Wilcox happy today?"

"I think so. Thanks," he said.

"Three even," she said. He paid her and she rushed back into the workroom. "Okay, I think I left you somewhere around 'meaningless nudity,' " Grace said.

"I didn't realize he didn't mean any of it," Iris said. "I was so inexperienced. I was a virgin. I figured it out when he clearly didn't remember it. By the time I got my clothes buttoned, he'd passed out. And when he asked me if I wasn't making too big a deal

116

out of that prom thing I knew — he had no idea. He'd blacked out."

"Oh, Iris. That's been hurting you all this time?"

"I don't know what hurt me more, his forgetting or the fact that I let it happen. But a couple of weeks ago he was cutting my grass on Saturday morning and I stormed outside to tell him to go away because I was sleeping. Sometimes I get a little crabby when someone wakes me up before I'm ready," she said. "And he said exactly the same thing that he said that night in the flower van. 'Come on, Iris. I need you.' And I totally lost control. I decked him."

Grace's mouth fell open. "As in hit?" she whispered.

Iris nodded. Her chin quivered.

"You hit a police officer?"

She nodded again. "Knocked him flat. A felony. Maybe."

The bell jingled. Grace looked at the ceiling of her little flower shop. "Am I being punished for something?" she said. She dashed into the store.

"Jeremy," she said. She sighed. Another infrequent customer who never bought much and loved to talk. Jeremy was one of the young guys from down at the marina, so in love with his pretty little wife but without much to spend. She'd been fixing him up with single blooms for a long time. "How are you?" she asked.

He puffed up a little. "I guess you could say I'm perfect. Janie had the baby! A boy! Just like we thought! And wow, is he big — over nine pounds, twenty-one inches, and we sat up through the night before he decided to come. His feet are so big they're like skis. I was there the whole —"

"I have just the thing," Grace said. She ran back to the workroom. She looked at her stash of accessories, grabbed a pair of blue baby shoes, pulled a length of blue ribbon from the ribbon dispenser, stuck the shoes in the arrangement she'd been working on, tied the ribbon around the vase in a nice bow, filled the vase half-full with water and ran it back into the shop. "Here you go, with my sincere congratulations!"

"Wow, that's pretty big. I don't know if I can —"

"From me to you," she said. "To celebrate the birth of your son!"

"You can't believe how hard that labor was and how much I really had to help," he said, holding the arrangement in the crook of his arm. "And the doctor said —"

"I can't wait to hear all about it, Jeremy!

Please promise to come back and tell me all the details when we both have more time. I'm in a rush and I know you want to get those flowers to your lovely wife." She walked around her counter, led him to the door, tried not to push him out too zealously, and flipped the Open sign to Closed. She locked the door and ran back to the workroom. "Okay, when I left you, you had just committed a felony. And I closed the shop."

"You closed?"

"I'm not opening that door again until I know everything! Did you knock him out?"

"No. But it sure surprised him. He had no idea why I'd do that."

A big spider suddenly appeared on the worktable, probably having hitched a ride in a flower shipment. Grace gasped and nearly fell over her stool trying to get away from it. Iris made a fist and slammed it on the spider without hesitating. She wiped her fist on her skirt.

"So I had to tell him," Iris said.

Grace reached for a paper towel to wipe up the squished spider. "Apparently you're a very physical person," she said, making a face at the mess.

"Didn't anyone ever tell you — you can't be in the flower business if you're squeamish or scared of bugs?"

"I'm fine with bugs. I just don't like them here. So you told him," Grace said.

"And just as I always suspected, he had no memory of it at all. He had no idea. He was basically doing it in his sleep. I could have been any woman."

"Yeah, I knew that about men. Did he say he was sorry?"

"Of course. He was devastated. He was worried that he'd hurt me, which he had not. At least not until he ignored me and forgot about me and about it. He thought I was mad about the prom and he got mad right back, saying it was stupid and melodramatic, that I knew he had a girlfriend and they'd just had a fight and . . . Well, you know all that."

"So, he's sorry, which of course he should be, but what do you expect of him now? Is he supposed to be more than sorry?"

"He's been sending me gifts all week and today this note came in a horn of plenty. It's beautiful, by the way. Will look great on my dining room table." Iris pulled the small note out of her pocket and passed it to Grace.

Grace read it. "That's very sweet," she said, handing it back. "Why does this upset you?"

"You have to know Seth," she said. "No one knows Seth like I do. He'd do anything for my forgiveness because he feels guilty about what he did, even though he was just a stupid kid and didn't mean to do it. He'd never intentionally hurt anyone. And now that he feels responsible for my anger, for my hurt, he'll do anything. He'll do whatever it takes to make it up to me. He'd marry me to make sure I know how much he regrets his actions."

"Gee," Grace said. "A girl could do worse. . . ."

"He'd sacrifice anything . . . everything to undo what he's done. At first I wouldn't tell him why I didn't want to be best friends anymore because I just couldn't face the humiliation. Then I didn't tell him why because I didn't want him to be nice to me out of guilt."

"Come on," Grace said. "You're thinking for him. You can't be sure all he feels for you is guilt."

"No, I can't. And I also can't be sure it's not."

"Iris," Grace said, leaning toward her. "You'd think a counselor would get over adolescent trauma by now!"

"That's why I'm in this business," she said. "You just don't know how hard it is to get beyond adolescent trauma."

"Yes, I do, but this is not about me. You should level with him. Again. Tell him why you're worried about his attention."

"Not in a million years!"

"Here's what you're going to do. Go home. Change into something that looks great on you, put on some fresh lips, go to Cliff's at seven and tell the man you forgive him. He didn't know what he was doing, it's been seventeen years and he's very sorry. Besides, what more can he do? What more do you want?"

"I don't want anything," Iris said. "I just want him to move on. I'm not strong enough for all this. I don't want to be his cross to bear."

"Iris, let him make his amends, accept his apologies and put him out of his misery."

"I'm afraid, Grace."

"Afraid of what?"

"Grace, I've wanted to fall in love since I was eighteen! Every time I met a guy with potential, I wanted so much to fall in love and be loved! But I couldn't. Because the only guy I've ever loved is Seth. I don't want to want him and watch him walk away from me again! I don't want to confuse his making amends for love and have my heart broken all over again!"

Grace stared at her, speechless. Finally she said, "Wow. Who knew you were so complicated."

"What am I going to do?"

"Go to dinner. Have a conversation."

"I just don't know what to say!"

"Talk to him. Tell him the truth. It seemed safer to drive him away than to make up only to watch him walk. Level with him. Be honest for once. Tell him that you're relying on him to also be honest."

"I can't," she said. "I just can't."

"Listen to me, Iris. Do you want to feel this way for another seventeen years? Confused and hopeful and angry and hopeful again? There's only one way to end this. Rip off that Band-Aid! Tell him, as a girl you loved him. You're not a girl anymore — you're a woman. Too old to play games. Too old to pretend. Tell him you need him to promise not to mislead you with stupid gestures. But also tell him he's forgiven for all the misunderstandings and idiocy of youth and he is allowed to let it go and walk away. Seriously, Iris — get it over with."

Iris sniffed. "And then?"

"And then, I can recommend the crab cakes. Nobody makes crab cakes like Cliff's."

Six

Iris dressed with care. She tried to examine her motives honestly and she wasn't sure if she wanted to torture Seth before telling him she was forever done putting up with his mixed messages or if she wanted him to be impressed and tempted. She wore gold slacks that accentuated her long legs. Not shimmering gold but more of a yellow-gold. She had a favorite cowl-necked black sweater that flattered her figure and she added a long gold chain. She risked a great deal by wearing her hair loose, falling to her shoulders. If she got caught in a big wind she'd look like Bozo the Clown with brown hair.

Her confidence restored, she walked into the restaurant and looked around. There was Seth at the bar. He turned, saw her and stood, looking across the bar at her. He smiled.

And right next to him, Troy stood. Also smiling.

Oh, this could be problematic.

Just to be safe, she looked around to see if any other eligible bachelors stood and smiled at her. Thank God, it was only two. But why did it have to be the two men she'd been trying to push away? She was trying so hard to build Troy into a good friend without romantic expectations and to keep Seth from leading her on and hurting her again. They were both making this difficult. She was running out of patience. If Troy had expected a quiet, private romantic dinner, Cliff's was the last place he should have chosen. If Seth wanted yet another round at working things out, he should be worried she might hit him again.

She realized she was just standing there while both men waited.

She moved toward them.

"You look beautiful, Iris," Seth said.

"You sure do," Troy agreed.

"Thank you. You have me at a disadvantage since I don't know who invited me to dinner."

Troy had just opened his mouth when Seth spoke. "You mean you came to meet someone for dinner without knowing who it was? Iris, that can't be safe!"

"In Thunder Point?" she asked. Then she lied. "I assumed it was Troy."

125

That made Troy beam with pleasure. "We have a table ready," he said.

God, it *was* him! Would he never get the message? Iris had a very brief and evil idea. She could act as if she was interested in Troy and see how Seth felt about that but the idea vanished very quickly as she imagined many more weeks of Troy trying to convince her they were meant to be a couple. But it would really serve them both right.

"What a nice surprise, Troy!" she said.

"Day late and a dollar short, as usual," Seth said.

"Huh?" Iris and Troy both said.

"I thought I'd come here after work, maybe eat some crab cakes at the bar or, if I ended up real lucky, I'd run into friends who felt like dinner. But I wouldn't want to intrude on a romantic evening," Seth said.

"It's not romantic," Iris said before she could stop herself. Well, she had to say that. She'd been trying like hell to explain to Troy she wanted to be friends but not lovers. It was beginning to look like she was going to have to do that the painful way. "Troy is a very dear friend, a colleague I depend on. We're not dating." She flushed slightly and couldn't bring herself to look at Troy. If his expression was crestfallen, she might weep

126

on the spot.

"Well, in that case, do you mind if I pull up a chair?" Seth asked, smiling.

"Gee, I don't know. Troy might have something he wants to discuss," Iris said.

"I'll leave you before dessert," Seth said, offering no way out. "Lead the way," he said to Troy. He followed them. "Did you like the apples?" he asked.

She stopped dead in her tracks and looked over her shoulder at him. "What? You gave me apples? There was no note, no card."

Seth maneuvered around them to hold Iris's chair for her. "I was up north over the weekend and it was harvest time. The apples were unreal, weren't they? As big as melons! Sorry, I should've thought of a card."

She sat down and looked between the men. "Cookies? Scarf? Wreath? Horn of plenty?"

"Cookies," Seth admitted. "I thought you'd recognize them. My mom made them. She always made those when we were growing up."

"Scarf, wreath and horn," Troy said, not happy. "Maybe you two can share more childhood stories. I really enjoy those."

Oh, he's asking for it, Iris thought. It was one thing for Troy to try being sweet, another to act proprietary when she'd specifically told him if he didn't stop with the romantic gestures they couldn't even be friends.

Cliff appeared at their table to take drink orders. Iris didn't hesitate. "Chardonnay. And hurry."

The men ordered beer and menus were placed before them.

"So, let me get this right. You were both leaving little gifts on my porch, both of you omitting notes."

"I just forgot," Seth said. "Really, I thought you'd figure it out — especially the cookies."

"I was trying to intrigue you," Troy said. "The dinner invitation was obviously mine. In *my* handwriting."

"It was *printed,*" Iris said in her own defense. And then she began to laugh. "Oh, my God," she said, laughing some more. "Well, here we are," she said, trying to regain her composure.

Seth was smiling but Troy was not.

"What?" she said, looking at Troy. "That was all very nice, Troy, but we're not dating. We've talked about this. We work together." A slight sound came from Seth and she turned to see he was smirking. "And don't you get all superior, because I'm not dating you, either. Although apples and cookies are very neighborly."

Like a man on a mission, Cliff delivered their drinks. When they were all on the table, Iris lifted her glass and toasted them. "To the two very nicest men," she said. "Friends," she emphasized.

Seth looked at Troy sympathetically. "Believe it or not, that's progress. For me, anyway."

Iris half expected Troy to say that in his case, he was backsliding. She sipped her wine but laughed into the glass. These two, both very handsome, sexy men, had no idea that she'd known both of them in the biblical sense. One of them couldn't quite remember it and the other one was remembering it too well.

She studied her menu but she barely saw it. No matter, she knew everything by heart. She was thinking about them. On the surface, there wasn't much that made one more appealing than the other. It was what had happened to her heart that separated them. After making perfectly satisfying love with Troy, she just wasn't swept away. She didn't long for more of him. After making completely *un*satisfying teenage love with Seth, a clumsy and inexperienced lover, she couldn't drive him from her mind for seventeen long years. How was something like that decided by a heart? It certainly wasn't intentional. If she could choose, she would adore Troy and tell Seth to go pound sand. Troy was safer, less complicated, had wanted her since almost the first second he'd laid eyes on her.

Cliff approached their table again and she closed her menu. But Cliff wasn't there to take orders.

"Deputy Sileski," Cliff said formally. "I'm sorry to interrupt, but I have a situation in the bar and it isn't pretty."

"What is it?" Seth asked, getting to his feet.

"Some love triangle thing that started as arguing turned loud and there's been a little physical stuff. Shoving. Struggling. I can call the cook, Ram, out of the kitchen. But since you're here . . ."

Seth walked to the archway that led to the bar and looked at two big guys on either side of a small blonde woman. One brawny man pulled on her left arm, the other pulled on her right arm. "They drunk?" he asked Cliff.

"I only served the guy on the left," he said. "The guy on the right came in just a minute ago, found them, started a scene. I don't know those people, Seth. They're not from around here."

"Did you call Pritkus? He's got the town tonight."

"He's on his way but he's maybe fifteen minutes away."

"Okay. Clear the bar area, then get behind the bar." He turned to Iris. "I'll be right back."

He walked into the bar and approached the two surly men, noting they were both big. He had his backup gun, a pistol, on his ankle, something he never expected to have to use, but it was there. If this had happened anywhere else, he'd wait for local law enforcement. But this was his town. The people here were his friends and he didn't want Cliff to lose any glassware.

"Gentlemen," he said calmly. He showed his badge. "I'm Deputy Sileski and I need you to let go of the lady and step apart. Right now. Ma'am, I'd like you to go over to that table by the window, away from these men, and have a seat."

"She's my wife! She's not going anywhere except home with me!" one of the men said.

"She's separated!" the other yelled. "We're just having dinner here!"

"Please, Carl, stop this," the woman said. "Paul, let go."

"Gentlemen, let go of the lady. *Now!*"

Carl was the one to make the first mistake.

131

"We don't need no goddamn Andy of Mayberry in our business!" he shouted. And then he took a swing at Seth.

Seth grabbed the man's wrist and, in the blink of an eye, twisted Carl's arm behind his back and pinned him to the bar. Seth met the eye of the other man, Paul. "Sir, I want you to sit at that end of the bar," he said, giving his head a tilt. "I don't want you anywhere near the lady. Ma'am, go where I told you to go. Now."

"But we are separated!" she said. "We haven't done anything wrong! And my husband is drunk!"

"This will get sorted out when Deputy Pritkus arrives. For now, everyone go to your corners."

"We've been separated for two days — because I caught the whore doing that bastard," the husband said from his compromised position against the bar.

Seth's phone vibrated in his pocket. "Do not move one muscle," he said to his captive. He glared at the other man, then the woman. "Did I speak a foreign language?" he asked. They separated.

Seth reached into his pocket with one hand, still holding Carl's arm with the other. "Sileski."

"I'm on my way. What've you got?" Pritkus asked.

"Twelve-twenty-nine in the bar, two males and one female," he said, calling it a domestic disturbance. "Light it up, will you? This is pretty inconvenient." Then he slid his phone back into his pocket. He leaned over the captive Carl. "You and I, we're going to walk outside and wait for the deputy on duty."

"No way," Carl said. "I'm taking my wife home and you can go fuck yourself!" He whirled around and hit Seth in the mouth with an elbow. In one fluid move, Seth shoved him back on the bar, facedown, pulling both hands behind him by the wrists. Seth gave a sharp jerk upward, causing Carl to yelp.

The place became very quiet. Seth reached up to his mouth with one finger and came away with blood. "And now you're going to jail." Holding both wrists firmly in one tight grasp, he reached down and pulled his gun out of the ankle holster and slid it into his belt at the small of his back. He straightened and looked at the man who was called Paul. "Do you want to go to jail, too?"

Paul, whose eyes had become very large, shook his head slowly.

"Good decision. I want you to put your hands on the top of your head and precede me out of the restaurant. Give me six feet so I can see every move you make and if you run, I'm just going to shoot you. I am not getting hurt in this ridiculous nonsense. Do we understand each other?"

The man stood and put his hands on the top of his head. "Like this?" he asked politely.

"That's very good, Paul. After you."

Seth straightened his suspect with a jerk on the back of his collar and by pushing up on his arms at the same time. "Behave yourself, Carl, or you're history."

Paul, very creative, used his butt to open the exit door. Seth used Carl. Once outside in the cold October night Seth directed Paul to his truck. "I want you to put both your hands on the hood and spread your legs."

"Am I in trouble?" Paul asked.

"Yes, but you're not in bad trouble. Yet. Be very careful." Then he opened the passenger door and reached into the storage box that separated the bucket seats and pulled out a pair of handcuffs. He applied one side to Carl's wrist and pulled him to the back of the truck, where he attached the other side to the trailer hitch on his hefty Tacoma. During this process, he watched Paul as best he could. Paul didn't seem to be moving.

Seth left Carl and checked on Paul. "I'm going to pat you down, sir," he said. Before doing so, he took a moment to dab his bleeding lip with his sleeve. All he'd wanted was to keep an eye on Troy and have dinner with Iris. This was pissing him off. "Anything sharp or dangerous in your pockets or on your person?"

"No!"

"Good," he said. "Spread 'em a little more." He ran his hands down Paul's sides, his hips, his legs to his ankles. Then, when he stood he saw the woman standing in the doorway of Cliff's. "You!" he shouted, pointing at her. "You want more trouble? Get back to your assigned seat before I put you in cuffs!" She disappeared.

He turned his attention back to Paul. "Fortunately for you, I don't have a second pair of cuffs. But you ruined my dinner and I'm pissed. Next time you want to date out of town so the husband doesn't see you, stay out of my town. Are we clear?"

"Yes, sir," Paul said contritely.

"Are you going to stay right here, hands on the hood and hope you don't go to jail or are you going to mess it up?"

"I'm staying," he said.

"Good decision. I hate shooting people. So much paperwork."

Seth went to Carl, who was bent slightly as he was attached to the trailer hitch. "So, Carl. Do you have weapons? Sharp objects? Anything that might stick me or hurt me and make me madder?"

"No," he growled.

"Very nice. Put your free hand on the truck, spread your legs." Then he proceeded to pat him down. When he righted himself he stared Carl hard in the eyes. "You are a pain in the ass, Carl. And you're going to jail. You really pissed me off."

"Go to hell," Carl said.

"Probably," Seth said. "But not over you."

Iris didn't wait a whole ten seconds before she dashed to the dining room archway that led to the bar to see what was going on.

"Iris, stay out of it," Troy ordered.

"Shh," she said, leaning around the wall. Of course, she could feel Troy right behind her, not about to be left out. As Iris peeked into the bar, the bar patrons were retreating to the dining room.

Seth was amazing. He wasn't her child-hood buddy anymore, he was a real cop. A real big, strong, handsome cop. He had two and a half agitators, the half being the woman, who wasn't helping things. But Seth clearly knew what he was doing. He was powerful, in fact. And who knew he had that gun? Did he always have that gun, just in case?

She winced when she saw him take an elbow to the mouth, but then she smiled when he secured his prisoner more forcefully, holding that big guy down with one hand. She watched the anger creep up his neck and into his face in a rose-colored stain that made his eyes glitter. And then she saw how he marched his prisoners out the door.

"Wow," she said softly.

"I bet they're method actors," Troy grumbled. "I bet he hired them to show up, create a disturbance and give him a chance to be a hero." He took her elbow to lead her back to their table.

Iris laughed at him. "If you'll recall, he didn't know I'd be here, so he couldn't have done that for me. Maybe he wanted Cliff to think he's a hero?"

Troy shook his napkin and put it on his lap. "I could've done that without bleeding," he grumbled softly.

The bar patrons drifted back into the bar. Some chose to leave. Iris wanted to peek outside to see how Seth was managing those two obnoxious guys, but he would see her and Troy might have a little tantrum. Maybe she could help, she thought with a half smile.

A few minutes later Cliff reported that Seth was still in the parking lot awaiting backup to transport all the naughty people. Cliff also went on and on about how great Seth was, how he didn't think anyone but Mac could do something like that, clear a bar of roughnecks single-handedly, but that Seth was taking this on without complaint, just like Mac would've done. And this sort of thing hardly ever happened, Cliff told them. And, if Seth hadn't been there, Cliff and Ram would have called 911 and tried to get the disturbance out of the bar themselves, so Troy and Iris shouldn't feel like they couldn't have a peaceful meal in the future.

Iris just smiled and ordered a Caesar salad. Troy followed suit and he was very quiet. A little grumpy. She understood completely. This was Troy's big play and he'd been upstaged by a deputy with a limp.

But Iris felt better. After all the worry and tension of the afternoon, it occurred to her that she was stuck with Seth. He wasn't going anywhere. He was going to be around every corner. They were going to be seeing each other no matter how she decided to behave. She could be mad, hold a grudge, refuse to get over her bad high school experience or she could let this play out and find out more about herself and Seth in the process.

Seventeen years. Well, the way she'd been dealing with her feelings hadn't helped her get over it. Or, for that matter, over him. Every time she heard his name, she felt a deep ache. She had never figured out how to move on. And what if she left herself open to him and he hurt her again? That wasn't going to be easier, but neither would it be harder. If he did something awful again, maybe her heart would finally get the message. . . .

Something about a glass of wine and thinking about the situation that way brought peace of mind, even though she had no idea where all this might be headed.

Two salads and a basket of bread arrived. Iris passed the basket to Troy. "Showing up here tonight, not knowing what was going to happen, not knowing where the surprise gifts had come from, was very uncomfortable for me," she said.

"Well, I didn't invite him," Troy replied.

"You know that's not what I'm talking about. Listen to me, please. I'm a pretty sure-footed woman. If my feelings for you change or grow, I'm capable of telling you so. I wouldn't hesitate to call you or ask you out. I know how to be direct. The truth is, I love you like a brother."

He leaned close and whispered, "You have done unspeakable things with your brother!"

She couldn't suppress a laugh and covered her mouth. "Give me a break here, Troy — I was *trying*! I wanted to fall for you! You're the most wonderful guy I know."

He buttered a piece of bread. "So, it just wasn't that good for you, is that it?"

"Don't put words in my mouth. It was wonderful. It wasn't love. It was hard to give up. Now stop screwing with me — you're only thirty, you're gorgeous, you're fun, you've had plenty of relationships that didn't last forever and you probably ended the majority of them. Not because there was anything wrong with the girls but because it just wasn't everything. In fact, I bet you ended a lot of relationships because she was way more into you than you were into her, and you can't let that happen. That's dishonest. Wrong."

"That's it, then?"

"Troy, what would you suggest?"

"We could keep going, see if it becomes better than perfect, because to me it was pretty perfect. . . ."

"I don't want that with you," she said.

"Why not?"

She put down her fork. "Because I really care about you, that's why. Because I really want to have you in my life for a long time. Friends with benefits?" She shook her head. "I'm not saying I'm too good for that sort of thing. But I wouldn't do that with you, Troy. I wouldn't use you like that. Not if I hope to have you as a good friend forever."

"I'm available to be used," he said.

She smiled at him. He was joking, she knew. She hoped.

"No," she said.

"Could you do that with him? Seth?"

She shook her head. "Never," she said. "I'd like to be your friend, but if we can't, we can't. Please say we can."

"We can," he said. "It would be easier without Deputy Dawg around, showing off."

She laughed again and concentrated on her salad. "Can I keep the scarf? I love the scarf."

"You could give me a lot of gifts," he suggested. "I'd be much more gracious."

They got back to their comfort zone, joking, laughing together, though Iris knew nothing would change his feelings. At least not right away.

They ordered crab cakes and while Iris really wanted to know what was happening with Seth, she didn't say so.

It was at least half an hour before Seth came back into the restaurant, holding a cloth-encased ice cube to his lower lip. The patrons clapped for him and he gave them a slight nod but went straight to Iris and Troy's table. A fresh beer was delivered and his old, warm and now stale beer removed.

"Let me see it," Iris said. He lowered the ice cube. "Ew. Ouch," she said.

"I've been slugged more since I came back to Thunder Point than in the past five years. In fact, I've been slugged more when I'm with you than at any other time."

"Really, I had nothing to do with the bar brawl," she said in her own defense. "You might need a stitch or two there."

"Seriously," Troy said. "You should go to an E.R. or something."

"It'll be fine," he said, taking a drink from his cold beer. He winced.

"In fact, you might want a plastic surgeon to look at that," Iris suggested.

"Why?"

"It could leave a miserable scar," she said.

He put down his beer and stared at her. "Iris, I have a three-inch scar on my cheek. What difference is it going to make?"

"Well, that scar really doesn't look too bad, you know. It's kind of, I don't know, manly or something."

He raised one eyebrow at her.

"I think it's ugly. You should get someone to look at it," Troy said. "It could put off women."

"Nonsense," Iris disagreed. "But, like with tattoos, you can go too far."

"Don't you like tattoos?" Seth asked.

"Oh, the right tattoo in the right place works for me," she said. "But when a person starts to look like a comic book, it's a little too much. Don't you think?"

He smiled but only slightly. "I have no real opinion about tattoos, unless they're prison tats. It comes in handy to know one when you see one."

"How long have you been a police officer?" Troy asked.

"Seven years."

"I thought it was longer," Iris said.

He shook his head. "I tested every time they opened testing for new hires, which wasn't that often. I wasn't hired the first three times."

"Did you have trouble with the testing?" she asked.

"No, I did all right. But despite doing all right, I have a slight disability. One leg is a little shorter than the other and sometimes I limp even with a lift in my shoe. I can stiffen up, but not badly. It doesn't hold me back. Even though I passed the written and physical tests, they didn't hire me. I think they finally took me on just to get rid of me. I was like a bad penny. I just wouldn't quit."

"Is that a fact?" Troy said, earning a glare from Iris.

"Was it hard? The testing?" she asked.

"Very hard. I studied and trained. For four years. After getting my degree."

"Did you always want to be a cop?"

"No," he said. "I always wanted to be a football player. After that was no longer possible I got very interested in police work. But it took a lot to convince them I wouldn't be a handicap. Hell, there are fat guys in the department that I could catch standing still."

It was very hard to imagine that his father didn't admire that. But right now she was looking at his lip, which had split open again. "Um," she said, pointing. He dabbed. "I think we should at least call Scott Grant, ask him to have a look. Maybe put a butterfly bandage on it."

"We?" he said.

"Well, since we're all having dinner together . . ."

"He can take care of his own lip, Iris,"

Troy said irritably.

"I'm an expert with butterflies. Besides, I want food," Seth said.

"Well, I can recommend the crab cakes, but they're a little spicy," Troy said. "You might want to go with something bland. Maybe pureed foods." He touched his lower lip for emphasis. "Clam chowder is pretty easy to eat."

"Are you being nice to me because I got slugged?"

Troy shook his head. "I was just being thoughtful. I get that way when people bleed in front of me."

Seth dabbed his lip again. "If you'd rather I just leave, I understand," he said.

"Oh, by all means, eat. If that's what you want to do," Troy said.

Seth stubbornly ordered a bowl of clam chowder and crab cakes. But it wasn't easy. The hot chowder made him wince and when he took a bite of bread, he left blood on it. "Fuck," he said, looking at the red-stained piece of bread he put back on the plate.

"You're bleeding on the bread, man," Troy said, barely hiding the pleasure in his voice.

"Yeah, that must hurt," Iris said. She got out her cell phone and dialed Scott.

"What are you doing?" Seth and Troy both asked.

"I'm going to help you, Seth. Because you can't help yourself." Then she spoke into the phone. "Scott? Can you hear me? Where are you?" There was a lot of crowd noise in the background.

"I'm in Bandon with the team," he yelled into the phone.

"I didn't know you went with them to away games," she said.

"Is this better?" Scott asked. "I put my jacket over my head."

"Much better. But I guess you're unavailable."

"Peyton's in Thunder Point," he said, speaking of his physician's assistant. "She's babysitting my kids, but that's okay. They're portable. What's up?"

"Well, I'm out to dinner with Seth and he had to break up a fight at Cliff's and got a split lip."

"Can you keep your voice down? Please?" Seth asked.

"Oh, sure," she said. "So, I think it might need a stitch or two. It won't stop bleeding. Not exactly hemorrhaging, but it's kind of a big cut. He's . . . uh . . . bleeding on his dinner."

"No problem. I'll call Peyton and ask her

146

to meet you at the clinic. When can you be there?"

"Fifteen minutes?"

"That'll work. She's good with stitches."

"That's great, Scott. Thanks. Oh — what's the score?"

"Twenty-one — fourteen, us! And it's their homecoming."

She laughed. "Way to go, Thunder Point!" When she disconnected, it seemed that all eyes were on her. "Twenty-one — fourteen, Thunder Point," she said to the dining room. A bunch of pleased sighs and soft laughter answered her. She smiled at Seth.

"I don't want stitches."

"Maybe she'll say you don't need any," Troy said.

"No, she won't. Doctors never do that. They love to cut and sew."

"Just a couple, Seth," Iris said.

"I hate needles." His voice was quiet. And very grumpy.

"That figures," Troy said.

"After all you've been through? After all those surgeries? You're afraid of needles?" Iris asked.

"I'm not afraid! I said I hate them! And why do you suppose I do? Could it be the number of times I've been stuck?"

"Well, don't worry. I'll be with you.

Peyton is very gentle and very nice. And if you start to feel weird, you can lie down and close your eyes." She looked at Troy. "Troy will come, too. We'll lend moral support."

"As fun as that sounds, I think I'm done here," Troy said. "I'm sure the two of you will be fine. I'm going to stay and finish my beer. Don't worry, I'll take care of dinner."

"Don't be ridiculous," Seth said. He raised his hand to flag a waiter. "You know what, Iris? You've always been very bossy."

"Oh, Seth, I don't think that's true."

He asked the waiter for the check and the young man shook his head. "Cliff says there's no check for this table tonight, Deputy. We appreciate the help."

Troy sat back and sipped his beer. "So, there *is* an advantage to sharing my date with you."

"Yeah, well let's not make it a habit, okay?" Seth stood and dug into his pocket. He fished a twenty out of his wallet and handed it to the waiter. "Tell him thanks, and here's a little something for the tip bucket."

Then with his ice on his lip, he escorted Iris out of the restaurant.

"Are you going to be good and follow me to the clinic?" she asked.

"What if I just drive out of town?" he asked.

"I'll call your mother," she threatened.

"You know, Iris, I had hoped to use this lip tonight. . . ."

"Well, get over it, Seth. You didn't have a hope of using it on me, so drive to the clinic and I'll be right behind you. Then you can go home, where I hope you have some ice cream."

SEVEN

Peyton's car sat in front of the clinic — she'd beat them. The lights were on and the door was unlocked when they arrived. "Oh, boy, I bet that hurt. Do you have any loose teeth?" were her words of greeting.

"No," Seth said.

"Well, if they don't get punched out, they'll usually tighten back up. Come on back. Iris, will you lock that door, please? And we'll leave the Closed sign as it is."

Seth followed Peyton and Iris followed Seth. Peyton led them to a room, the largest patient room, where there was an exam table, a sink and a cupboard that reached from floor to ceiling stuffed with supplies. It also came with two little kids in their pajamas. The boy was sitting on the doctor's stool and the little girl was on the only chair in the room.

"Will and Jenny, what are you two doing in here?" Peyton asked. "You're supposed to be in the lunch room."

"Can we watch?" Jenny asked.

"If we're quiet?" Will added.

"I don't know," she said, looking at Seth. He shrugged.

"Okay. Seth, sit on the table for me. This isn't going to take much. Or long. You'll be done in ten minutes." She put on a pair of rubber gloves and touched the laceration. "Not too bad. But it definitely needs a few stitches. Maybe five or six . . ."

"Six?" he asked loudly.

"Here's what I'm going to do. I'm going to clean it — just a little Betadine, a surgical disinfectant. Then I'll put a couple of stitches on the inside where your teeth cut it and then a couple outside on your lip and skin. That way the wound won't heal on top first and leave scar tissue underneath that will give your lower lip a misshapen look. A lump. You don't want to look like you're pouting for the rest of your life."

"I don't care," he said, clearly pouting.

Iris crossed her arms over her chest and stared at him. She was sending him a message not to be juvenile, but she had no confidence he was receiving it. Men were all alike in so many ways — he could take on a couple of big men who wouldn't mind beating him to a pulp, but the idea of a few little stitches had him running scared.

Peyton put a drape around Seth and swabbed his lips with brownish-red liquid. Then she drew a syringe and Seth went completely pale. Iris wasn't the only one who saw it. Everyone saw it.

"I'm just going to numb it," Peyton said.

"Just a little stick," Jenny said.

"Like a mosquito bite," Will said.

"You know what?" Peyton said. "I'll have a better angle if you lie down here. Go ahead, just lie down." While she was talking, she was holding the syringe behind her back. She eased him back and suddenly snaked the syringe out. Holding his head down with one hand, she gave him a little stick with the other.

"Ouch!" he said.

She gave him two more sticks in a rapid movement, then pulled his lip out and gave him two more before he could complain. She put the syringe on a tray. "You'll be out of here in a few minutes," she said. Opening a sterile package containing her materials, she picked up a hemostat and touched Seth's lip. "How is it? You feel that?"

"Feel what?"

"Never mind. If you'll just be still for another minute . . ." She picked up a curved needle with the hemostat and stitched —

one, two, three — on the inside of his lip. She knotted and cut. Then one, two, three on the outside, knotted and cut. A small bandage was applied, she snapped off her latex gloves, all her accoutrements were tossed on the tray and covered with the drape that had protected his shirt. "You can remove that bandage in the morning. Be careful shaving. Come in and get the stitches out in seven to ten days. You're good," she said. Almost as an afterthought, she touched the scar on his cheek. "Whoever did this did a beautiful job."

Seth sat up. "Considering the EMT said he could see my molars through my cheek, not bad, huh?"

Will was standing in front of Seth, holding out a lollipop.

"A parting gift?" Seth asked.

"You get candy if you get through it," Will said.

"Do you need help cleaning up?" Iris asked. "Or locking up?"

"No, I'm fine. It won't take five minutes. Then the kids and I are going to go home, finish our movie and they're going to bed," Peyton said.

"Thanks for opening up," Seth said.

"Aw, you'd do the same for me," she replied.

Iris and Seth stood on the sidewalk outside the clinic. "You were very brave," Iris said. Then she laughed.

Seth just unwrapped the lollipop and stuck it in his mouth. "I had higher hopes for this evening."

"It couldn't possibly have been more entertaining," she said. "I'll take you out for ice cream. Come on. If we go back to Cliff's, we can probably have it for free."

"I'm not going back there." He looked at his watch. "McDonald's is still open. Let's go there. We can eat it in the car. You drive."

"All right, that's not too much to ask," Iris said. "Then I'll drop you here to pick up your truck. And, Deputy, be sure to mind your manners or we'll be putting stitches in the other side of your mouth."

"Do I look crazy? I don't want to tangle with any more scary people tonight."

After going through the drive-through, Iris and Seth sat in the McDonald's parking lot with their soft ice cream. He had vanilla. She had vanilla with chocolate, strawberry, sprinkles and whipped cream. Since the football game was out of town, the parking lot wasn't crowded.

"Troy was hoping for an evening alone with you," Seth said.

"Nah," she said.

"He was. I screwed up his plans."

"At great cost," she said. "Why did you come back here?"

"Here?"

"Thunder Point," she clarified.

"Besides the fact that it's home? Well, there's lots of unfinished business."

"Me? Am I some of your unfinished business?"

"Definitely, but I had no idea how unfinished it was until the day I cut your grass. Another reason is my father. He's seventy-two and he's not mellowing. Just the opposite, I think. He's still angry with me, too, but the reasons are entirely different. I really want my father to let go of that if he can, for my mother's sake. It makes her so unhappy, having Norm resist me and act hostile toward me the way he does."

"I don't understand why he's so angry."

"Because he thinks I had the world by the balls and threw it away by getting in that wreck. Norm was really disappointed — he expected so much more from me. When I left Thunder Point for college, the whole town was proud of me. I had a great freshman year, short-listed for the Heisman, ending with a pro contract. I don't think it ever occurred to my dad that just because I was a good football player in high school and my one year of college, there was no guarantee I'd perform in the NFL. Hell, I might've wrecked my knee or my head in my first season. It's a risky game."

"You also could've been hit by a bus in Seattle. Then would he be mad?"

"Probably. I've tried letting it be Norm's problem, but I don't think it's good for him and I know it isn't good for my mom. My brothers have had about enough, too. Norm doesn't make family gatherings very soothing. I'll do what I can with him. I realize there might be nothing I can do."

"But you're going to try."

"I'm going to try," Seth affirmed. "I love my father. I don't enjoy his company very often, but he's my father. And the pain in my ass."

That made her laugh for a moment, but she grew serious. "What about Sassy? More unfinished business?"

"Seriously?" he asked, stunned. "Iris, I didn't even know Sassy still lived here."

"I think she left and came back more than once. She was done with this one-horse town."

"I had no idea she'd married Robbie Delaney," he said. "I just found that out since coming back!"

"Twice," Iris said. "I'm not sure of any of the details. We've never been friends. But she married him for a short time when they were real young, got divorced, married him again, got divorced again. I think there was another husband in there somewhere, but I'm not sure. I did see you talking to her down on the field at the last football game. . . ."

"She found me," he said. "I tend to stand out these days. Especially in uniform."

"You didn't look particularly annoyed," she pointed out.

"I'm the town cop," he said, spooning ice cream past his stitches. "I'm going to do my best not to look annoyed no matter who talks to me, no matter how annoying they are. But I did tell her that I'm not going out with her for any reason, not to catch up, not for coffee, not for anything."

"She *did* ask you out!"

"Iris, I haven't given Sassy a second of thought since high school. We dated for a few months in high school, I remember it as mostly horrible."

"So do I," she said in a fairly quiet voice. She cleared her throat. "She's not fat and she's not missing a tooth in front."

He grinned. "That put me in a bad spot," he said. "The first time I ran into her was at

157

Cliff's, at the bar. I was meeting Mac and she was picking up some takeout. I couldn't drive the image you'd painted of her out of my mind and I couldn't stop laughing. She accused me of laughing at her and stomped off. It was embarrassing," he said, laughing, rubbing his eyes. When he looked up, he found Iris smiling. "I mean, hell, she does have pink hair. And she dresses like she's still in high school."

"Sorry," she said.

"No, you're not. You always liked getting me into trouble."

"Not that much. Why are you bringing me gifts, leaving them on my doorstep?"

He lifted his spoon of ice cream. "I'm warming you up. I made a lot of mistakes and I get it, but, Iris, you're chilly. And so fucking unforgiving."

"I forgive you," she said. "Now stop."

"I'll stop when I'm convinced," he said. "Besides, I didn't do as much of that as Troy did. I'm going to show you I'm not that kid anymore. I'm going to get you back."

"You can't talk to me that way, Seth," she said seriously. "You can't. You have to stop it. You're going to hurt me."

"I'm not going to hurt you," he said. "You're going to trust me again."

"And when you have a change of heart?

Walk away and can't remember what happened or . . . or who I *am*? When you get another bout of amnesia?"

He was shaking his head. "You have no idea how much that loss of memory haunts me because I always wanted that to —" He stopped. "Listen . . ."

"Stop," she said. She turned toward him, holding her ice cream. "I have a couple of things to say. Things that need saying." She took a breath. "Seth, I was just a girl. I've since become an expert on girls and let me tell you, they don't get over things like that easily. I didn't get over it easily. I'm ready to accept your apology, ready to move on, ready to say it's finally in the past and go forward. I'm all grown up now, but I'm no better at being used or treated like crap. Do you hear me, Seth? Because if you mess with my feelings again, there's no guarantee I'll let it go. No simple apology is going to make it go away. In fact, we could become sworn enemies."

He was quiet for a moment. "I know, Iris, and I wouldn't blame you. I never would have deliberately hurt you in the first place. I sure won't in the second place."

"Good. Be careful, then."

"I promise."

"No monkey business," she said, taking a

big mouthful of ice cream.

"We'll just go to dinner one night. Not in Thunder Point," he suggested.

"No," she said. "That would be monkey business."

"No, it would be dinner," he said. "You had dinner with Troy. A friendly, non-romantic dinner . . ."

"Troy is different."

"Troy can give you gifts but I can't?"

"That's right, you know why? Because Troy didn't steal my virginity and break my heart and Troy is a colleague and friend. We have an *adult* relationship."

"Troy loves you," Seth said.

"Now you're being ridiculous," she said. "I have an understanding with Troy."

"Oh?" he asked. "Friends with benefits?"

"Ack," she said, punching him in the arm. "I don't have benefits with anyone!"

He rubbed his arm. "That's encouraging," he said. "What is it about me that makes you want to hit me?"

She shook her head. "I don't know. I'm not like this with anyone else. I think when I'm around you I regress to my eight-year-old self."

"Try to get a handle on that, will you? You're stronger than you look."

"I could've helped you tonight, you know,"

she said, grinning suddenly. "I could've taken one of the men and held him while you managed the other one. We did it back in the day. Playground justice — we stood up for each other."

"We were really young then, Iris. I don't want you to defend my honor anymore. And I'd like you to stop slugging me!"

"You were so scrappy, but I could take you," she said. "It's good that you gave Keith Urban his haircut back, though."

"Do you really want to bring up the subject of hair, Miss Brillo?"

"Now see, I could be damaged for life from careless comments like that!" But she laughed very happily. "You really did look like a wild child. Some throwback rescued from a jungle or something with your long golden hair when everyone else had buzz cuts . . ."

"My mother loved my hair," he said. "By the way, you can't take me anymore so stop slugging me!"

"You did good tonight, Seth. I watched from the dining room."

"Watched me take one in the face?" he asked.

"It was just an elbow," she said. "Kind of an accident. You managed very well. It was impressive, actually. I think you actually grew after high school. How tall are you, anyway?"

He stared at her. "Six-one and six-two, depending which leg I'm standing on," he said, raising a tawny brow.

And she melted into laughter.

They sat in the parking lot and laughed like fools. The ice cream was long gone or long melted when Iris took him back to his truck parked in front of the clinic.

On Saturday Grace was busy with weddings so Iris didn't even have time to report in that the Friday night confrontation had been beyond interesting. Then Seth called on Sunday morning. He had a most charming lisp that left her struggling not to laugh. "Can we try dinner pleath? Maybe out of town where no one knowth uth? Like Cooth Bay?"

She held her hand over her mouth for a moment. "How is your lip?" she managed to croak out.

"Ith fat. What about dinner?"

"Sure. In a couple of weeks. I'm not going to make this real easy for you, Seth. I'm pretty wary."

"I gueth I don't blame you."

She crumbled into hysterical laughter. In fact, every time she thought about him all

162

weekend she smiled. Sometimes she just laughed out loud. From the grumpy way he insisted on eating even though he was bleeding on his bread, to his fear of needles to finally saying a nice good-night after ice cream — it all reminded her how much she had missed his company. But she was determined to guard her heart. He'd ripped it out once, she wasn't going to help him do it again.

But she was still smiling on Monday morning even though it was chilly and wet with a steady drizzle under gray clouds. She wouldn't be riding her bike to school many more days this year. It was definitely a driving day.

She stood in the hallway outside her office doorway, smiling and saying good morning to the kids. This was where she felt at home; this was where she knew she belonged.

Rachel Delaney walked by and said good morning. She had a fat lip, too. Not unlike Seth's, except she was fortunate enough not to have stitches.

Iris snagged Rachel's sweater. "Hey, how's it going?" she asked.

Rachel smiled a lopsided smile, her hand going self-consciously to her mouth. "It's all good, Miss McKinley."

"Got a boo-boo?" Iris asked, looking at her lip.

Rachel chuckled. "Blame Cammie. We were working on a few cheers and moves over the weekend and I took a knee to the face. Pretty gross, huh? I guess it could'a been worse. She could'a broken my nose!"

"I hope that particular move is out of the routine now," Iris said.

"I think we can get it," Rachel said. "But I think I'll be the jumper and not the catcher next time." She tried her smile again.

Brett Davis sauntered toward Rachel, his eyes all sleepy and sexy. He came up behind her and slipped his arm through hers. "Morning, Miss McKinley."

"How's it going, Brett?" she asked. Unless she'd missed some breaking news, Brett was the big man on campus. He was a popular football player in a town where football was king. He was a year older than Rachel. They looked so perfect together, a regular Barbie and Ken, but they were sexy. Iris knew all about this yet would never get used to it, these children filled with heat and phero-mones.

"Good, good. We killed Franklin High in Bandon Friday night," Brett said.

"I heard. Congratulations!"

"Thanks, it was awesome."

Then he led his girlfriend away down the hall, affectionately nuzzling her temple, slipping his arm around her waist. He was very like Seth had been — polite, good-looking, attentive. As far as Iris could see from her close watch on the academics of the team, he was also a good student. She wondered if Rachel helped him with his homework the way Iris had helped Seth.

Rachel seemed very good-natured and kind, and Iris had been watching. Her mother, Sassy, had been conceited and superior, dismissive of girls she deemed lesser and only interested in having a large collection of boys. Rachel hadn't seemed to inherit that — points to Sassy for raising her well.

Iris stood in the hall until the bell rang. Then she tackled her desk. Each year in the fall, seniors were looking at colleges, at scholarships — sports and academic and those based on financial assistance — while Iris was scheduling testing. The sophomores and juniors were taking their first stab at SATs while seniors who hadn't done well were trying one last time. She had prep classes scheduled. She was meeting with students in large groups to take aptitude quizzes to help them decide on a study path. There were college applications and selection for seniors. Besides graduation, this was the busiest time of year.

At midmorning, Troy stood in her doorway. "Got a minute?"

She looked up. "Of course."

"She has a fat lip," he said.

Iris smiled at Troy. There were few teachers who cared as much about every student as he did. He tried to convince his friends in town that he got a teaching degree because it was easy and that his real interest was in recreation, as much as he could fit in, his choices being particularly expensive. But Iris considered him an überteacher. He was excellent in absolutely every aspect.

"I spoke to Rachel this morning. She explained it as a cheer practice accident. She was trying out a new routine with her friend Cammie. Some kind of lift or throw or something and Cammie's knee hit her mouth. Sounds reasonable."

"Uh-huh. She seems to have one of those accidents every other week or so."

"They're kids, Troy. They're careless sometimes. Do you notice other things? Depression? Isolation? A lack of freedom from home — like not being allowed out with friends or not being allowed to attend school events? Anything?"

"Not yet," he said. "I smell an ill wind."

"I'm watching. And I appreciate that you're watching, too. I asked the gym teacher to keep an eye — they're stripped down pretty much in their little gym uniforms and if there are lots of bruises, she'll see them. But so far she says all looks normal to her."

"Don't stop the watch, please," he said. Then he pulled a piece of paper out of his pocket and handed it to her. The name Misty Rosario was written on a spare hall pass. "Do you know Misty?" he asked.

"I know who she is but I don't believe we've had much interaction."

"She's a sophomore. I have only one sophomore class and they're a pain in the ass, mostly. But Misty has been a delight. She's very smart. I suggested she sign up to take the SAT or ACT early just to get a feel for it while there's plenty of time to take the prep course and maybe retest next year. She said she won't be taking the test. She's also become very quiet and sad just lately. I tried to talk to her but I have to be very careful."

"Of course," Iris said.

"She's a fifteen-year-old girl," he added, though no explanation was necessary. Troy couldn't and shouldn't speak to her privately, it could suggest impropriety. "But I can send her to you so you can ask her why she isn't interested in the college entrance test. And maybe figure out why she's sad."

"Sad, awkward, unhappy, self-conscious, nervous, afraid, lonely . . ." Iris ran down the list. "Don't those words describe the majority of teenage girls?"

"On some days all teenagers act out those emotions," he said. "But with Misty it's most days. I almost never see her laugh anymore. She walks alone to class."

"Why don't you tell me what you suspect and cut right to the chase," Iris said.

He shook his head and shrugged. "I wonder if she's being picked on. I haven't seen anything suspicious, but these days school isn't always where it happens anymore. It could be on the internet. Of course, it could be other matters — illness in the family, economic issues, her own health. It's not academic, that's for sure. She's very smart. But she's different."

"Different how?"

"Withdrawn but not shy. Sad but not morbidly depressed. Her history class is full of troublemakers, which is how I have them all, I think. Many of them are older than Misty. But she'll answer questions confidently without so much as a blush. She'll talk to other students but stays alone. Frankly, she acts like someone who's keeping her brain tumor secret from the world."

"Send her to me," Iris said. "Tell her I want to discuss the SAT with her. In the meantime, I'll pull up her transcript. And we'll go from there."

"Will you tell me what you find?" he asked.

She smiled at him. "Maybe. It depends."

"Wanna grab a beer after work?" he asked.

"Jeez, it's only Monday!"

"I'm not working at Cooper's tonight. I don't have many of those nights."

"Okay then. Where? The beach?"

"Nah, it's too cold and wet to sit on the deck. Let's meet at Cliff's."

She'd been putting in a lot of time at Cliffhanger's lately. "You're on. Five?"

"Four-thirty, c'mon. I'm going to be so ready to be out of here by four, but I can hang out and clean chalkboards for a little while."

"All right," she said with a laugh. "See you there."

And he was gone.

In a little town like Thunder Point, great teachers were hard to come by. The pay was on the low side because the budget was small and the town didn't offer much beyond rugged coastline and quiet neighbors. And yet, they had some excellent, dedicated educators. Troy was one of the best. He'd taught junior high math for a couple of years in a private school, but he was a history major and had taken the Thunder Point job a couple of years ago. For a young guy, he was pretty worldly and seemed to know all the tricks and signs with the high school kids. He was devoted to them; he never missed a thing. When they were talking about the students, they were completely in tune.

Why couldn't she love him? It would be so much less complicated. She was quite sure Seth was right — Troy loved her. He could be an excellent partner given a little encouragement.

But, curse the luck, she was still stuck on the guy who broke her heart years ago.

EIGHT

Misty Morning Rosario was a very small, thin, flat-chested fifteen-year-old. Unsmiling, as she was at the moment, she wasn't very pretty. Iris had to concentrate to keep herself from making assumptions about what her issues might be.

"I bet everyone asks you about your name," Iris said.

"Am I in trouble?" Misty asked.

"Oh, gosh, no. Not at all. Are you worried about something?"

Misty just shook her head. When Iris held silent for a minute, Misty finally answered, "It's supposed to be Misty M. on my school paperwork. My parents, they were kind of hippies or something and I was born on — guess what? A misty morning. Could you think of anything more lame?"

"Well, my mother was a florist and named me Iris. I think I've finally made peace with it but growing up, I hated it. You know what really surprised me? Even girls who had regular names confessed to hating them! I think every twelve- or thirteen-year-old girl has fantasies about changing her name."

"Really?" she asked.

"Even the girls named Kate and Mary and Sue," Iris said. "How long have you lived in Thunder Point, Misty?"

"Two years, I guess. Since the start of eighth grade."

"You've had such good grades. Are you the oldest child in your family?"

She nodded. "I have a little brother. His grades aren't as good because he's a screw-off."

Iris laughed and could see Misty beginning to relax. "Did you know that most firstborn children are the most accomplished, especially academically? They show the most leadership skills, which I guess should be obvious." They talked for a while about the deli Misty's parents owned and operated in Bandon. It was bigger than Carrie's deli and had tables for diners. Misty helped out on the weekends. Her dad was Portuguese and a lot of their deli items were his family recipes. They talked about everything Iris could think of — dogs, grandparents, babysitting.

"I was asking Mr. Headly about you

earlier today. He mentioned that your grades are so good that he suggested taking the SAT this year and you . . ."

Misty's eyes went downcast. She shrugged and clutched her hands in her lap.

"What is it, Misty? What worries you? You're bound to do well. And depending on your score, you could retake it next year after a prep course and really kill it. Or, if the results are excellent, you could let it stand."

She just shrugged again.

"Let's talk about college, Misty. Are you worried about the cost? About leaving home? About college studies being harder?"

"I'm just not very interested in college," she said softly.

"I'm so surprised. But that's not a decision you have to make now. In fact, you don't even have to decide next year. More to the point, since college isn't required, you can decide at any point that it's not right for you. But it makes sense to be prepared in case you decide to give it a try."

"It doesn't feel right now," she said.

"It probably seems a long way off," Iris said. "Misty, will you look at me?" Iris asked gently.

Misty lifted her eyes and Iris was not surprised to see she was near tears. Oh, Troy was right. Something was wrong. "What's bothering you, honey?" Iris asked. "You can say anything in this office and it will go no further."

"Not even to Mr. Headly?" she asked softly.

"Especially not Mr. Headly," she said. "Just you and me."

"You won't get it," Misty said.

"Oh, I don't know. I've been a counselor for a while now. There isn't much I haven't heard. Plus, I bet I had some of the same worries when I was your age."

The girl hesitated a long moment, contemplating by chewing on her lower lip. And then she spoke. "I'll just be alone," she whispered. "Why should I go away to a big school just to be alone?"

Iris was completely surprised by this. "Why would you be alone?"

Yet another self-conscious shrug. "I won't have any friends."

"How can you be sure of that?" Iris asked.

"You ever had a best friend?" Misty asked. Iris nodded. "Sure."

"You ever have a best friend drop you?"

"Well, as a matter of fact, I have. It's very painful. Is that what happened, Misty?"

She nodded and her eyes filled with tears. It was a miracle they weren't flooding over.

"My best friend since eighth grade got a better friend. And they don't like me."

"Misty, are you being bullied? Picked on?" Iris asked. "It's okay to tell me."

She shook her head. "She . . . Stephanie . . . was my best friend. I mean, we liked other friends, but she was my best friend. For like two years. Now she's Tiff's best friend and I'm out. She does everything with Tiff — we don't even talk on the phone or text anymore. They sit together at lunch, assembly, games. If I just show up and sit by them, they talk and laugh and ignore me. They do things together after school and I'm not invited."

Iris frowned. "Do they say or do mean things?"

"Sometimes Tiff does and if she does Stephanie tells her to stop it, but she still wants to be Tiff's friend and my ex-friend. It just sucks. I'll get over it, I guess, but it just sucks."

"Because it hurts," Iris said. "I'm sorry. I don't know why three never works, but it seems to never work. Is that why you aren't interested in the SAT?"

"Pretty much. My mom says to just get over it, that I deserve better friends, that in five years I won't even remember it."

"Well, your mom could be right, but just

getting over things isn't exactly easy. That takes time. I understand completely. You might change your mind about friends and college and SATs, if not this year, maybe next year."

"I don't need another place to not fit in," Misty said. She sniffed and wiped at her eyes. "I have to be honest with myself. I'll never be cool."

Iris pushed the tissue box toward her. "That's not true. You have everything it takes to be well liked. You're a nice person, you're smart, you're considerate."

"I'm the size of an ugly sixth-grader with no boobs."

"Be honest with me, Misty — is there any pushing, shoving, pinching, knocking books out of your arms, chasing you down online, sending mean texts or anything like that? Any bullying?"

She shook her head. "No. Steph is just done with me and Tiff hates me, that's all. If you tell anyone, I will *die.* Because I am *not* a baby!"

Oh, Iris wanted to pull those girls into her office and just slap them senseless. It would never help Misty but Iris knew that if Tiffany was mean, she was probably troubled. Probably insecure. Or maybe spoiled. Or she lived in a home where cruelty was an acceptable way of life. Mean girls. There were always mean girls. They lasted a lifetime.

"I wasn't expecting this at all," Iris said. "And while you're trying to work this out, trying to make new friends, better friends, I actually have a totally unrelated question for you."

"What?"

"Do you have a study hall?"

"Fifth period, right after lunch. Why?"

"Do you need that study hall for schoolwork? Homework?"

"Sometimes I get my homework done in study hall, sometimes I like to read. My classes are all hard — please, I don't want another class."

"No, sir! I looked at your transcripts — you're in accelerated classes, a straight-A student, I might add. I was wondering if you'd like to work in the office during your study hall. Primarily, my office." She indicated the credenza behind her desk — it was stacked with notebooks, papers, folders. "This is material for the SAT prep courses, college requirements, scholarship information — all stuff I'm trying to get ready and keep up with. It needs to be sorted, stapled together, put into the right folders. I have to make sure every student has all the necessary information. Since you're not taking the prep class, would you like to transfer your study hall to my office and give me a hand?"

Misty frowned and looked at Iris with suspicion. "Do you think if I do that you'll convince me to take the test?"

Iris laughed. "I thought if you did that to help me, I might eventually catch up! I need an intern and I don't have one yet. I need another counselor and I don't have one of those, either. I work a lot of nights and weekends and I'd rather read. What are you reading right now?"

She looked away a little shyly. "Some romance called *The Rosie Project* . . ."

"I *loved* that book!" Iris said. "Well, if you're interested I can find space for you, a cubicle at least, and on days you have homework you need to do, just do it. On days you have time to help me, I'll set you up with a project. No pressure — it's your call. But hey, if you're busy ignoring your ex-friend and her new clique, maybe we could help each other out."

Misty thought about this for a moment and finally smiled. "I could maybe try it for a little while, see if it works."

"That would be great. I have two other students helping me — one is a junior and she comes in during second period and the other, a senior, is here sixth period. I think maybe I'm going to be able to solve my intern problem!"

"Are you just being nice to me?"

"*Just?* Oh, please, can't you see I'm drowning? I have other girls to ask if you need to keep your study hall sacred — that's up to you. But, Misty, it's really all right if someone is nice to you. Regardless of how Tiffany and Stephanie have made you feel, you're a very smart, nice person. If I were fifteen again, I think I'd want you for a friend."

"That's nice of you to say, I guess."

"I'm going to show you something private." She opened her desk drawer and pulled out a picture of an extremely homely girl — fuzzy, wild brown hair that had a misshapen look to it, bushy brows, the biggest teeth in the world, thick glasses and a few zits sprinkled on her nose and chin. "Me. Eighth grade."

"Wow," Misty said. "Your hair isn't like that anymore."

"I learned a few things about hair, but that's mine. And I eventually grew into my teeth. I wasn't small, I was large. Taller than all the boys in my class. If that wasn't bad enough, I had two left feet. I'm not what you'd call coordinated. I tried out for cheer-leading one year — it was a catastrophe. Right here at Thunder Point High. The mean girls had a good laugh at that."

"You had mean girls?"

"Misty, mean girls have been around since God was a boy. So have girls like me, who have to grow up, get smarter, make it in a tough world. By the way, there are still mean girls when you're an adult, but with every year it gets a little easier to say, 'You're not a nice enough person for me.' When I went back to my class reunion a few years ago, the mean girls were still there. They were still pretty, still getting lots of attention, still making snide remarks about people. But I was reacquainted with some classmates I hadn't paid much attention to in high school, girls who had gone on to have remarkable careers and had either grown very attractive or had finally developed the confidence they needed to *appear* very attractive. I keep this picture close at hand to remind myself who I was, how far I've come and what all the girls in my school go through at one time or another. It keeps me honest."

"My mom says someday this will be unimportant," Misty said.

"Maybe so," Iris said. "But right now, to

you, it's very important. I'm right here anytime you need to talk about it, do a feelings dump, get it off your chest. . . ."

Misty laughed. "I don't know if I can spare it," she said, looking down at her chest.

"Yeah, you'll be all right. So, do you have time to help me? If you don't think you do, I understand. And if you start and it's just too much, you can stop."

"Yeah, I can probably do it. So, Miss McKinley, when your best friend dropped you, what did you do?"

"Oh, I was pretty miserable for a while. Seemed like it took me a long time to get past it and even when I didn't think about it every day, I still never forgot it. It made me very fussy about friends. I'm cautious — I have no interest in being hurt. It's worked out all right — I've made some wonderful friends."

"Thanks," Misty said. "So you want me tomorrow?"

"I can make that work if you can," she said. "Have you ever been a student assistant before?"

Misty shook her head.

"We have a lot of them in these offices. The school nurse has three. The assistant principal has at least three. There are several in the secretary's office. We're a pretty good team. I don't think we could make it without students."

"And what if Tiffany decides she wants to work in the offices?" Misty asked.

Clever girl, Iris thought. Already looking for potential conflicts and figuring them out. She smiled. "It kind of sounds like Tiffany is too busy to help out."

At four forty-five Iris entered Cliffhanger's and knew that Troy would be there, anxious as he was to be done with work for the day. She ordered a beer and some potato skins. "This might be dinner," she told Troy.

"Works for me. How's Misty?"

"What a delightful young lady. Very mature, isn't she? Not much gets by her. I looked at her grades — no wonder you wanted her to take the SAT. Accelerated classes for years and never gets less than an A."

"So, did you convince her to take the SAT?" he asked.

"No, she's not interested in that right now. Don't worry, she has plenty of time. Not a good idea to pressure a teenager with too many adult responsibilities, especially if they're showing some resistance."

"I saw her last period in the hall. She was

talking to a couple of kids and appeared to be in a very good mood, so what did you do?"

"I just talked to her, didn't hear anything I haven't heard before, reassured her. And then I gave her a job."

"What job?"

"I asked her if she was interested in working for me during her study hall and helping me get through my paper jungle. She seemed interested — she said she'd try it for a while. I assured her if she had studying to do, all she had to do was say so and she could use the time on schoolwork. We have a couple of extra cubicles in the office used by students who are helping out — they sort, file, stuff envelopes, you name it." Her beer arrived. "Misty makes three student helpers for me. I really scored, thanks."

"And that's it? You talked to her and gave her a job?"

"Uh-huh. I think she was flattered. It'll help fill her bucket."

"Huh?"

"You know — the bucket . . ."

"What are you talking about?"

"Well, the elementary school teachers talk about the bucket a lot. Everyone has one. When people say nice things to you, do nice things, make you feel better about yourself, they're filling your bucket. When people are mean or insulting or hurtful in any way, they're emptying your bucket and you don't want to go around with an empty bucket. It makes you sad and cranky. And you don't want to be emptying other peoples' buckets — that also makes you unhappy. The best way is to fill all the buckets you can and keep yours nice and full by looking for positive people and experiences." She smiled.

Troy leaned his elbow on the bar and rested his head in his hand. "What do I have to do to get a job with you?"

"Master's degree in counseling." She took a sip. "Easy peasy. You'd be great."

The weather turned wet and cold at the end of the month, rain washing the colorful leaves off the trees. Iris stood in the hallway outside her office every morning and listened to the kids cough and sneeze and hack as they passed. The homecoming game was held in the rain a week before Halloween and Iris sat in the stands with a plastic tarp over her head like most of the town. Snuggled up beside her was Troy, who kept saying *God bless the rain!* On Saturday night everyone dried off and donned their best clothes for the big dance.

Iris was not surprised to see Seth at the

dance. She figured he would be there, if not in an official capacity then in a semiofficial capacity. He'd had his stitches removed and was wearing a suit rather than his uniform. In fact, there weren't any uniformed police officers at the dance but there were some outside in the parking lot, despite the nasty weather. And now that she knew a little more about the new Seth, she knew about that gun on his ankle.

Iris's job at a school dance was to watch for student problems. She kicked some girls out of the restroom for smoking, confiscated what looked like a flask from a sixteen-year-old boy, stopped an argument between two boys over a girl and did it all without taking a shot to the face. She lifted her chin and gave Seth a very superior smile.

At around ten, a good two hours before these die-hard kids would give up the dance and leave, Seth made his way to her side. "I had my stitches out. Wanna go out for a drink after the dance?"

"Where?" she asked. "Cliff isn't open this late, I'm not going to Waylan's, the beach would be insane in this weather . . . I did confiscate a flask, but even I'm not that daring."

"How about your place?" he asked, grinning.

"Nice try," she said. "Actually, I have a headache."

"Are you just practicing?" he wanted to know.

"I do have a real headache," she said. "Blame the weather and the class of 2015. You think your work is dangerous?"

"How about if I call you tomorrow?" he asked.

"I might not be answering the phone tomorrow. I might need a day to myself. I really do have a headache. Right here," she said, giving her temples a brief massage.

"I could take you home, rub your temples. . . ."

"You're doing it again," she said. "Coming on to me. I thought I explained, I don't really need your bullshit."

"Which is why I'm being careful not to give you any! Sooner or later you're going to trust me again!"

"Later," she said.

Iris was at the high school gym until midnight. She was supposed to be part of the cleanup committee, but she talked Troy into taking that on for her. She bundled up, went home and left her clothes on the floor when she got into her flannels and crawled into bed. At four in the morning she started coughing a little. At six she wheezed and sneezed. At eight o'clock she felt like she had swallowed razor blades so she took Advil and gargled. It went downhill from there.

NINE

Seth called Iris in the early afternoon on Sunday. He got the cell phone number from his mother, officially breaking the rule of not allowing her to be in any way involved in his relationship with his childhood friend. It sent Gwen into a whole series of hopeful flutters. And questions about whether they'd finally been talking again. "Stop," he said. "I just want to ask her something. Not another word about it."

Seth called from his mother's home phone. Of course, her name popped up on Iris's caller ID.

"Iris," he said.

"I'm sick," she croaked out. "Go away." She hung up.

There was no logic to laughing at that, but he did. God, he'd missed her. She was so feisty.

On Monday he called the high school and asked for Ms. McKinley and was told she wasn't in. He called her cell phone at about three in the afternoon. "Still sick," she wheezed. "Flu. Get lost." And she hung up.

Again, he smiled and just shook his head. He went to the pharmacy section of the grocery store, then to Carrie's deli. He loaded up on supplies and told Carrie that Iris was sick and he needed chicken soup. Gwen would have been honored and probably a little too excited to make soup for Iris, so he refused to ask her. "I can drive to the deli in Bandon but I'd rather have yours," he told Carrie.

"Don't you dare feed any of my people Bandon soup!" she nearly roared. She went to the back of the deli and pulled a yellowish brick wrapped in plastic from the freezer. "Just put this in a pan, add a cup of water and put it on a low flame. Here are some biscuits to go with it. How sick is she?"

"I haven't seen her yet," he said. "She attempted to answer her phone a couple of times and it doesn't sound pretty. Maybe you better get some more soup ready — Pritkus called in sick and said two of his three kids are down."

"Oh, dear," Carrie said, turning away from Seth and going to the back again. She returned with another frozen yellowish brick. "Drop this off at the Pritkus house, will you, Seth? Steve's wife is smart and adorable but there is no worse cook on earth. You can't get well out of a can of soup. This is the real thing. I'll get started on a new supply. Sounds like they're dropping like flies out there."

"What do I owe you?" he asked.

"Forget about it. Save as many as you can."

He made a final stop at Pretty Petals and asked for a cheerful bouquet. "For your mother?" Grace asked.

"Not this time," he said. "Iris has the flu."

Grace stepped back with a look of fear on her face. He was surprised she didn't make the sign of the cross. "Tell her I hope she gets better soon and not to come around me until there's not a germ left in her body. If you're smart, you'll leave this on the doorstep."

"I don't scare that easily," he said.

Armed with his supplies, he went to Iris's house.

Of course she wouldn't open her door so he called her from his cell phone. "Open up, Iris. I brought you medicine."

"Go away," she rasped. She hung up.

Risking prison time, he picked the lock on the back door and let himself in. Even though this was Thunder Point, she definitely needed better locks. *Whoa,* he thought, looking around. Iris definitely wasn't sick in a tidy way. The kitchen and dining room were a mess and one peek into the living room exposed a blanket and pillow on the sofa, dirty tissues on the coffee table, floor, side table. There was a small trash can overflowing with tissues and maybe other stuff. And there was a bucket. *A bucket?* This could be worse than he feared. The TV was on though no one was watching it. The dining room table had dirty bowls, juice glasses, more tissues. And then Iris came out of the bedroom. Make that stormed out of the bedroom with her wild hair and plaid flannel pajamas that were buttoned off-kilter. "What are you doing?" she barked. And then she fell into a coughing fit that really sounded like she might not be long for this world. She had to sit on the couch before she could get under control and tears were running down her cheeks. Her red cheeks.

Part of him felt very bad, putting her through that. Part of him was now convinced he'd done the right thing. She needed him.

She looked up at him from the sofa. "What are you doing here?" she whispered.

"I'm going to get you well," he said.

"Please," she begged. "Go away."

Seth put his bags down on the table and pulled out a box. He opened it and extracted a gizmo. A thermometer. It didn't look like a regular thermometer with a silver end and mercury inside. "You don't have a thermometer, do you?" he asked.

"Somewhere," she said with a careless wave of her arm. "Maybe."

He approached her cautiously. "Don't hit. Just look up." He ran the rubber tip over her forehead. She coughed and wheezed while he tended to her and tried not to breathe her air. "Ew," he said. "You have a fever."

"Big shocker," she said.

"You're sick."

"Like I've been telling you for two days."

He leaned closer, listening. "What is that noise? Hear it? Like a motor?"

"What?"

"Do you have a pet? Like a kitten or puppy under your shirt? Purring? Growling?"

"It's my *chest*!" she said, coughing again.

"We might need reinforcements."

"Jesus, Seth, will you just leave me alone? I'm *sick*!"

"You don't have anything in the house to help you get better, do you?"

"Like what?" she asked, and coughed horribly again.

He shook his head. He went to the kitchen, found a puny bottle of Advil. He filled a clean glass with water. "When was the last time you took anything for the fever and stuff?"

"It's been a few hours," she admitted. "All I have is Advil."

"Take this," he said, giving her a cold-and-flu capsule that promised to cure at least seven of the prominent symptoms. "Then go take a very long hot shower — the steam is good. Find clean jammies. You might have to burn those. I'll start your soup and straighten up."

"If you touch my trash, you're going to get the flu."

"I have rubber gloves."

"I so hate you right now."

"By the time I leave you're going to love me."

"Don't count on it."

But she turned and walked away from him. He allowed himself to chuckle very quietly, very carefully. She looked like shit. No one he'd ever known in his life could be quite as appealing and look that bad. Jesus, she might be dying she looked so bad. And he felt so soft toward her right now.

When he heard the water running, he called Scott. "Hey, Doc, I'm at Iris's house. She's got a bad case of the flu with a fever and a nasty cough. I gave her some over-the-counter stuff and I brought Vicks and soup. I wonder if you should check her? Make sure she's just got the flu?"

"Hmm. Maybe. I gave her a flu shot. How high is the fever?" Scott asked.

"One-oh-two and change."

"That's not too good. Let me run a couple more people through here and I'll come over and have a look."

"It's ugly, Doc," Seth said.

"It's never pretty, Seth," Scott replied. "Should I bring anything?"

"All your antibodies."

Before the shower turned off, Seth had searched for clean sheets and got Iris's bedroom in better shape. He wasn't sure it had any effect on curing the flu, but his mother always did that for him when he was a kid and something about getting scrubbed and in clean sheets just worked. He even spread a fresh sheet over her sofa. He started heating the chicken soup and went through the kitchen, dining room and living room, scooping up dirty dishes and trash. He did wear the rubber gloves. Whatever she had, he wanted no part of it.

By the time she came back to the living room in clean pajamas, the place was tidy and a delicious aroma that Iris wouldn't be able to appreciate wafted through the house. She sounded all stuffed up but obviously her nose was dripping, ergo the tissues all over. In fact, he was a little concerned that her red, chapped nose might actually fall off soon.

"Sit down here, Iris," he said. He had poured her a glass of orange juice and put it on the coffee table. He gave her a large spoonful of cough syrup — an expectorant. She made a terrible face and shuddered. He had all his medications lined up on the coffee table. "Don't you have any of this stuff on hand?" he asked.

"I hardly ever catch anything, even though I work in a petri dish and the kids all have something."

"You need this stuff," he said. "Thermometer, cough medicine, cold medicine, decongestant, Advil, et cetera."

"Bag Balm?" she asked, picking up the old-fashioned green tin.

He touched her red nose. "For this. The best."

"I used to have some of this," she said. "I just cleaned the house. Some of the expiration dates on over-the-counter stuff went way back. To grade school."

He chuckled and lifted her feet onto his thighs.

"Now what?" she asked.

"VapoRub," he said, peeling off her sock. "You're going to like this."

"On the feet?"

"Neat trick," he said, gently massaging it into the sole of her foot. He smiled to note her eyes rolled back in her head. "Nice, huh?"

"Ohhh," she agreed.

She flopped back onto the pillow on her couch and just moaned softly, with a rattle in her chest, while he massaged her feet. When he thought he was done, she wiggled a foot to suggest a little more. He laughed and obliged.

"I'll get you some soup. And then —"

There was a knock at the door. "Now what?" she asked.

"Very few possibilities," he said, putting her sock back on her foot. "Either my mother, demanding to know why the deputy is at your house in the middle of the day, or Dr. Grant, whom I called."

"Why'd you call him?"

"Because you're sick. He might have some miracle cure in that little bag of tricks of his."

"I could make do on more VapoRub," she whined.

Seth laughed on his way to the door. Who knew the way to Iris's heart was through her feet. She was playing with fire here, he thought. If she didn't have a completely disgusting virus, he could take complete advantage of her. In fact, he looked forward to it.

"Hey, Scott," he said, when he opened the door.

"Hey, Seth. How's the patient?"

"Very low on gratitude. Why don't you have a look while I dish up some chicken soup."

"I'll do that," Scott said.

While Seth was in the kitchen rummaging around for a bowl, tray, other necessary items, he listened to Scott and Iris. "Bad flu, huh?" Scott asked.

"I think you need higher quality vaccines, Scott. Obviously it didn't work."

"Or maybe it worked and if you hadn't had the flu shot you'd be way sicker."

She coughed and wheezed. "When you get sicker than this, you die."

"I'd like a throat culture, please," the doctor said.

"Just look at it, check out the razor blades. That should be enough." She opened and said, "Ahhh." Then she gagged, which led to more coughing.

"Ick," Scott said. "Try not to breathe on anyone. Absolutely no kissing anyone."

"Look at me," she said. "You know anyone that stupid?"

"I'm not sure," he said. "How invested is the cook?"

"I'm not kissing her," Seth yelled from the kitchen.

"Good," she yelled back. "I wouldn't let you!" And, of course, she coughed.

"Can I listen to your heart and lungs, please?" Scott asked. "Deep breath?"

Seth was bringing the chicken soup into the living room when Scott was putting his stethoscope back into his bag. "You have a nice little rattle in there, but I don't think we need a chest X-ray. If your throat culture is positive, I'll bring you some antibiotics. For now it looks like you have everything you need. Have some soup and, Iris, would it kill you to drink more fluids?" He pinched the flesh on the back of her hand. "I know it hurts to swallow, but you have a fever, probably because you got a little dehydrated. That happens when you have a sore throat. Drink about a gallon of orange juice and water, all right? And maybe some tea. Any nausea?"

"Nah. All my troubles are from the chest up."

"What's the bucket for?" he asked.

"I filled up a trash can with tissues and didn't have the energy to empty it and the bucket was right under the sink."

"Ah. Take a couple of hot soaks or long hot showers — steam is good. If you can stand it, gargle with warm salt water. It will do wonders for your throat. It's kind of amazing, how it heals. Need anything else from me?"

She shook her head.

"Eat some soup," Scott said, patting her knee. "I'll let you know about the throat, but I think it's just irritated from coughing."

He got up to leave and Seth walked him to the front door.

"It was nice of you to check on Iris," Scott said.

"We look out for each other when we can," Seth said.

"I see that." Scott smiled. "Lip looks good. Peyton did a good job."

When Seth went back to the sofa, Iris was balancing the tray holding the soup on her lap, spoon in hand, tears running down her cheeks. "Aw," he said. "Sore throat?"

She shook her head. "I think the Advil

kicked in. It's not too bad."

"But you're crying. Iris, you almost never cry. Like, twice in your life, and both when I'm around . . ."

"I just feel rotten. . . ."

"But you're going to eat soup, drink orange juice, smear Bag Balm on your nose, sleep through a bunch of chick flicks and feel better," he said.

"Uh-huh," she said, crying through another spoonful of chicken soup.

"I'm going to be in town late tonight," he said. "Half my staff is out with the flu, which means two guys, leaving only me and Charlie. I'm going to run over to my house, get some clothes and a clean uniform and spend the night next door. I'll have my phone on all night. I can check on you later and if you need anything . . ."

She looked at him through her filmy eyes with her Rudolph nose shining. "Why did you come over?"

"Oh, I don't know. I thought you might be really missing your mom today, being sick and all. My mom drives me crazy, but all the things she does make me feel better. After she leaves, at least." Then he chuckled. "So I'll leave."

"I did. I do," she said. "I miss my mom. It doesn't happen a lot but there are times when . . ." She wiped her eyes with her paper napkin and coughed.

"When what, Iris?"

She took a breath. The tears ran. "When I realize . . . I have no one."

He was silenced and motionless for a moment. He had his mom, his brothers, his cranky father and Oscar. There had been times he felt alone, felt he'd let everyone down and had driven them away, but somehow they always reminded him they were still around. When he was literally dying in a Seattle hospital his mother came and sat at his bedside night and day; his dad and brothers had visited even if they didn't sit vigil like his mom had; his teammates from the Seahawks came; his coach from Thunder Point High was there once. He had family, flawed though they might be.

He patted her knee. "You have me," he said. "You will always have me, though I realize that's not much. Stop crying right now or I'll hug you and risk contamination and then who will you have?"

"You brought me flowers," she said, dabbing her eyes again.

"Grace said flowers are a hard habit to break. She also said you should drop in when you're germ-free, or something like that."

Iris laughed, which sent her coughing again.

"I'm going to go," Seth said. "You finish your soup and juice and get some rest. I'll be next door if you need me tonight. I can heat soup, take out trash, whatever. I could check on you?"

She shook her head. "Not tonight, okay? Let me burrow in and kick it."

"Sounds like a plan. I'll call tomorrow. Not early."

Scott went back to the clinic. It was barely five, but dusk was already upon them and the day had been dark to begin with. The end of the week would bring Halloween and he just hoped it wasn't cold and rainy — no doubt that would bring another flood of fall colds. He went inside and hung his damp jacket on the coatrack.

"How's Iris?" Peyton asked.

"Miserable," he said. "I did a culture but I'm pretty sure she has a bad cold that took up residence in her chest. Like half the town that sat through the last football game in the cold rain."

"As did you," she reminded him.

"I have the constitution of an iron man," he said. "I think we should lay in some of Carrie's chicken soup, though."

"Feeling vulnerable?" she asked.

"No, but Iris had some and God, did it smell good!"

"Done," Peyton said. "I went next door to buy dinner and she'd just started a fresh batch. She gave me some she had in the freezer. So, Scott, how do you feel about spring?"

"Like it can't get here fast enough," he said.

She laughed at him. "I agree, but I meant for a wedding. On my family's farm. First of May everything will be blossoming. The planting will be done. We can call in the family, have it catered by my Basque relatives . . ."

"May? Can't we do it earlier than that?" he asked. "How about a Thanksgiving wedding?"

She pulled him into her arms. "Paco is being very strong, turning a blind eye to me living with you," she said of her father. "But when it comes to the wedding, he will have his way. Let's not ask too much of him."

"Oh, he's being very brave, all right," Scott said. "He mentions our living arrangement every time we talk. I half expect to hear from the Pope. Or at least an archbishop. Doesn't your mother have anything to say about this wedding? Don't *you*?"

"I want to be married on the family farm when it's at its best," she said. "When I was eighteen I couldn't wait to get off the farm. Now I want to get married there, wear a dress the color of pear blossoms, eat until I can't move and have a long weekend of fun. Anyone who can borrow, rent or buy an RV or fifth wheel is welcome, how about that? And really, Scott, you haven't lived until you've been to a Basque wedding."

"I just want to get into bed with a Basque woman, how about that? The sooner, the better." He looked around. "I guess you would have told me if we had patients?"

"We have kids," she said. "Devon picked them up and brought them here. They're in the break room with their little movies."

"Ew, I hate having them here with all the viruses we've had running through the place. . . ."

"Scott, most of those viruses came from the schools. They're probably safer here — we wipe everything down with disinfectant and wash our hands fifty times a day. But if you're willing to close up, I'll take them home and get the soup started." Her eyes twinkled. "I have chocolate cake for dessert."

"The kids can have that. I'm having you for my dessert."

■ ■ ■ ■

Seth stayed busy in town after fetching some clean clothes. He had dinner at the diner. With his patrol unit parked outside, everyone knew exactly where to find him if he was needed. He left the usual note on the office door when he locked up: For Assistance Dial 911. He didn't go to his mother's house until nine o'clock. His father had already turned in but Seth consoled himself that his dad hadn't taken an early bedtime to avoid him. Norm typically went to bed early and rose early.

Seth had noticed one dim light inside Iris's house, but that didn't mean she was awake. Likely she was dozing on the couch. He liked the "early to bed and early to rise" philosophy, too. But on this night he didn't find sleep until almost midnight. He had too many thoughts spinning around in his head to fall asleep. He was remembering when Iris had learned the facts of life, when she'd learned about her father.

Iris got the biological details about where babies came from when she was around eleven or even younger, but for whatever reason she didn't put together what that had to do with her parents. When she'd been very young and asked where her daddy was, Rose had a simple explanation. "He's not with us anymore, angel." Iris had taken that to mean he was dead. But puberty brought more detailed questions — what was his name, what was he like, where had he lived, who were his people?

Even though they were best friends, Seth hadn't had any idea that Iris was burdened with such curiosities. As for the birds and the bees, Seth had been given the facts much earlier because his two older brothers, Nick and Boomer, never spared a single detail — from puberty on they were obsessed with girls and sex, not necessarily in that order.

When Iris was fourteen and constantly asking questions, Rose had to come clean, explain to Iris the truth about her father. It was a dark family secret, she said. Rose had been a young secretary when she'd fallen in desperate love with her married boss. They'd dallied. Iris's mother never came out and called it an affair, which it was. The boss was older; his children were teenagers. When Rose got pregnant, they worried about what to do for a while because Rose's married boyfriend was very successful in the community and respected in his church and clubs. And his wife was mighty angry.

Ultimately, Rose was settled with a generous sum of money, enough to go somewhere and start over with *her* child. Rose struggled for a couple of years, alone with a baby and no family support. She finally chose Thunder Point and turned an old print shop into a flower shop. That alone would explain Rose's struggles to eke a living out of the place — she had no experience operating a small business and she wasn't much of a flower arranger, at least in the beginning.

When Iris first learned the truth about her biological father, she'd wept. Of course, the only person she would lean on was Seth. At the time, when Norm was so proud of him, he couldn't imagine being abandoned by a father.

But Iris, being Iris, was down about it for around three days before coming to a decision. "Screw him. Who needs him? As far as I'm concerned he's dead, which is what I've believed all along anyway."

It wasn't until Rose fell ill that she provided Iris with the name of a businessman in Wichita, Kansas. Iris didn't confide any of this to Seth, of course — they weren't friends anymore. But when Seth took his mother to Rose's funeral and spent a couple of days at his childhood home, he'd asked questions about Iris. The facts were whispered to Seth by his mother, along with the promise that she'd never told another living soul. "Did she go find him?" Seth had asked. "No. Iris told Rose it was his loss."

Seth thought about that part of Iris's life story. That Iris — she was so strong, so independent and fearless. It took something like being felled by the flu to make her emotional, to make her say, "I'm all alone."

In Seth's opinion, she'd have been wasting her time seeking out her biological father. If he hadn't made an appearance in thirty-four years, he wasn't likely to now, if he was even alive. There could be siblings, but were they going to bring her decongestant and Bag Balm when the flu hit her? Not bloody likely!

So it was down to him — he would be her family.

If she'd let him.

Staying at his mother's house, right next door to Iris, was a simple matter as he had a great excuse to be there. Steve Pritkus was still under the weather, coughing up a lung. Pritkus suggested he was ready to come back to work and couldn't still be contagious, but Seth asked him to stay home so they wouldn't all have to endure his watering eyes, dripping nose and horrible cough.

Besides, he was quite happy to use the time to keep an eye on Iris. His other deputy, Charlie Adams, was on nights and the third, Rusty Sellers, had just succumbed to something — cold, flu, whatever. It was Seth and Charlie. And a real nice, quiet town.

"You still paying rent on that place in Bandon?" Norm asked.

Seth grinned at his father. "You tired of my jokes already?"

Norm grunted in response.

When Seth asked his mother to put together a little extra dinner he could take to Iris while she was sick, Gwen clutched her chest. "Of *course,*" she said.

"Don't get all excited. We're just being neighborly," he said.

"An excellent starting point!"

Gwen would have been delighted to have her son at the dinner table, but she was even more pleased to think of Seth sharing an intimate dinner with his childhood friend, a girl she already thought of as a daughter. Even if Iris was too sick to get cozy, they were spending time together again. Every day Seth took something to Iris and stayed to share it with her — a little pot roast, carrots, potatoes and Gwen's favorite cucumber salad, which was basically cucumbers and onions in a vinegar dressing. Or Gwen's spaghetti and meatballs, something Norm liked to have once a week. Or her pork chops baked in cream of celery soup with a side of mashed potatoes and peas. He also took his old Yahtzee game and Scrabble set. They played a couple of games after dinner until she started looking tired.

Seth realized he really owed his mother for this. But he was going to hold off on thanking her.

TEN

After a couple of days of steamy showers and self-medicating, Iris felt worlds better. Despite the fact that she had tons of work on her desk at school, she also had a very annoying cough that would frighten the students and her colleagues, so she stayed home all week. Day after day, she opened the door to Seth and his mother's food. "You don't have to do this, you know," she said. But, secretly, she loved it. It wasn't just the meal, which was always good in a very comforting, homey way. It was also Seth, who was taking his dinner break with her.

Seth wasn't the only one dropping by with goodwill offerings. There were students, as well. Krista, her senior student helper, came bearing cookies her mother had baked. "I'm so glad to see you," Iris said. "I've been wondering how the office is holding up and how Misty is getting on there."

"Fine, as far as I know," Krista said. "Are you worried about anything?"

"You mean besides the fifteen tons of paperwork on my desk?" Iris asked with a laugh that had her coughing. When she was under control again she told Krista what was happening. "I've been worried that Misty is feeling a little out of place, being new to us and all. In general, not just in the counselor's office. If you get a chance to ask her how she's doing or if she needs help, will you? I haven't even been in the office to train her."

"Of course, Ms. McKinley. I have my lunch hour the same time as Misty — I'll check on her."

"Oh, that would be so helpful. And thanks for the cookies! I'd hug you but —"

Krista laughed and stepped back. "That's okay, I can feel the love from here!"

"Cute," Iris said.

A couple of other students came by — one brought crocheted slippers. A secretary from the school office brought brownies. Troy showed up and she asked him if he would mind bringing her the SAT prep course portfolio after school the next day. "I don't dare show my face around there, looking and sounding like I do," she said. "I bark like a seal!"

"You look great," he said. "What else can I bring you? Do you have food? Juice? Soup? Everything you need?"

"I'm all hooked up," she said with a laugh. "My neighbor has been making me dinner every night."

"That's a lot of trouble," he said. "Can I bring you something from Cliff's or Carrie's?"

She shook her head. "Gwen is so happy to be doing it. She was my mom's best friend and took me under her wing long ago." And right as she said that, Seth came walking across the yard, wearing oven mitts, carrying a casserole. His department SUV was parked at his mother's house and he wore his uniform.

"Hey, Troy," he said cheerily.

"Seth," Troy said. "Delivering dinner?"

"Chicken something," he said. "Join us?"

"You're eating, too?" Troy asked.

"Well, I guess I could go home and eat the same thing with my mother and Norm, but frankly, Iris is better company." He smiled. "Even in her condition."

"Very nice, Seth," she said. And then, of course, she coughed.

"I'm doomed," Seth said to Troy. "Pritkus is down with half his family, my other deputy has some variation on this bug, Iris already contaminated me, half the town is sneezing and everyone who goes to the clinic has time to stop by my office and list their symptoms for me. I'm so grateful."

"I've been tempted to wear a mask to school," Troy said.

"Want to join us for this chicken something?" Iris asked.

"I don't know. . . ."

"Make up your mind, man," Seth said. "I only have a half hour for dinner."

"I think I'll pass," Troy said to Iris. "You have the plague and I think Seth could be a carrier. I'm going to take my chances on Pizza Hut. I'll bring you your SAT prep folder after school tomorrow. If you need anything else, text me."

Like old roommates, Iris and Seth put out plates, flatware and napkins. The casserole sat in the middle of the kitchen table. She grabbed a little leftover salad in the fridge, something she'd thrown together for lunch, and Seth pulled two rolls wrapped in plastic wrap out of his jacket pocket, making her laugh. She remarked that the "chicken something" was wonderful and he said she sounded much better. Their conversation wandered, as it had the past few nights. She told him about some of the student issues — no names — that she'd been challenged with. He asked her what she'd been doing on holidays since her mom passed away.

"Various friends," she said. "Last year Grace and I teamed up with a turkey breast and gravy from the jar, but the year before I drove to Eureka and spent three days with my college roommate and her family. What about you?"

"I've been a junior deputy, then a junior sergeant for as long as I can remember so I end up working most holidays. On the few I can sneak away, Boomer has it at his house in North Bend. He's got two kids."

"They still call him Boomer, do they?" she asked.

"Everyone calls him Boomer, even his wife and kids. I think he likes it."

"And Nick?"

"New woman every time I see him. I don't know if he'll ever find one that sticks with him."

"Really? It's been a long time since I've seen him, but he's a very sharp, good-looking guy and what a smile!"

Seth smiled. "Better than this?" he asked.

"Miles better," she said. "Kind of crazy that all you boys have handsome smiles when old Norm last smiled a few years ago. . . ."

"Was it that recently? Too bad no one got

a picture. So, since I'm working in Thunder Point this year, Boomer's family has agreed to come to town for Thanksgiving. I'll have to work, but we divide up the day so everyone on duty gets turkey. I'll at least get a long lunch break to have dinner with the family. Will you come?" he asked. "My mother would be thrilled. So would Nick and Boomer."

"Ah, I don't know, Seth. That's very sweet, but I wouldn't want to give the wrong idea to anyone. And there's Grace. And Troy. Troy has family in San Diego but he hasn't said anything about going home."

"Bring them," he said. "My mom would be so happy to pack 'em in for her holiday meal. She won't admit it, but she hates it when her daughter-in-law is in charge — she wants to control the meal. And I don't care what ideas they get — we used to have Thanksgiving together every year."

"When it was me and Rose. It hasn't been me and Rose in a long time."

"I haven't been in Thunder Point for a long time," he said. He touched her hand.

"You've been here for an hour and a half," she pointed out to him.

"Have I? Time flies . . ."

"You told Troy you had thirty minutes."

"I lied," he admitted with a shrug. "I'm

216

the boss. I'm on the clock all the time. My phone is on. If the phone chimed, I'd have to leave in the middle of the chicken whatever-it-was."

"I believe it was chicken tetrazzini."

"You have amazing taste buds." He smiled at her. "How about a game of Scrabble?"

"Don't you have to work?"

"Sort of," he said. "I've been in this uniform since six this morning. Believe me, they get their money's worth. Hey, when everyone is over the flu, I'll teach you to play chess. If you want to . . ."

"You play chess?"

"I learned when I was rehabbing my leg. I just didn't have much stamina, especially after a really demanding session. But my brain needed to be kept busy, so I learned."

She smiled sweetly. "You've changed so much."

"I hope so. But I hope I'm the same guy in the good ways."

On Halloween Seth called Iris. "Do you have something you can warm up for dinner? Because I'm afraid I'm not going to get over tonight until late and my mom didn't cook. I forgot — Halloween is different."

"Don't worry about me," she said. "I'm

snacking tonight. There are little goblins due any second."

"And I have to keep an eye on the goblins around town."

"You do that."

Seth hadn't been back in Thunder Point on Halloween since his senior year in high school. He didn't remember it ever being a major holiday among the locals and yet, what he witnessed was an extraordinary display. On this clear and cold night, the town was alive with celebration. Everyone had their porch ornaments displayed, from corn stalks to pumpkins; there were witches and ghosts flying in the trees, orange and black candles lit the windows. Three separate neighborhoods had haunted houses or graveyards with spooks that jumped out at expectant kids. Seth's mother was dressed as a scarecrow and was standing stone-still at the end of her sidewalk until a little one passed and then she suddenly came to life, startling them, sending them shrieking and giggling up and down the sidewalk and street.

Seth drove around town slowly, occasionally shining the SUV's spotlight on trick-or-treaters. Now and then he'd flip on the siren for a couple of startling *whoop-whoops*. As soon as darkness had fallen, when it was still early, parents had the little ones out. He could see mothers and fathers standing along the curbs socializing while princesses, sci-fi creatures, spacemen, animals, robots and hobos ran up to front doors. The under-seven crowd and especially the under-four crowd wore bulky jackets with their costumes. Little girls had all colors of makeup on their faces and wild, jeweled and colored hair; boys had helmets and masks.

The business district was all done up — there were garlands, lights, harvest decorations and jack-o'-lanterns everywhere. Private business owners like Stu from the diner and Carrie from the deli, folks who were licensed food handlers, handed out things like candied apples and cookies. Rawley Goode was helping Carrie and while he wore no costume save his denim jacket and ball cap, he was still a little spooky. Down the street there was a wild and crazy witch, cackling and prancing all over the sidewalk — she wore black shoes with curled-up toes, red-and-white striped stockings, a black dress with little bells sewn onto the hem, a scraggly gray wig and a very tall black hat. She had a pointy chin, a wart and three blacked-out teeth. It took a moment but Seth realized it was Grace.

He pulled over and got a picture of her

with his cell phone. Then he decided to snap a few more — Stu was a pirate, Carrie was a gypsy — and there were kids everywhere who were happy to pose for the town deputy. Even though it was a small town, none of the kids would get to every house and his mom and Iris would enjoy seeing pictures of the ones they missed.

A three-foot-tall Spiderman tugged on his pant leg and asked him if that was a police costume. The little mermaid, Ariel, asked him for a ride in the police car. Waylan, dressed like a bloody butcher and standing in front of his bar with a bowl of candy, invited him in for one on the house. Seth declined with a laugh and a *whoop* of his siren.

He was strangely touched by the celebration, by the many kids, by their parents socializing while the kids ran wild. He knew the drill — one parent took the kids while the other stayed home with the candy bowl. This wasn't his first small town. His last assignment was just northeast — a town of only six hundred — and he'd stayed out on Halloween night just like this, patrolling, making sure it was a peaceful celebration of spooks and witches. But back here in his hometown, it kind of tugged at his heart. He remembered years of his mother dressing up, his neighbors scaring the little kids, all the candy. When he was eleven or twelve he and his buddies did a few reckless things — tipped a couple of trash cans, soaped a few windows, smashed a pumpkin or two. *Bad boys,* he thought with a chuckle. Nothing a broom and dustpan or a little Windex wouldn't fix, but if they'd been caught there would have been holy hell to pay.

He wouldn't mind the challenge of it all, he realized. Kids. A wife and permanent home. In fact, he thought he might be good at it.

He drove up the hill and parked in a quiet place where he had a good view of the neighborhood. As the night grew later and darker, the little kids with parental supervision were giving it up and the slightly older kids were coming out. It was around eight-thirty and he noticed the costume change as the kids were bigger — now there were hatchets through heads, bloody knives protruding from chests, ghouls and headless monsters. He remembered that, too — the evolution of costumes. He remembered when his brothers had graduated to bloody beasts and killers while he was still dressed as a pirate. He couldn't wait until he could paint his face white, with blood dripping from his mouth like the undead instead of some lame pirate or cowboy.

A couple of kids walked down the street — a mummy and a karate black belt wearing his white gi. He figured them for about eleven. Maybe small twelve-year-olds. He could imagine how big a fight they had to put up to get permission to go out without Mom and Dad. It was always a bit of a worry, but Mac had confirmed if there was any real Halloween trouble, it was more likely to come from the bar or maybe a house party. The kids were pretty safe here. They sent out all the standard safety pleas to the community — stay in groups, don't eat unwrapped candy, don't get in any car except your parents' and don't go inside any houses.

A couple of ninjas approached the mummy and karate kid from behind. Could be nothing, of course. But Seth exited his car, locking it, and stood in the shadows. The trick-or-treaters were about fifteen feet away from him when one of the black-clad ninjas sprinted forward, grabbed the bags of candy and kept going.

Seth crossed the street at a jog just in time to grab the fleeing ninja by the collar. He gave him a shake and he dropped the bags of candy. Seth looked around in time to see the other ninja take off, cut through the yards and disappear behind the houses while other trick-or-treaters stood rooted to the spot.

Seth gave his captive a shake. "I saw that," he said.

"Lemme go! I didn't do nothin'!"

"Nice try," Seth said, dragging him away from the spilled bags of candy. "Hey, you boys," he yelled to the victims. "You want your candy?"

They stepped forward hesitantly. Seth had to hang on to the squirming ninja for a long moment. He pulled him back so the smaller kids would have plenty of space to retrieve their candy. He could see they were very nervous. They just scooped spilled candy into the bags without investigating it closely.

"Do you know this kid?" he asked the victims. He ripped the stocking cap off the ninja's head. The kids, a year or two younger, just shook their heads. "You know what it means when someone rips off your Halloween candy on a dark street?" Again they shook their heads. "It means it's time to go home. It means the party is over. Want me to follow you home, make sure no more ninjas are waiting for you?" Still silent, they continued to shake their heads. "Then go," he said. "Fast."

They ran like greased lightning.

Seth dragged his ninja to his patrol car and stood him up against it. "Here's what I need from you," he said. "Your full name, your address, the name of your accomplice and his address."

His culprit, a freckle-faced kid of about twelve, just a big kid, stared at Seth in sheer terror for a second. And then he lunged and made to run. Seth took a couple of long-legged steps and grabbed his collar again. "Sorry, pal. That's not going to work. Do I need cuffs?"

The kid shook his head. Then he started to cry.

That's better, Seth thought. "Your name?"

"Robert," he said. "Bobby."

"Last name?"

"Delaney," he said. He sniffed and wiped his nose on his sleeve.

I'm cursed, Seth thought. He sighed. "Your parents home?"

"Just my mom."

Crap, he thought. *Just what I need.* "All righty then, let's go see your mom. I'll need an address, if you please."

"Aw, man . . ."

Seth put him in the passenger seat and told him not to touch anything if he wanted to keep that arm.

Charlie Adams had come on duty at five

and was going to be in town, doing the same thing Seth had been doing until trick-or-treating was over for the evening. He called his cell rather than using the radio. "I'm going to be out for a few minutes, delivering a juvenile to his parents."

"It's not one of my juveniles, is it?" Charlie asked, in reference to his own teenagers.

"I haven't had any problems with Adams teenagers tonight. This is a Delaney. I don't think it'll take him long to explain to his mother that he's been assaulting little kids and stealing their candy."

Bobby Delaney groaned and slid down in his seat.

"May the force be with you," Charlie said.

Seth drove eight or ten blocks to the house. It wasn't a very big house. Two-story with a porch. He'd heard it was Sue and her three kids plus Sue's sister, brother-in-law and their two kids living there. Eight people would be a crowd in that space. The place looked pretty quiet. There was a light on in the living room but it was otherwise dark.

Bobby preceded him across the porch and opened the front door. He heard Sassy's voice shout, "Who's home?"

"Ma?" Bobby called.

Sassy walked into the living room from

downstairs. She was all made up though she wore two fat curlers in her white-blond hair with the pink tips. She wore skin-tight black pants with high-heeled knee-high boots over them, a silky low-cut top that flattered her cleavage and a shiny vest. She frowned when she saw Bobby and Seth standing just inside the door. "Seth?" she asked.

"Tell your mother why I brought you home," Seth said.

"I boosted some kid's candy," he said quietly.

She took another step closer. "You stole it?" she asked. "You stole some little kid's candy?"

"He wasn't that little," Bobby said defensively.

"Two kids," Seth said. "Both smaller than Bobby. He came on them from behind and then was going to run, but guess who was right there to chase him? The law."

Sassy glared at her son. "Go to your room." Then she looked at Seth. "What do I have to do now? Pay a fine? What?"

"How about you keep him in to think about consequences. You might want to make him apologize to his victims and their parents."

"Fine. Whatever."

Seth frowned. "You on your way out?"

"Maybe, I don't know."

"Can I just suggest, you should do something about this. Your son could've hurt those kids."

"He's a pain sometimes, but he wouldn't hurt anyone," she said.

"Wherever you were thinking of going, you weren't thinking of driving there, were you?"

"Why? What's this about?"

"About your breath, which is pretty high-octane right now." He sniffed the air. "Wine, I guess. And a lot of it."

"I've had one glass of wine! And I'm over twenty-one!"

"Is that your car in the drive?" he asked.

"Yeah, why?"

He shrugged. "Just wondering what to be on the lookout for. Listen, maybe you should get Bobby's dad involved, make sure he gets the message that his little prank is actually against the law, not to mention it's a real bad kind of bullying and stealing to ignore. You don't want him getting the impression it's okay. It's not okay. If I hadn't been there, I can't guess what might've happened to those little kids. Plus, Bobby wasn't alone — there was another kid with him who took off. I wouldn't have brought him home to you if I didn't take this seriously. You understand me?"

"I understand you still hold a grudge from high school," she said, giving her hair a flick over her shoulder.

"Sorry? What?"

"You know what I'm talking about, Seth. We were going steady, we were first loves, broke up badly and it was probably my fault and you're not over it. That explains the way you've been acting."

He frowned. "How have I been acting?"

"Like you don't care. Like you don't dare take a chance on me now, even though we're years older."

He continued to frown and shook his head. "I think you've got the wrong impression, Sue. Now, about Bobby —"

"Bobby's fine," she snapped. "This is about you and me and you know it!"

"There is no you and me," he said as patiently as he could.

"So you keep saying, but you never forget your first time. . . ."

"I think you are drunk. No matter what, don't drive tonight. And if you're smart, you'll call Bobby's father and tell him the boy is in need of a strong moral influence."

"Right," she said. "Sure."

"Sue, listen to me. Listen very carefully. There was a very brief time we dated when we were kids. It was a long time ago. You weren't my first and I *definitely* wasn't yours. And I haven't thought about you once in seventeen years. I didn't even know you married Robbie Delaney because no one mentioned it and I didn't care enough to ask. There's nothing. There won't be anything. Not in this lifetime. Now let it go, drop it, and if you love your boy at all, concentrate on being a decent mother to him!"

Seth left the house, his boots striking the wood of the porch and steps loudly. He got into his car. Before pulling away from the curb, he called Charlie. "I'm done here," he said. "How's the town?"

"Quiet. The only residence party I saw seems to be breaking up early, most of them leaving on foot. Not many kids out anymore. I checked in on one noise complaint — just music and they apologized and turned down the volume. The Knudsons' haunted house is still open but in the past twenty minutes there haven't been any kids around there."

"Business district?" Seth asked.

"Under control the last time I looked. A few adults and teenagers wrapping things up."

Seth looked at his watch. It was after nine.

"If you don't need me, I'm going to get off the clock and get something to eat."

"Sure thing, boss. I'll give you a call if anything important comes up, but I think we're good."

Seth drove slowly down the street toward the pizza place, now pretty busy with teenagers. He phoned from the car and ordered a large pizza and for the next fifteen minutes he just hung around in front, talking to people. Then he went in for his pizza and took it a few blocks up the hill to Iris's. He wanted to see Iris to escape the nasty feeling Sassy had left on him.

Funny thing about Sassy. He'd thought she was his first until Iris had informed him about that night before the prom when he'd lost his virginity in a drunken stupor. Of course he'd known about Sassy's reputation, he'd heard the talk. He hadn't really cared that much whether she'd been with other boys before him. She'd made a lot of assertions about her virginity and he'd just let her. It's not like he owned her. What happened before they'd started dating wasn't his business. Besides, their relationship had been short and troubled.

He phoned the dispatcher and clocked out for the night. Then he called Iris from the car and when she answered he said, "I hope you're up."

"Sure. What's going on?"

"I've been on duty since early this morning. I've taken pictures of a lot of little goblins and princesses and witches, plus I have a pizza in the car because I'm starving. I'm done for the night."

"Well, bring that pizza in here!" she said.

Just the sound of that made him feel better. He couldn't get in there fast enough. He pulled his squad car right into her drive and parked.

ELEVEN

Troy worked at Cooper's bar on Halloween night. Cooper had been snagged by his wife to go to town to trick-or-treat at a few spots with their three-month-old daughter, who was dressed as a little duck and didn't have a clue how they were exploiting her cuteness. Rawley had gone into town to help Carrie hand out treats at the deli and it wasn't likely to be busy at the bar, not with the weather as cold as it was and all the real action in town.

He wasn't particularly sentimental about Halloween, but he did have to admit the kids he saw were pretty hilarious. The doctor's kids came out to the beach for a little show-and-tell before going house to house in town with Devon, the coach and their kids, Mercy and Austin. The little girls were, predictably, princesses. Austin was a zombie and five-year-old Will was with SEAL Team Six.

By seven o'clock Cooper was back and by seven-thirty the coach and his kids were done for the night. It wasn't even nine when Troy had swept, mopped and put everything straight. He headed for town, looking for a little diversion. He'd chosen to walk to work since it was a dry night. Going back to town across the beach, he passed a pretty big bonfire and a bunch of high school kids bundled up and chasing each other around the sand. When they saw him there was a lot of shouting. "Hey, Troy, hey!" It made them feel so cool to call him by his first name when they weren't at school and when he wasn't with other teachers. He got a kick out of them. He did manage an adult move and told them to be careful around that fire.

Troy had a small two-bedroom apartment in town in a pretty ratty and cheap building — one bedroom to sleep in, one to store toys. Besides semi-decent furniture the only thing he'd done to improve his surroundings was reinforce all the locks — his toys and sports gear were valuable.

He walked past his street and up the hill toward Iris's house. Parked in front of her house was the Sheriff's Department SUV. That was pretty blatant. Usually Seth at least parked in his parents' drive, though that was just about as close to Iris's back door as her own drive. Even though they insisted theirs was merely an old friendship, Troy could pick up the vibes. He wasn't convinced either Iris or Seth would admit it, but Troy could see what was happening. There was some kind of chemistry going on there that was more intense than friendship.

He turned around and walked back down the hill. He could head to Cliff's or maybe even Waylan's. He felt like having a beer. Maybe a little distraction. He should've thought it through before taking a job in a little town like this because as far as single women went, they were few. The chances of finding himself lucky on Friday were pretty slim. Of course, when there was snow on Mount Hood, he could head up there and after a day of skiing he would usually find someone to flirt with.

He'd met Iris soon after moving to Thunder Point and had congratulated himself on both good taste and wisdom — she was pretty, smart, funny and sexy. It didn't take him long to ask her out. Figuring he could enjoy a long time with someone like Iris, he'd settled into the little town very happily. But it didn't work out for them. Troy had been around the block a few times — it happened that way sometimes. He was disappointed, but he told himself that would pass.

He wasn't sure what he wanted to do with himself. Waylan's door was standing open and the tinny sounds of oldies from an antique jukebox drifted out. Waylan's wasn't a bad place but there was no conversation there. There were a few old boys who drifted in after work because the drinks were cheap, but night usually brought out a solitary and tight-lipped crowd who just wanted to drink in peace. He decided to see if the mini-mart was still open, grab a six pack and —

And then he saw the witch sweeping her sidewalk and pulling in her harvest decorations. "Hey," he called out.

She turned toward him and cackled a little wildly, grinning broadly to show her blacked-out teeth.

He laughed at her. "I thought you were going to dress up this year?" he said.

"Funny. I put a hex on you. When you get up to pee in the morning you will be very surprised at how little your thing is."

"You are evil."

"You shouldn't beat up on witches. We're sensitive."

"But are you thirsty, that's the question."

She leaned on her broom. "I don't know. I'm pretty worn-out — I've been putting curses on people all night. . . ."

"Is there a whole town full of little wangs?"

he asked.

She grinned again. "Some people got big ones."

"Wow! What do you have to do to get a big one?"

"Sometimes just be a bitchy girl. That'll do it."

"You are a bad, bad witch. You could get thrown out of the witch's union. Come on, let's get your stuff off the sidewalk and stop in at Waylan's for a cold beer. No one will notice the costume in there."

"I guess that's supposed to be a plus," she said. "Can you pull this stuff in while I brush my teeth? I need to be free of this black stuff. I'll be right back."

"Don't change clothes, Dillon," he said, using her last name. "Now that I think about it, I want to buy a drink for a witch tonight. It fits my mood just right."

"I've never been in Waylan's," she said.

"It's right across the street!" he said.

"It looks a little . . . seedy."

"It's completely seedy. And very forgettable. But the beer is cold. Hurry up."

Troy did as he'd been told and pulled in the flowers, jack-o'-lantern and other decorations and took them back to the workroom. He looked around the shop and workroom appreciatively — Grace kept a nice little shop. It was very tidy and classy. There was a huge glass-fronted cooler that stretched the length of the back room and it was filled with flowers. On the other side of that room was an office space and small bathroom. The floors were shiny wood, the walls painted cheerful yellow and shelves were stuffed with supplies, all neatly arranged. Troy heard a stomping sound and the back door opened. Grace entered and locked the door behind her.

"Where were you?" he asked.

"Upstairs. The stairs are in the alley behind the shop."

"What's up there?" he asked.

"Me," she said. "There's a little space. Very little. Rose used it as storage. She even let other people rent cheap storage from her — like some of the other businesses. I cleaned it up, made a couple of minor improvements and I live up there." When she smiled, her teeth gleamed. He thought he might miss those black patches.

"Come on, witchy. Let's get a drink across the street."

The inside of the bar was dark and gloomy and smelled like years of spilled beer and stale smoke from back when people were still allowed to smoke in bars. That was the real reason Waylan always had the door propped open, unless the cold wind howled or sleet blasted the windows. The lights were dim and there were only three people at the bar, with a lot of space between them. There was one couple in a booth near the back of the place, sitting very close, nuzzling each other. Other than that couple, there were only men, all of them apparently alone. The place was a dump, really. But the bar itself was nice and the mirrored shelves behind the bar were pretty classy.

"Wow," Grace said.

Troy pulled out a bar stool for her to occupy. Once she was on it and he was beside her, she leaned close to him and whispered, "My feet were sticking to the floor."

He laughed. "Don't let it worry you. We'll get bottled beer."

"Good idea," she said.

He asked the unsmiling Waylan for two Heinekens in the bottle and some peanuts.

"I just swept," Waylan said.

"Then bring an empty bowl and we'll be careful with the shells, how's that?"

"We'll try it," he said. "I don't like my odds. Bet I have to sweep again."

Two beers appeared quickly, a couple of square napkins slapped down beside them. Troy leaned an elbow on the bar, lifted his beer and grinned. "So. Come here often?"

Grace twirled some strands of her gray witch's wig. "I think I have the same hairdresser as Waylan. Do *you* come here often? Because that could be a red flag."

"There are three places to get a cold beer in town and I work at one of them. If you're in the mood for a beer, you better be in the mood before eleven."

"Want to know what's odd about this place?" Grace asked. "No one is looking at me. I'm the only witch here, right?"

"You fit right in," he said.

"I'm kind of hungry and I think Waylan forgot about the peanuts."

"Want to wander down to the pizza place?" he asked.

"Tell you what. I don't have any beer at my place but I do have food. If you get us a couple more beers to go I can make us grilled cheese."

"Grilled cheese?"

"With bacon and tomato slices? A side of chips?"

"Waylan," Troy hollered. "Two more Heinekens, leave the caps on. We're going to take them home." He stood and reached into his pocket for his wallet. He put some bills on the bar just as Waylan put the bottles there, then they walked out carrying two beers each. They went through the flower shop and out the back door to the stairs.

"Kind of dark back here," Troy said.

"I look around before I lock up. I never see a problem."

"What if someone's hiding behind the Dumpster?" he asked.

She stopped on the stairs and turned to look at him. "Thanks for that, Headly. That should cost me a little sleep."

"I'm sure you're safe here," he said. "Especially here."

She snorted and led him up the stairs into a very small loft. They entered directly into a little kitchen that blended right into a living room. It looked like everything a person needed was right there — small sofa, comfy chair, two narrow side tables, a modest wall unit that held a TV and shelving for books and pictures. Except one thing was missing.

"Where's the bathroom?" he asked.

"Through that door. Help yourself," she said, putting the unopened beers in the refrigerator.

He didn't need a bathroom, but he wanted to see the rest of the place. He handed her the two opened and still half-full beers and headed through the door that was not really a door but more of an arch. Through that arch was an extremely small room with a

Murphy bed pulled down and neatly made up and a bathroom with a sink, toilet, shower and a little cupboard space. Very little. In the bedroom there was one small chest of drawers and a freestanding armoire.

He walked back to the kitchen. Grace already had food on the table for two and a frying pan on her two-burner stove. There was just the bar-sized refrigerator and microwave. "This is actually very . . . cute," he said.

"Thank you."

"Is there space over all the shops?"

"Space, yes, but pretty useless space. No other apartments that I'm aware of. This was an unfinished room but I saw great potential here. It needed plumbing and a little finishing. The windows to the street are in the closet-sized bedroom. It's very cozy, but I'm one person. And I have an office downstairs in the shop."

"That's a mighty small refrigerator," he observed.

"I've been known to leave a couple of bottles of wine in the flower cooler," she said. "Would you mind slicing this tomato and microwaving this bacon while I excuse myself for just a moment?"

"Sure. My specialties — slicing and microwaving."

As he prepped the food, he considered that he'd never even been curious about Grace before. He'd been in her shop exactly twice — once to order flowers to send to his mother for Mother's Day and once to buy Iris a bouquet, though he'd never mentioned it was for Iris. He had run into Grace around town, usually with Iris — they were girlfriends. He hadn't known she'd made this little storeroom into a home, didn't know who her friends were. He'd found himself in her company a few times recently because they'd been in the same place at the same time and neither of them seemed to have anyone else. And she was a good second since Iris had rather firmly cut him loose.

When she came back to the kitchen, she was wearing jeans and a T-shirt, socks on her feet, her hair pulled back into a ponytail. "There," she said. "I was all done being a witch."

"You were a good witch, but I'm still going to check in the morning and make sure you're powerless."

"Won't you be surprised. . . ."

"Do you live here alone?" he asked.

"Of course! There's no room for another person here."

"Why are you so tidy?" he asked.

"I like tidy," she said. "Aren't you?"

He shook his head. "I scatter. I live among piles. I don't mind a mess at all. Do you ski?"

She looked down and began fussing with bread, margarine, cheese slices. "Not really," she said. "It's been years. Why?"

"Well, because I'm thinking of going skiing my next long weekend. Not far — just Mount Hood. You could come along," he suggested.

"I don't have skis."

"They rent 'em. Boots, too. You'd have to have your own jacket and stuff. . . ."

"I don't think that's in my budget," she said. "Especially not for one time on the mountain."

"I had to ski in jeans and a parka for a long time. My dad did maintenance for the city and my mom was a teacher — we didn't have much money for all the things I wanted to do. Some long underwear, jeans, borrowed gloves . . ."

"Yeah," she said. "I could manage that, maybe. . . ."

"I don't have a long weekend anytime soon. Like maybe a month. But think about it. Could be fun."

"Could be. Want a pickle with your grilled cheese?"

"What I'd really like is tomato soup," he said. "I'm sure that's out of the question, but growing up I used to dip my grilled cheese in tomato —"

She opened a cupboard where she stored about twenty cans. One of them was tomato soup. She smiled at him and he was a little overcome with how pretty she was.

He'd really never noticed that before.

Seth devoured the pizza while Iris checked the pictures on his phone. She laughed at the costumes of the Thunder Point shop owners, especially Grace, and cooed over the little ones. "I didn't even take pictures," she admitted. "I was doing good to get to the door with candy before they started yelling! Halloween is cute but honestly, it wears me out!"

She'd pick up a piece of pizza, take a bite and chew, put it down and go through the pictures again and again. By the time she was finally ready to concentrate on the pizza, he'd consumed half of it.

She handed him back his phone. "You got it all greasy," he said, wiping it off with a napkin.

"You're very quiet tonight," she said.

"Oh? I'm sorry, was there time for me to speak?" he asked.

"Very funny," she said. "It was a quiet night, wasn't it?"

He shrugged and took another bite, though he didn't really feel hungry all of a sudden. He put his pizza down. "Got a beer?" he asked.

She cocked her head and gave him a half smile. "In uniform?" she asked. But she grabbed a beer from the fridge.

"I logged off for the night. I just haven't changed yet." He opened the beer and took a pull. "Ahhh," he said. Then he looked at Iris. "I had to deliver a twelve-year-old home to his mother. Sassy."

Iris put down her pizza slice. "Oh?"

"He ripped off candy from a couple of younger boys. He didn't hurt them, but I was right there and caught him. I'd like to think he wouldn't have hurt them, but I will never know for sure. That's a bully move. I hate that."

"Kind of soured you on all the Halloween fun, I guess."

"Yeah, but it's Sassy who sours me more. The way she talks. She thinks there was something between us. Something meaning-ful." He shook his head. "I don't get that. I remember it as painful. Short and painful and better forgotten."

Iris was very quiet for a long stretched-

245

out moment. All the way through him wiping off his hands, taking another slug of beer, wiping his mouth with the napkin. Then he looked at her and said, "What?"

"That's how I was sure you thought of us," she said.

"Iris, I didn't know there was an *us*. At least, I wasn't sure what kind of us there was. I was grieving a lost friendship without knowing there was more to it. There was a good reason you were so hurt and angry. It's not like that with Sassy. She's been married at least three times since high school and still talks as if we should give it another chance."

"I guess that's how she feels," Iris said. "Maybe she's felt that way for years."

"If she has, she's delusional. Look," he said, then he paused at length as if thinking about things. "I'm bound to screw this up. I was an ass and an idiot. I was a teenager. I thought I was a gentleman, my mother drilled good behavior toward girls into my thick head. I did have the occasional gentlemanly act. But honestly? I was drawn to Sassy because she exuded sex and opportunity. I couldn't have put words to it then, but that's what it was. And it was a miserable experience that filled me with shame and jealousy and frustration."

"And broke your heart," she added.

"For fifteen minutes, until the next pretty girl came along. The next one broke my heart, too. So did the one after that. I was quite a bit older before I was clear on what mattered, what was genuine. Sassy was never a friend, never a girl I trusted. That's not right, Iris, but that's all I had at the time. And guess what? That's all she had. I haven't lost a second of sleep over her since."

"That doesn't mean she isn't hurting over it now," Iris said.

"There's nothing I can do to help her with that. It's time for all of us to grow up and move on. She might not have admitted it yet, but she's got bigger problems than whether one of her old high school boy-friends wants to date her. If she doesn't pay attention to her kids, at least one of them could get real mean. He's a big kid and he could get in some real trouble."

Iris sat up a little straighter. "Um, could we have a professional conversation? High school counselor to deputy sheriff? Confidential and all that?"

"Sure. But what — ?"

"There's a girl at school I worry about a little. Could be she's just kind of klutzy. She's got an excuse for each of her bruises, perfectly logical excuses. There's just some-thing a little suspicious and I . . . Not just me, other teachers have been wondering what's going on. I never thought about a younger brother being responsible for her injuries, but what if a brother is fighting with her? Knocking her around?"

Seth shrugged. "I fought with my brothers regularly. Nick and Boomer got into it a lot — my mother went after them with a broom, swatting them till they gave up. But they usually came away with bruises. The occasional black eye. I wouldn't call either of them abusive. Just stupid. And siblings. For that matter, you and I used to go at it pretty good. You beat me up!"

"You totally had it coming," she argued. "Besides, you could've taken me. Why didn't you? Now that I think about it, if you could beat up Robbie Delaney, you could beat me up, but you didn't. . . ."

"I wasn't allowed to hit girls," he said. "And we were young then. That never hap-pened when we were older, like teenagers."

"This is a teenage girl," Iris reminded him. "A sweet girl. She's not a scrapper, not someone who would pick a fight and end up with injuries."

"What kind of injuries?" he asked.

"Bruises on her neck. Shoulder. Split lip

and black eye. How many times can you get kneed in cheerleading practice or run into a wall?"

Seth frowned. "Black eye? Bruises on her neck?"

Iris nodded. "Troy brought it to my attention and I've been watching her. Seth, it's Sassy's daughter. And now I know she has a younger brother who could be a bully."

"Shit," he said.

Twelve

When Iris was in high school and John Garvey was the school guidance counselor, there was a girl in her class named Laura. She was popular, but not mega popular like the homecoming queens and such. She was a cheerleader, was in lots of clubs and worked hard on school projects, like the dances. As Iris recalled, she rarely dated, which might've been one of the reasons they were friendly — it seemed as if it often got down to Laura and Iris stringing up crepe paper and balloons for dances they wouldn't attend.

Laura came to school one morning crying her eyes out. She was so upset she couldn't go to first period so she hid out in the bathroom near the gym, a spot no one would really notice because there wasn't a lot of traffic in there once classes started.

John Garvey, the dumbest counselor who ever lived, summoned her and demanded to know what was wrong. He refused to let her go to class without telling him; he said he'd keep her in his office all day if necessary. Laura said she'd tell him if he promised not to tell her parents what she said.

Laura told Iris about it later. They weren't really close, not the kind of girlfriends who walked to class together or talked on the phone at night, but they had always liked each other. Mr. Garvey promised never to tell anyone and so Laura told him her father had pitched a fit that morning. He was probably hungover, she said. He was mad about everything and everyone. He'd been out of work for a couple of months and was angry in general. That morning, he screamed at her, grabbed her by the hair and knocked her head into the front door, cracking the glass in the small diamond-shaped window. He was pissed about that and threw her school-books out onto the front lawn, which was very wet and icky. He screamed at her that she was a worthless piece of shit and she walked to school without a coat because she wasn't going back inside for anything.

Mr. Garvey listened very patiently, Laura said. He comforted her and, within about thirty minutes, she had recovered and went on to class with a late slip written and signed by Mr. Garvey. That afternoon when Laura went home and walked into the house, she walked into a fist. "So I hit you, do I?" her father bellowed. "Now you're hit, you sniveling little cry baby!"

When Laura went to school with a fat lip the next day, she said her little sister accidentally opened a cupboard door in her face. And she told Iris, "Never trust that bastard Garvey — he's a liar and a creep."

When Iris told Seth that story, he was appalled. "My God, don't you take an oath of confidentiality or something when you become a counselor?"

"If someone is in danger or is a danger to others, we really do have to step in and do something proactive, but tipping off the abuser isn't on the list of recommended actions. John Garvey thought he knew everything and frankly, he did a lot of damage. I wonder what's become of Laura? I hope she's hugely successful and brilliantly happy and sticks pins in a John Garvey doll every day."

"Do you have any idea how much time Robbie Delaney spends with his kids?" Seth asked.

She shook her head. "He hasn't lived in Thunder Point for years. I have no idea when he officially left town — I was away at school for a long time after graduation. I heard through gossip that Sassy left, was back, left again, was back. Her sister and parents lived here and when she's been on her own, she moved in with family. At least that's what I heard."

"I might try to have a conversation with Robbie, unless you think that's a bad idea," Seth said.

"Handle it delicately," she said. "We don't want him to act out on the kids because . . ." She took a breath. "Because what if he's the abuser?"

"Well, here's the thing I can't do, Iris," he said. "I can't have any unnecessary traffic with Sassy. She just gets all the wrong messages."

It was nice to have someone like Seth to talk to for a lot of reasons. They were on the same professional team, to start with — both of them concerned about abuse and neglect and all manner of violence. It was also nice to have a friend to talk to about everything from silly, funny things to serious matters to global issues. And someone who shared your past was extremely comforting. The one thing that continued to worry her was that she still had a dangerous attraction to him. She was afraid that when it all played out and he told her the truth, that he wanted to restore their friendship but had no romantic ideas, it was going to sting. And sting bad.

But for now she let that worry slide as she dug into how to handle the situation with Sassy's bruised daughter.

She waited patiently for another sign, and sadly it didn't take long. The phys ed teacher reported that Rachel Delaney had dark bruises on her biceps that resembled the strong grip of someone who might've grabbed her. Whether the abuser had been male or female wasn't certain, but four fingers and a thumb on each arm looked pretty obvious.

Iris launched into action. She summoned Cammie Munson. She sent a note asking her to drop by during her study hall or right after classes ended for the day. It was around midday that Cammie stopped by.

"You wanted to see me, Ms. McKinley?" she asked politely.

"Yes, thanks for coming by. Have a seat," she said, rising to close both her doors — the one that led to the offices and cubicles and the one that opened to the hall where all the students passed. When that outer door was closed, a do-not-disturb sign automatically slid into place. "I was looking at the SAT scores — you did so well. Are you happy with the scores or do you want to try to do better?"

Cammie sighed. "I don't know," she said wearily. "I could probably do better, but do I have to? I mean, I can get into an Oregon college with the scores I have, right? Because the thought of another prep course and another whole day of exhausting testing . . . God, it sounds just awful."

Iris couldn't help it, she smiled. "I understand completely. Unless you're looking for a little additional scholarship help for an out-of-state school."

Cammie shook her head. "There's no way I'm going out of state," she said. "It's going to be hard enough managing an Oregon school. We don't have a lot of money. I'm applying for financial aid."

"I understand that completely," Iris said. "I got through college on loans and aids. Lucky for me, I chose to stay and work in Oregon. That reduced the balance on state loans. Kind of like working in the trenches, you know?"

"Really? I didn't know that," she said, scooting forward in her chair. "Because I don't want to leave Oregon. To travel, maybe, but not to live!"

"So we're pretty good on that issue, are

we?" Iris asked.

"I think I'm good to go," she said. "I'd so love to cheer for the Ducks, but I hear it's really hard to get in that squad."

"But I've watched you and you're good. I like your chances."

"Thanks, Ms. McKinley, that's really nice of you to say."

"Oh, I'm not just being nice, Cammie — I think you're very talented in a lot of areas. So, let's talk about something else, since we have time. Your best friend is Rachel Delaney, am I right?"

"Right, yes," she said.

"You two could be sisters, you look that much alike. Tell me why you think she has so many accidents," Iris said, stabbing the subject with a sharp point.

Cammie was momentarily speechless. "I don't know what you mean," she finally said.

"Yes, you do, Cammie. She gets hurt a lot. Bruises, black eyes, soreness, one day her lip was cut and swollen. What's up with that?"

"I don't know," she said with a shrug, looking into her lap. "She got hurt in cheer one day. . . ."

"Here's what we have to do, Cammie. We have to level with each other before something really bad happens. I can help her if she needs help without it coming back on you. She either needs some kind of intervention to stop the abuse or she could use a consultation with a neurologist to find out if she has some condition that throws her off balance, like multiple sclerosis or a brain injury. I suspect, however, that someone is hurting her. And if I'm right, I can give her some ideas of how we can stop it without anyone being mad at her. Okay?"

Iris could barely hear Cammie's voice, soft as butterfly feet. "I promised," she whispered.

"And I promise you, Cammie, I will keep your secret."

"But if I'm the only one who knows —"

"Well, that's very unlikely. You come to understand that as years go by — there are no secrets. Not really. But that's beside the point — if someone is hurting her, I can get around the secret part and get her out of a bad situation."

Cammie shook her head and her pretty blond hair swayed. "I don't think so. I don't think you can. I can't talk about it."

"Here's what I want you to do. Think about this for a day or so. Think about what's more important — telling the counselor so Rachel can be helped or keeping this secret and having something worse happen. And also think about this — it's part of my job to investigate if I think something dangerous is happening. I don't have a choice. I have to try to figure out what's going on."

"No!" she said, suddenly panicked.

"Yes," Iris said. "Yes — which is better than having something really bad happen. You can tell Rachel if you feel you need to — tell her that I'm worried about all those accidents and I want to know who's doing that to her. Tell her she can come to me. She can trust me."

"She won't," Cammie said.

"Don't let this go on, Cammie. Will you at least think about it?"

She nodded weakly; she looked overwhelmed with doubt.

"Check back with me in a day or so. Let's get this taken care of for Rachel's sake. She's a wonderful, sweet girl. She has such a bright future, just as you do. I want you girls to have it all, you know. A great graduation, a great college experience, good lives, friendship for a long time."

Cammie stood. "Here's what you don't get. If I tell, if someone gets involved, it's going to be so bad. So much worse."

"Not always. Sometimes when someone gets involved, solutions are found. You'd be surprised."

"Do you want me to leave this door open?" Cammie asked.

"Yes, thanks," she said.

Iris sat at her desk, thinking. She hadn't been completely honest with Cammie. When a kid was in an abusive situation at home, the child could be saved, but usually at a great cost that would make her wonder just how good that solution was. It often meant breaking apart a family, getting police involved, foster care, all kinds of interventions that, for at least a little while, seemed worse than the abuse. Years later they might look back and think, *Thank God someone was brave enough to step in!* But getting there often felt like the pain was only escalating.

If Rachel's twelve-year-old brother was beating her up badly enough to leave black eyes and bruises, the children would have to be separated. Maybe counseling could help both the victim and the abuser, put them on a better path.

Of course, it might not be Bobby at all. Maybe it was Sassy or Rachel's father or one of the many other family members they lived with. But it was now beyond doubt as far as Iris was concerned. Someone was isolating Rachel and pounding her. Those

259

situations didn't get better spontaneously.

She heard the laughter of girls and it was like a balm for her worried spirit. She opened her other door, the one that led to the offices and cubicles. She went in search of the laughing and, in a small cubicle set aside for her use, Iris found Krista and Misty sorting and stapling papers and laughing hysterically.

"I must have missed the joke," she said, leaning into the little room.

Krista looked up and had tears on her cheeks from her laughter. "Oh, Ms. McKinley, it was hilarious!"

"You know Butch Sandler?" Misty asked. "He's such a slob anyway, but he was making milk come out of his nose! Totally gross."

"We didn't laugh in front of him," Krista said. "That would only encourage him."

"But we had to bring our ice cream back here to finish because it was just impossible to eat it in the lunchroom with that going on. Really, I thought I was going to die."

"Did you two just finish lunch?" Iris asked.

"It's my study hall and Misty's lunch period, so I worked in here during lunch and went to lunch during study hall so we could eat together. A bunch of my girl-friends have this lunch hour so we can all eat together. That's okay, isn't it? Because you said —"

"Of course it's okay," Iris said. "You can manage your schedule. Both of you do so much for me and it's appreciated." She squinted at Misty. "Did you get a new haircut?"

Misty beamed. "Do you like it?"

"Very sharp," Iris said. She looked like a new girl. Not a hint of sadness or stress. She even looked more mature.

"Oh, by the way, I signed up for the PSAT without the prep course, just to see where I stand without a lot of studying ahead. That's what Krista did and it worked out for her."

"It was perfect," Krista said. "I took it again the following year and did great."

"Good," Iris said. "But let me ask you this — is the syllabus for the prep course ready for me to pass out? It's coming up soon."

"All ready," Misty said, pointing to a neat stack of papers on the bookcase.

"You are lifesavers. I hope I'm paying you enough for all this hard work."

They melted into laughter all over again.

I couldn't have planned that better if I'd planned it! Iris thought.

Seth could count on one hand the number of people from his childhood who'd kept up with him after the accident and Robbie Delaney wasn't one of them. Of course, most of their lives, from grade school through high school, they were rivals as much as friends. It seemed to Robbie that Seth got every break, Robbie was clear about that.

Now, so many years later, Seth was trying to figure out a little bit about Robbie. He'd been seen around town regularly, going to the occasional football game, but he had a small business in North Bend and had lived there for years. Robbie painted lines in parking lots and cut down trees. His cell phone number was on his business card and internet advertisement.

Seth called him. "Hey, Robbie, it's Seth Sileski. From Thunder Point. How are you?"

"Good, good. Need some lumber cut?"

"No," he said. "But I do need to talk to you. Can we get together?"

"What about?" Robbie asked.

"Well, about your boy, as a matter of fact. Nothing too serious, but . . . Sassy didn't tell you I gave Bobby a lift home the other night?"

Seth heard a heavy sigh. "No, no one mentioned that. What happened?"

"Look, can I just get a half hour of your time?"

"I'm real busy today. I like to get a lot of work done when the sun's shining. Why don't you just lay it on me. He in some kind of trouble?"

Seth didn't answer. "You break for lunch?"

Robbie was quiet. "I'll meet you at the casino. I'll be the guy in the truck in the parking lot with the line painter. I can't take a lot of time, Seth. But if that's the only way you're going to tell me about my boy, we can meet there."

Seth went to the sandwich shop and got a couple of subs and a couple of drinks and pulled slowly into the casino lot. It was easy to see where Robbie was working — a big area was sectioned off with orange road cones and tape. The line painter was a hand-held piece of machinery about the size of a large lawn mower and Robbie had his head down, watching his work, the painter chugging along.

Seth parked outside the tape and carefully made his way over to Robbie, watching the wet white lines. Robbie finally looked up, raised his visor and turned off his machine. Seth was struck by how much Robbie looked like his dad — he was large and a little overweight. Then he gave a half smile and pulled off his cap, wiping a hand over his balding head.

"I brought lunch," Seth said. "I know you're on a tight schedule."

"I'm painting lines," Robbie said.

"In the sunshine." Seth handed him a bag. "I bet it's a good business."

"It's not like I carry a gun or anything," he said.

"You could, if you wanted to. It's not as if you're likely to use it. I haven't used mine and I'm hoping I never do. Let's go sit under that tree. Might as well enjoy the weather. It's not going to stay warm and dry much longer."

Seth was barely settled when Robbie spoke. "Hard to believe Bobby did anything bad." He opened the bag and pulled out a thick sub. "He's a really good kid. He helps me on weekends and he's easy to be around, easier than I was at that age. He's nice, you know? Good-natured."

"Might not have been as much bad as a stupid prank," Seth said as he pulled out his sandwich. "But it might be something you want to talk to him about, just to be sure. It was Halloween night and I was sitting in the dark on a street just keeping an eye on things when I saw a kid dressed all in black charge a couple of smaller kids and grab their candy bags. He wasn't alone, he was with another boy, also dressed in black.

I caught Bobby while the other kid got away. I made him give back the candy and took him home." He took a bite of his sandwich, chewed and swallowed. "I suggested to Sassy that she tell you, get you involved in talking to Bobby, make sure he's not headed down a bad trail."

"Sue Marie didn't say anything," Robbie said, reminding Seth that Sassy had a name preference. Robbie ate a little more. "But then, we don't communicate very well."

"You're divorced?" Seth asked.

"Might as well be, but it isn't official. She left a couple of years ago. She works here," he said, pointing to the casino. "She's a cocktail waitress. Hard work."

"I didn't know that," Seth said. "I knew she lived with her sister, is that right?"

Robbie nodded. "Look, I'll talk to Bobby. I see the kids all the time. Not Rachel so much anymore — she's sixteen, got a boyfriend, does a lot of babysitting, cheerleader, all that. But the boys are with me almost every weekend and they're good kids. The little guy, Sam, he's only nine and a real kick in the pants, but what a sweetheart. I'm no hotshot cop or anything, but I do the best I can and those kids are good kids."

Seth laughed. "Like I'm a hotshot cop? I'm a deputy in a little bitty town, Robbie.

It's not a big job, it took me about four years to convince the Sheriff's Department to hire me. But it's my little town and every once in a while I feel like I do something that could matter. Like taking Bobby home before he got in more trouble."

"Hmm," Robbie said. "What did Sue Marie say when you brought him home?"

"She sent him to his room. I hoped she meant to talk to him later, get the drop on him if he was up to no good. But I think she was getting ready to go out or something and was a little . . . She was distracted. You know?"

"Drinking? Was she drinking?"

Seth measured his answer. She hadn't seemed drunk and as far as he knew, hadn't done anything wrong. "Well . . ."

"It was a problem for us sometimes," Robbie said. "We got married so young. Sue Marie is still young and pretty. She likes to party. Sometimes she can hit that wine kinda hard." He took another bite. "Was she planning to go out with you?"

"Me?" he asked. "No. Why would she be going out with me?"

Robbie shrugged. "She mentioned you were back in town about ten times and said you'd gotten together and she thought . . . I guess she thought you'd be dating any that."

"I don't know where she got that idea. I ran into her one night at Cliff's when she was picking up takeout, but no, there was no getting together. That night I ran into her, I was meeting someone. I'm seeing someone."

"You are?" he asked, suddenly a little more interested and slightly more friendly. "Who?"

"I shouldn't say," Seth said. "We're really new. And I don't think she knows yet, even though I'm at her house almost every day."

Robbie laughed. "Who?" he said. "Someone from town?"

"I shouldn't tell you," Seth said. "At least not until I put down some stakes. You have a bad reputation for going after other guys' girls."

"Come on, that's not right. It was just Sue Marie and it was high school. You ever lose any other girl to me? Besides, I'm not exactly tempting these days. I'm married with three kids even if I'm the only one who knows it."

"When did you and Sue Marie get married?" Seth asked.

"Right after high school. She got pregnant with Rachel. We didn't either one of us finish even the first year of college. Not like we planned it that way, but I was okay with that." He got a very wistful look on his face. "That little girl, Rachel, she was the best thing ever happened to me. You seen that girl? She's pretty and smart and the sweetest kid. Everyone likes her. I don't get to spend as much time with her since I don't live with Sue Marie, but we're still close. She tells me what she's doing, where she's going, if she needs something she calls me. She's everything to me. I gotta be honest, maybe I didn't amount to that much, but those kids are everything to me. Sue Marie, too. She doesn't really believe it, but she is."

He really loves her, Seth thought with some surprise.

"You wouldn't ever knock her around or anything, would you?" Seth asked. "Like maybe grab her and give her a shake if she's not listening?"

"What are you talking about? You don't touch a woman that way, man! How many times did Iris knock the shit outta us and we weren't allowed to hit back? Jesus, Sileski, *you* never hit back, did you?"

Seth laughed in spite of himself. "Naw, she flattened me every time. Sue Marie isn't a hitter, like Iris was, is she?"

"Naw, the only thing Sue Marie ever hits

is the bottle. Aw, I shouldn't't've said that."

"It's not going anywhere, buddy. By the way, it's Iris. Iris is the girl I'm chasing. But could you try not to tell anyone? Because Iris just isn't getting it yet and I'm going to have to up my game."

"Whoa," he said a little excitedly. "Iris? You always hung out with Iris, but I didn't think . . . You know."

"I know. I seriously didn't think much back then. So, you gonna talk things over with Bobby?"

"Oh, absolutely," Robbie said. "I don't want him picking on younger kids — that just won't wash. And hey, I shouldn't have made it sound like Sue Marie is a bad mother or anything. She takes her wine a little seriously sometimes, but she's a good mother. Maybe she'll even think about things and . . . Well, I don't get my hopes up about that. But I will definitely talk to Bobby."

"Tell him I'm his friend," Seth said. "Tell him if he ever needs anything and you're not available, he can call me."

"That's good," Robbie said. "That's real good. Hey, thanks for lunch. It was good to see you. Good to catch up."

"For me, too," Seth said, shaking his hand. "Call anytime I can help."

THIRTEEN

After being told about Seth's conversation with Robbie, Iris was left with very few options but to question Rachel about her frequent accidents, her bruises. Cammie had not come forward with information and Iris was not about to sell her out.

At first, Rachel was quite convincing, telling Iris that her frequent injuries were not related in any way to any form of abuse or neurological disorder. No, she had never thought of herself as one who bruised easily or someone perpetually off balance. In fact, she assured Iris, if she looked around, all athletic girls suffered their share of scrapes, bruises and mishaps.

And then Rachel had yet another fall and sustained a concussion. Iris found out about it after the fact — Rachel's aunt was concerned because she had hit her head slipping on the icy walk, had a headache, then started throwing up. She took her to see Dr.

Grant, who wasted no time admitting her to the hospital. But Rachel was examined, observed and released before Iris even heard about it.

"It's right under our noses," she said to Seth. "Something is happening to that girl — something medical or abusive or something. I can smell it."

Seth agreed. "Keep watch. Don't drive her further away with too many questions. You can call Child Welfare if you want to," Seth said. "But in my conversation with Robbie, I didn't hear anything that made me suspect anyone in her family would hurt her. Robbie's gone positively sweet — he's not the Robbie I fought with for years growing up."

"Sassy hasn't gone sweet," Iris said. "But she seems to be very proud of Rachel and Rachel is a nice girl. She's protecting someone. Uncle? Aunt?"

"Where'd you leave it when you talked to her?"

"On a positive note, I hope," Iris said. "I want her to know I'm not there to make her life difficult. I'm there to help. I made sure she had my cell phone number."

The Thunder Point football team made the state playoffs, but they didn't make it far. They were a ranked favorite and lost the second game. A pall fell over the town even though a couple of players had such a good season they had great scholarship potential.

Iris returned to school after her flu for the busy season of prep courses for the SAT and then the tests. Students who signed up were allowed a full day for the prep and a full day for the test. There would be another chance after Christmas and again in June. Most juniors liked to test in the spring of their junior year and the fall of their senior year. She had been busy with this since school started and she was back to bringing work home.

And Seth had started showing up with either ice cream or maybe a bottle of wine. Iris stopped him from bringing his mother's dinner every night, but she couldn't seem to get rid of him. It was even harder to make him go away since she enjoyed every second he was around.

After a couple of very busy weeks, she stopped by the flower shop on a Friday afternoon to see Grace. "I remember this as the best time of year, but my mother thought of it as the worst time," Iris said. "Business was kind of down. But so was work and she didn't need me in here as much."

"There's plenty to do right up to the night

before Thanksgiving, then there's nothing until about the second week in December. It would be a good time to take a break if I took breaks," Grace said.

"Don't you ever think of going back to Portland to visit friends?" Iris asked.

"Oh, there's a standing invitation, but I'm very cozy here."

"Would you like to spend Thanksgiving with me?" Iris asked. "Like we did last year?"

"Well, I might have plans. I'm still mulling it over. Troy is going skiing up in the Mount Hood area. He said I'm welcome to join him, though I don't have any gear or the right clothes. You could come, too. We could share a room."

"So, you're going?" Iris asked.

"I didn't say yes yet. I could rent skis and boots, but I'd have to ski in jeans."

"I have a bib and jacket you could borrow," Iris said. "I have extra gloves and mittens and hats."

"But then you couldn't go! I don't want you to be alone! I'd rather have Thanksgiving with you than think of you being alone."

"This is a nice conundrum. Seth invited me to his mother's — I guess his brothers are going to be there and it will be a big family gathering. The invitation is extended to you and Troy, too. But I'm having a real problem with this. I don't think it's a good idea."

"Why not? You've been close to the Sileskis your whole life, even through all that time that you and Seth were on the outs. You love Gwen! She's like a second mother to you."

"I do love Gwen," Iris said. "Ever since I had the flu, Seth has been hanging around his mother's and coming over almost every night. I don't think he does more than visit his town house in Bandon and I keep trying to put a stop to it, but he keeps showing up."

Grace leaned on her worktable. She smiled. "Want to come upstairs for dinner? I have chili in the Crock-Pot."

"Aw, I don't know. . . ."

"I have wine, Iris. And it would keep you away from your house for a little while."

Iris thought about that for three seconds. "Yes," she said. "That's right. Okay."

"And you can tell me why you want to get rid of a guy whose company you enjoy so much."

Grace locked the shop and they went up to Grace's apartment. When a glass of wine was in Iris's hand, it was only too natural to tell her closest friend about her dilemma.

"I wish he'd spend more time with his family, with his other friends, with his deputies. It's nice to see him and, I admit, it's great to be on good terms again. But he's been at my back door almost every day for weeks now. It was understandable when he was playing nursemaid to my flu, but I'm all better. I'm not used to being with someone so much."

"Need more space, Iris?" Grace asked.

"I'm starting to get used to him," she said. "That's not a good thing. He doesn't understand — I have feelings for him. I probably always will. There's nothing I can do about it. Fighting with him didn't work so I'm just going to have to accept it. But if he hangs around every day then on that day he moves on, I'm going to feel hurt. Grace, I don't want to feel sad over him. Friends need to keep it friendly."

Just as she said that, her cell phone rang. It was Seth.

"Hello?"

"Hi. Are you going to be home tonight?"

"A little later. I'm having dinner with Grace."

"Good. Then I'll go home, shower, change out of my uniform and see you in a couple of hours."

Iris paused for a moment. "Okay. See you then."

When she disconnected she looked at Grace. "I guess I'm going to have to try to explain to Seth, huh?"

"I can't wait to hear this explanation."

"What am I going to say?" Iris complained.

Grace just sighed and dished up two bowls of chili. She put a box of crackers and a small bowl of shredded cheddar on the little table. Then she sat down. "Iris, of all the people I've ever known, you not only have the biggest aversion to lies, you have always known how to be direct with the truth and still gentle and diplomatic. You're the only person I know who can tell a fifteen-year-old girl that the way she's dressing isn't doing her any favors and make her feel like she's just been given a compliment and motivate her to cover her body more appropriately. This is what you do, Iris. You speak the truth kindly, unreservedly, with complete candor. It's your job and you've mastered it."

"I don't feel as confident as you make me sound."

"You love Seth. You don't want to be exploited and disappointed. You need boundaries — friends are friends, not romantic partners, and when the line is blurred people get hurt and getting hurt is not a good agenda. Come on, Iris," Grace said. "It's only fair, what you want to say."

"It's only fair," she agreed. "What if he doesn't understand?"

"Iris, he doesn't have to understand, he just has to comply. Tell him you want a boyfriend, not a boy who's a friend. Tell him whatever you told Troy to get him to back off."

"You know about that?" she asked Grace.

"I don't know what I know. I mentioned that I thought Troy was still looking for a way to go out with you and he said that you put him straight, that you were just friends and he shouldn't presume any more. So? I don't know anything."

"I did do that. And you know why this is harder? Because I really don't love Troy. I mean, I like him a lot and I wish I could love him because he's so great. But I don't. With Seth it's all confused."

"Well, give it to him straight, the way you do so well. And don't back down."

The night was cold, but Iris didn't care — she walked from Grace's apartment. Even though her car was in her carport, the house was dark and it was obvious she wasn't home. Yet Seth was parked right behind her car, sitting in his SUV, waiting. She walked right up to his window and tapped.

"What are you doing?" she asked.

"Waiting for you to get home," he said.

"Why aren't you at your mother's house?"

"It would have been awkward," he said. "Me sitting there expectantly, maybe peeking out the window to see if the light's on yet, maybe texting you a lot. I didn't really want to sit with my mother in front of the TV. I just wanted to see you."

"Why?" she asked.

"Same reason I come to see you whenever I want to, because you're more fun than my mother. And I brought wine."

"I've had two glasses of wine," she said.

"Good thing you don't have to drive anywhere." He let himself out of the car. "There could be a special on crafts on the shopping channel or something and that would have been torture. My mother enjoys explaining what we're watching on TV. I was happier waiting in the car."

"Seth, what are you doing coming over here every day?"

"Being cheerful, helpful and friendly," he said.

"Oh, brother." She shook her head. "Come in. Let's get you a glass of wine."

"Do you have a beer?"

"Why would you bring a bottle of wine if you want a beer?"

"Because you'll want a glass of wine, maybe, and I'm accommodating."

"What you are is confusing. Yes, I have beer. And you can have it while we have a serious talk."

"Another one of those?"

"Just listen, then," she said. She unlocked the house, opened the door and let him in. "Kitchen table," she instructed. She gave him a beer and sat down at the table. Looking at him. He was smiling patiently. She loved his soft brown hair. He took a drink from his beer bottle. "Well?"

"Are you going to listen to me?"

"Of course, Iris. I always do."

"All right, here's the thing. It's nice to be friendly again. I'm glad we sorted through our more serious issues and can be on good terms. We have a really complicated history, you and me. When I stop to think about it, the odds were against us patching things up. So this is good — we patched things up. But now we have to have some boundaries."

"Whatever you say, Iris," he said, tilting the bottle against his lips again.

"You can't come over every night," she said.

"Why not? You busy?"

"Most nights I bring work home."

"I know. And most nights I work kind of late. Or I run or work out. But I'll do what you want. We could have dinner before you do schoolwork or I could come over a little later. But we always have a lot to talk about, we have a good time."

"Seth," she said, leaning toward him, elbows on the table. "I can't have this. I can't have you here every day, being my buddy, my pal, getting me so used to having you around, relying on your company. Because you're going to come over one night and tell me you met a great woman. And you'll want me to meet her. You'll want me to get a date so we can go out together. You'll want to talk about her all the time and you'll expect me to be so happy for you, that you found the right woman. And I'll be alone again, just like before. I'll be sitting in front of the home shopping network, reading through reports from school and you'll be making love somewhere with the perfect woman. Don't you get it, Seth?"

"I get it, but that's not going to happen. I'm not a high school boy anymore."

"Oh, underneath it all, you're still that guy. But I'm not the girl you could count on to be a buddy anymore. See, I'd be disappointed. I'd feel kind of abandoned. I don't need any more friends, Seth. I mean, in the friend department, I have Troy."

"Troy seems nice. I guess that didn't take?"

"He's a *friend*! That means we see each other at work and maybe an evening a week, sometimes with other teachers. I don't want it to be any more serious with Troy because I just don't. It just isn't there. I feel about Troy kind of the way you feel about me — like I love him madly except not in the right ways."

"You think that's how I feel? And you don't want it to be any more serious with me?" he asked.

"I just don't see that happening. And don't misunderstand. I must admit I appreciate that you wanted to straighten out our situation, that you wanted to make amends and be friends again, friends like we used to be. We can do that, Seth. But you have to stop coming around all the time. I still have feelings for you. If you keep paying so much attention to me, I'm going to be broken. Oh, damn, that was hard to say. Don't make me say that again."

But Seth wasn't listening. "You have feelings for me? What kind of feelings?"

"Right now I have feelings like I'd love to

shove you in a hole! Don't you hear what I'm saying? I had a big crush on you, all right? And you let me down. I know it was a long time ago and I know you're sorry and I accept your apology, but all that being said I still don't feel like going through it again. So we can be friends, all right? But not every damn day — it sets me up for a major letdown. And I want to be free! I'll never find the right guy if you keep slogging up my brain like you do."

"I do?"

"You do! You are not boyfriend material. You are pal qualified and that's about all."

He took another swallow of his beer. "That's perfectly understandable, Iris," he said. "I'll be more careful about that." He stood. "Thanks for the beer." And then he let himself out the back door.

She heard his car start.

"That went well," she said to no one. "Thanks for the advice, Grace!"

Seth drove about four blocks to the alley behind the flower shop. He left his car running while he ran up the stairs and pounded on Grace's door. She opened it cautiously; she was in her pajamas.

"I need flowers," he said.

"What kind of flowers?"

"It doesn't matter, but I need some right this minute. They're for Iris."

Her eyebrows shot up. "Really?"

"Come on, could we hurry up here?"

"Iris likes calla lilies. I might have some in the cooler. . . ."

"Today, Grace?"

"Let me get my keys."

She locked her back door, ran down the stairs and let herself into the shop. It took her about five minutes to gather the flowers, put them in a vase, tie a ribbon around it and walk into the alley to give them to Seth.

"What do I owe you?" he asked, reaching for his pocket.

"I'll run you a tab. I'm not opening the register tonight. But it's going to be expensive."

"I'll stop by tomorrow or Monday and settle up."

"Sure," she said. "I hope she likes 'em."

I hope she likes *me,* Seth thought. He drove back to Iris's house, backed into her driveway and hurried to her front door. She was used to him coming to the back door, but he rang the bell and knocked.

Iris opened the door. She held his beer in one hand and a tissue in the other. "What the —"

He pushed his way in, sliding an arm around her waist, holding the flowers in the other hand. He leaned his forehead against hers. "I'm back," he said. "I don't want to be a pal. I want to be more. Way more."

"You better not be lying," she said with a sniff.

He kissed her. It was clumsy at first. She backed away a little. Then she moved forward and let him cover her lips with his. He felt the initial resistance and then the submission. He moved his mouth over hers for a moment and then, against her lips, he whispered, "You're going to let me in, trust me, give me a chance and eventually you're going to love me as much as I love you."

"You . . . ? Love . . . ?"

"I do, Iris. I've always loved you but I didn't know what love was. I think I've got it now." He reached behind him to set the flowers on the table just inside the front door, then wrapped both his arms around her waist. "I wasn't fooling around, I was just giving you time to get used to me again. I've missed you so much. I think we're right together."

Her eyes teared up. "Seth, why didn't you act like it?"

"I tried to let you know without getting clocked," he said. "I'm coming over every day and not to be your buddy. You have to give me a chance."

"Oh, God," she said, putting both arms around his neck to hold him closer. She promptly poured half a cold beer down his back.

"Ah!" he said, shouting and arching.

"Oh, God!" she said, righting the bottle in her hand. She made to pull away but he pulled her right back.

"Iris, how long are you going to continue to torture me?" he asked her. "Can we put down all the weapons and just make out for a while?"

"I suppose, but shouldn't we get you out of that wet shirt?"

He smiled, lifted one eyebrow, reached for the vase of calla lilies and poured the water down the front of her shirt. She gasped, arched away from him, then started to laugh. She emptied the rest of the beer on the front of his shirt while her lips were pressed against his. He poured a little more water from the vase down her back.

And then the laughing stopped and the kissing grew more intense. Hotter. And deeper and wetter.

"Just take me to bed, Iris," he whispered. "And I'll never ask for another thing."

FOURTEEN

It was like old times and yet completely new. It was fun and games and then it was desperately serious, Iris thought. The first thing Seth did was take the beer bottle from her hand. "Are you finished with this?"

"I think so."

"You were crying and drinking my beer?" he asked.

"Don't flatter yourself, I didn't cry that much. But I did drink a little of your beer."

He touched her lips with his again. "Good idea," he said. He ran a tongue over her lips. "You have excellent lips, Iris. Just excellent."

As they made their way to the bedroom, he pulled her wet shirt off, then his own, tossing them both on the floor. He kissed her; he unsnapped her jeans and pushed them down over her hips, never letting her go. "Sit," he said, sitting on the edge of the bed himself. While she kicked off her pants, he took some time to remove his shoes and that secret gun he wore around his ankle. He started to put it on the bedside table, then cast a narrow-eyed glance her way, lifted a thoughtful eyebrow and moved the gun to the dresser across the room.

"I can still get to it there," she said, laughter in her voice.

"With you, I have to worry. If I don't perform well, I might get shot."

He pulled his jeans down and stood in his plaid boxers. "Sexy," she said.

"Be careful. It's the family tartan."

"The Sileski clan has a tartan?" she asked.

"I didn't think I was getting lucky tonight. I also didn't think I was getting thrown out. A guy has to be ready for anything with you, Iris." He lifted an edge of the covers. "And I am. Crawl in."

He slid in right beside her, pulling her close. They were face-to-face, nose to nose, forehead to forehead. His hands ran up and down her back, over her hips. "Iris, you're wearing fancy underwear," he said.

"I always wear nice underwear. Sometimes downright slutty underwear . . ."

"I'm on board for some of that," he said with a sigh. "Iris, you have no idea how long I've wanted to do this, to feel you against me like this. Still and close." Then he slid her panties down and unhooked her bra.

"Hmm. This is even better," he said, pulling her against him, feeling the length of her in his arms. "Please say you're on the pill."

"I am, but what about you?"

"Clean as a whistle, no danger. I have a condom if you're concerned."

"I can trust you?"

"Not only has it been a long time, I was screened recently. I'm disease- and virus-free. But beware, I could be potent as the devil." He smiled against her lips. "I want you. I want to do things to you."

Her hands were on the waist of his boxers. "In the family tartan?"

He let go of her just long enough to ditch the boxers. "You're right. We don't need anything between us."

"If tomorrow comes and you've forgotten . . ."

"Honey, I lost more in that disaster than you did. Things would've been so different if I'd remembered. I don't know how, but I know everything would've been different. Now, you have to do something for me, Iris. I need you to shut up for a while." And with that he was hard on her mouth, crushing her against him. With a bent knee, he separated her legs and his fingers gently investigated her inner thighs, her lower belly, her soft butt, her damp center. Just as he began to probe a little bit, his lips dropped to her breast.

She moaned and arched slightly, wanting more of him. With his mouth on her sensitive nipples and his fingers on her, in her, she was squirming with pleasure. His touch was so sweet, so powerful.

He moved slowly until he was over her and her knees were spread, his mouth on hers again, his kiss deepening and his tongue inside her mouth at the very moment he entered her. He lifted himself, looking into her eyes. "God," he whispered. "Iris . . ."

Then his mouth was on hers again and he began to move inside her, slowly and deeply. She drifted away as she clutched at him — every nerve in her body was focused on their coupling and she rocked toward him just as he pushed harder into her. His mouth was everywhere — on hers, on her neck, on her breasts, on her mouth again. She began to pant, she mewled in anticipation of the payoff. It didn't take very long; she felt a molten heat gather in her core and then there was the beautiful clench and throb she'd been searching for. He pushed deeper and was still, holding her tight against him, mouth to mouth, pelvis to pelvis. He hummed softly as Iris saw stars.

Then she felt him pulse inside her just as he groaned deep in his throat.

It was a long time coming down from that. It seemed to last forever. And it was so good.

There they were together again, forehead to forehead, nose to nose, kisses coming softer and sweeter, panting a little and breathing each other's warm breath. He held his weight off her while keeping them so close that not even a sigh could come between them. They were like that, still and quiet and close, for a long time.

"Iris, I love you," he said.

"How do you know?" she asked in a whisper.

"I've known for a long time," he said. He gently left her body, rolled onto his back beside her and pulled her into his arms so that her head rested on his shoulder. "I thought about the fact that I never forgave myself for hurting you years ago. I didn't even know the extent of that hurt, yet I never got over it, either. Then, a couple of years ago I started letting people in the department know that I was looking for an assignment in Thunder Point. I told them it was my hometown, that I grew up here, that my parents lived here. I didn't think it would help my case to tell them there was a girl in Thunder Point I couldn't forget, but you were one of the reasons I wanted to be here. Right here where you are, where I'd see you every day so I could figure out how to have you in my life again."

"What if I hated you?"

"In fact, I thought you did. I didn't know you had a crush on me in high school — how would I know that? But that aside, you loved me once. I didn't think you loved me the way I wanted, but what the hell, Iris — it was a place to start. Because I couldn't forget you — you were always on my mind. I dreamed about you, for God's sake!"

She pushed herself up to look into his eyes. "Yeah, about that . . ."

"The dreams. I dream about women from time to time — sometimes strangers, sometimes celebrities, sometimes random women I'd seen a time or two, but you were the only encore performer. I even had dreams that we had sex in the flower van. Maybe I remembered it in my sleep but not when I was conscious." He smiled. "It was much better for me than it was for you."

"That part of your memory is correct," she said.

He growled in some shame but kissed her neck. "How did you ever manage to forgive me?"

"Reality eventually sank in. You're not

much of a drinker, Seth. At least you weren't then. You were practically sleepwalking. And then you passed out. It was a crappy set of circumstances, but I don't think I was wrong and I don't think you were malicious. I think we were in different realities. I wonder what would have happened if I'd told you the very next day, the second I realized you didn't remember."

"I don't know," he said. "I'd like to think just knowing, we would have gotten together. But were we mature or intelligent enough for that? You had a crush — were you capable of dealing with a seventeen-year-old athlete so self-centered and arrogant the world revolved around me? That's a big job for any girl. And I cared about you so much, but was I mature enough to know the responsibility of that? I don't know, Iris. I know everything would've been different, but I don't know in what ways."

He rolled her over so he was looking down at her again. "I know that after all we've been through and after the years we've put in, we should know now. What do you think?"

"I think I love you," she said. "I always loved you, but I think we would've screwed it up seventeen years ago. We might've ended up in the same place as now — making amends and promising to do better. Or we might've been estranged forever."

"I'll do better, Iris," he said. "I'm not saying I'll be perfect, I know better. But there's one thing — you're one woman I never forgot. Never got over. That's got to mean something." He ran a big hand down her body and she shivered. "It means a lot right now."

The next thing she knew, she was sighing and arching again. Then she was exploding, a shower of sparkling stars raining down on her while he pulsed inside her. Then there was the panting, the sighing, the gratitude neither of them spoke of. And that precious closeness. They were quiet in the dark for so long.

"Are you leaving now?" she finally asked.

"If you want me to, I'll go. But you have to promise me we'll see each other tomorrow and we'll be all right."

"But don't you have to go? Your car is in my drive and it's —" She looked at the clock. "It's after midnight. People will know you spent the night."

"I want people to know I spent the night. I'm not hiding anything, I'm an adult and this was consensual. And beautiful, it was beautiful. But if it makes you uncomfortable, I can leave. We can be more discreet. You're a high school counselor."

"I'm an adult, too," she said. "I know you won't be upset to learn you are not the first man in my life. Nor the first to stay overnight."

"I have no trouble believing that."

"But your mother lives next door," she reminded him, as if he needed reminding.

"Even more reason. My mother is probably typical — she has a hard time remembering her sons are not twelve. Even if you lived a mile away, don't you think she'd find out? And soon? She's very nosy. A good mother, but very nosy."

Iris giggled. "I have a confession. I've only slept all night with a man a couple of times. College and once later. And I didn't sleep well."

"I suppose it takes getting used to."

"You suppose?"

"I've had a few girlfriends, but I never lived with any of them. They were perfectly nice, terrific girls, but it just wasn't that serious. We didn't do sleepovers. I didn't want to stay over."

"God, we're pathetic," she said.

"How's that?"

"Thirty-four, never married, never had sleepovers, never got serious . . ."

He snuggled closer to her. "Maybe this sleepover will be okay," he said. "It's completely up to you."

"I'm in," she said. "Stay."

It was no grand test for Seth. He slept like a baby. Somewhere in the dark of night he felt Iris stir and get up. When she came back to bed, she brought him a glass of water. Then she reached for him, kissing his shoulder, his ear, his neck. He roused to her naked softness against him and he rolled with her, devouring her all over again, taking her, loving her until she cried out. Then he cradled her, covering her with soft kisses all over her body, holding her until her breathing came deep and even. He nuzzled against the delicious smell of her skin and slept. He was pressed up against her, spooning her or holding her through the night.

He'd never felt more at home, more at peace.

He'd thought he was in love a couple of times before, or maybe it was more accurate to say he wanted to be in love and hoped to be. But this was so different and no one had ever explained it to him. He felt his love for Iris deep in his bones. He felt it in his soul. His life would be half a life without her. He wanted everything with her. It was like he'd waited for a woman like her. He wondered if it would terrify her to learn how much he wanted. He was ready for everything with her — commitment, family, a lifetime. It was going to be hard to go slowly.

He woke at the same time as Iris. Someone was at the door. He looked at the clock and it was seven, a rare hour for him to be asleep. But then the woman beside him had been greedy and tired him out. She mumbled and started to get out of bed. "No, let me," he said. "Stay right where you are."

He pulled on the family tartan and headed barefoot to the front door. His limp was much more pronounced when he didn't wear shoes with a little lift in the heel. He looked out the window in the front door and saw only the top of someone's head, but her hair was curly and silver.

He opened the door and she jumped. "Seth!" she said.

"Who did you expect?"

"Well, I wasn't sure, but I saw your car and you hadn't come home and —"

"Because I'm here," he said.

"But . . . where's Iris?" she asked.

"Where do you think she is, Mom?"

"Oh! Oh, dear."

"I think from now on, you should call

when you feel like popping over. What do you say?"

"I . . . ah . . . I . . ."

"That's right, Mom. You have the number so if you need something, just call. Or you can always call my cell — I'll let you know that everything is all right. Okay?"

"Yes! Of course! But I . . ." She shook her head. "Oh, the hell with it. You might warn a person! I went out to get the paper and saw your car, but I couldn't find you!"

"I'd like you to consider it a pleasant surprise, say no more about it and go home. I'll call you later."

"Yes," she said. "Yes, call later."

And she turned to waddle down the walk, crossing the yards to her front door. He chuckled and went back to bed. He slipped under the covers and pulled Iris close. "Check that one off. Gwen has found us out."

"Oh, Seth!"

"What? It was bound to happen. At least it's over with. Now maybe we can sleep in. Although, you might be bad for my career — I never stay in bed this late in the morning."

"Oh, God, that was your mother at the door! That's like a dating nightmare! The worst kind! She thinks I debauched her little boy."

"Would it help if I told her I debauched twice and you only once?"

"Ack," she barked, slapping him on the arm. "That was your *mother.*"

"Yes, it was. I sent her away and told her to call ahead next time. She's old enough to know better."

"I'll have to say something to her," Iris said. "What in the world am I supposed to say?"

"Tell her you're sorry you missed her this morning, but you were naked, warm and hoping to get laid again before breakfast."

"Seth!"

"I slept like the dead. Right up until your greedy little hands were on me, teasing me, getting me up. Literally." He grinned. "Best sleepover I've ever had. I think I'll do it again."

"You're not the least bit troubled by her early-morning visit, are you?"

He shook his head. "Not the least."

"What are we supposed to do now?"

"I think we should at least go steady, but that's about the most patience I have. For two cents I'd take you right to the justice of the peace and stake my claim. I love you, Iris. And you sleep very well."

"You're in a bit of a hurry, I think."

"I am, I guess. Sorry. Take your time, Iris. Don't let me rush you."

"What is it you think you want?" she asked.

"Everything. I want all of you. Happily ever after, a couple of kids, a permanent home, waking up together in the morning, fighting over who has to get up to get breakfast for the kids, arguments over chores and finances and then make-up sex and then we do it all over again. I want to be the person you love the most, get mad at most often, make up with because you can't help it. I want to be the guy you laugh with, lean on, cry on, yell at, reach for. I can do it, Iris. I can be the one."

"Seth, everyone is going to think this is too sudden," she said.

"Screw 'em. Even not counting the past thirty years, we've been working our way back to each other for a couple of months. No one knows me like you do — there's no woman in the world I will ever know the way I know you. Take your time, Iris. I'm ready when you are."

"What if I decide this is just not for me?"

He was shaking his head. "After last night? Bullshit."

She curled up close. "I think you should

try to convince me one more time. Then we'll shower and go get breakfast. Then I'll think of something to say to your mother."

His hand moved smoothly over her breast. "Please don't talk to me about my mother while I'm making love to you. I want to be able to do my best."

And she laughed until he successfully stopped her.

Iris found it was a transition that took minutes, not weeks. Seth took her to the diner for breakfast where they sat at the counter together and no one blinked an eye at them having breakfast together on a Saturday morning. They ran into Dr. Grant and his little boy having breakfast. They got to hear all about how Scott and Peyton had set a date and there was to be a big Basque wedding at her family's farm in the spring. Mac stopped by to check in with Gina and get a shopping list from her so he could make a store run, but he paused for a cup of coffee. Eric from the service station came in for a late breakfast and there was a little small talk about classic cars taking up residence in his body shop. Then Seth said he had some paperwork and told Iris to come over when she was ready for a lift home.

"Don't be silly," she said. "I'm walking. In fact, I might take a long walk across the beach."

"I'll talk to you later." He kissed her on the cheek as he left.

"That was nice," Gina said after he had gone.

"*He's* nice."

"So, you two?"

"Recently, sort of. Except that we've known each other since we were four. So it wasn't exactly a blind date."

Gina laughed. "A couple of old friends getting together has great odds. Mac and I were best friends for years before we became Mr. and Mrs. Mac."

"That's right," Iris said. "I had forgotten that."

"I didn't think this town would ever forget," Gina said with a laugh. "They had all been taking bets while we stumbled around trying to get together."

"I wonder how many in town have been watching me and Seth. . . ."

"Oh, I think many," Gina said, smiling. "You don't look unhappy."

"Just a little nervous," she said. "His mother is going to need an explanation for why his car was in my drive this morning."

"Child's play," Gina said. "We had to deal

with two sixteen-year-old daughters! Talk about nerves!"

"But I'm an expert on sixteen-year-old girls," Iris said. "I'm definitely not an expert on sixty-five-year-old mothers!"

"Same principles apply, I think," Gina said.

Iris popped her head in the flower shop and met eyes with a grinning Grace. "How'd those calla lilies work out?"

"Very well. You're quite a clever matchmaker."

"I had nothing to do with it! I was in my pajamas and had just plunged headfirst into a smutty novel when he came pounding at the door, a desperate man, demanding flowers for you. What in the world did you do to him?"

"I told him he had to go away."

"I'm going to remember that move," Grace said with a laugh. "In fact, I'm going to call Sam Worthington and tell him to leave me alone! And that I'll be right here if he's upset."

Iris bought a beautiful carrot cake from Carrie's deli and walked up the hill to her house, except she went next door and knocked on Gwen's back door. When Gwen opened the door, Iris immediately flushed pink. "Hi," she said, holding out the carrot cake.

"Come in, Iris, come in. Bearing gifts?"

"And maybe an explanation," she said a little timidly. "About this morning . . ."

"Shh. Seth would have a fit if he knew you were trying to explain. Besides, I've been hoping for years that the two of you would find each other. I don't know what happened between you, but you and Seth sure stumbled around for a long time."

"I was angry with him, Gwen. We had a fight in our senior year. It was all a horrible misunderstanding. Of course, it was mostly his fault. . . ."

"Of course," Gwen said.

"I brought you this cake. Have it for dessert. Norm will love it. I know you could bake an even better one, but this will give you a couple of hours to yourself instead. And about last night . . ."

"Shh," she said again. "I'm dying to know everything, but you better keep it to yourself. Let's just say I have a feeling those spare shirts he's been keeping here are going to move out."

Iris blushed again and felt so juvenile. "Possibly."

"I can't believe I went pounding at your

door! He's been so adamant that you're just friends that when I saw his car there in your drive, I wondered if something had gone wrong! I didn't even think! I just wanted to know he was all right!"

"That's completely understandable," Iris said.

"No, it's not, it's completely ridiculous. I know you kids think I grew up wearing poodle skirts to the soda shop, but that was the generation ahead of us. I was born in '49 — I came of age in the sixties! Free love, Haight-Ashbury, Vietnam, make love not war . . . Please, we were wild and daring. I married a man seven years older than me — I thought my parents were going to die! He didn't have two nickels to rub together, either, but he just romanced me and I was sunk."

Norm? Iris thought. Rule number one for Seth — he was not allowed to turn into a crabby old fart who just ignored her.

"At least you and Seth have some advantages. You have educations, good jobs, have known each other forever," Gwen said.

"I've always loved Seth," she said. "But, Gwen, we just admitted our true feelings last night. What if it doesn't work out? Again?"

"Ach, don't borrow trouble — if it's

304

meant to be, it works out. If not, just break an old woman's heart and think no more of it."

Iris burst into laughter. "You have a very mischievous side."

"So it's been said. I just want you both to be happy, together or otherwise. He's my baby and you're like a daughter. I've wanted this for longer than I can remember. And I promise — I'll stay on my side of the fence."

Iris was surprised to feel her eyes blur. She suddenly sniffed.

"Iris, what is it?"

She pursed her lips and shook her head, trying to gather strength. "I miss my mother at the strangest times," she said. "I wish the two of you were sitting here with me, listening to my lame explanations and excuses and . . . and letting me tell you how much he's always meant to me. I've missed him, Gwen. Seth is a good man."

"I know, sweetheart, I know. And it's good you've finally realized it. He desperately needs help picking out some undershorts!"

Iris laughed. "They're awful, aren't they?"

"I bet they were on sale. He's a good boy, but he's a little tight like his father."

Seth called Iris in the early afternoon. "Why don't you do whatever Saturday chores you have, then come over here. I'll cook and you can see where I used to hang my hat before I found a way to stalk my obsession in Thunder Point."

"Are you trying to avoid your mother? Because I talked with Gwen and she's not going to be a problem if you're at my house."

"No, there's no avoiding my mother. She'll notice if my car is at your house and she'll notice if your car is gone all night. And I hope your car will be gone all night. I just want to spoil you a little. I'm not a bad cook."

At six o'clock she walked into a simple but classy town house in a nice little complex just north of Bandon. He had a yard the size of a postage stamp, a patio that could hold two people comfortably, a living room, dining room, kitchen and two upstairs bedrooms. After seeing the family tartan boxers, she was a little concerned about his furnishings, but it turned out he'd been friendly with Pottery Barn and had quite decent furniture.

There was no sign of another woman here. No distinctly female touches. And it seemed Seth was willing to spend hard-earned money on some things — like his furniture and his mattress — but there was no question he'd purchased his towels and dishes on sale.

She kicked off her shoes and sat at his small dining room table, letting him serve her. He, of course, wore his shoes. That simple thing filled her with great tenderness for him; the shoes kept him even and steady.

They each had wine and she touched his glass with hers. "We've really overcome quite a lot in our lives, haven't we? Multiple losses and adjustments," she said. He'd had his losses, his career plans shifted, the trials of dealing with a disability. As for Iris, she'd been raised an only child by a single mother, then had buried her, leaving her very alone.

"I think we cut them in half by moving forward together," he said. "What do you think?"

"I think I'd have a real hard time turning back now."

"Good. That's exactly what I want to hear."

FIFTEEN

Iris went to Thunder Point High on Monday morning, walking on rainbows. It was when she was standing outside her office door, saying good morning to students, that she realized with some shame she hadn't thought about Troy all weekend. Well, she'd been on her honeymoon! And she hadn't broken up with him or cheated on him or anything like that. But still . . .

She knew how Troy felt about her, how much he hoped she'd change her mind and try again with him. It was pretty irrational of him and she had convinced herself that it all boiled down to the fact there wasn't much of a dating scene in Thunder Point once you graduated high school. That was how their first date had started — they were colleagues, both single, and he'd asked her if she wanted to go hiking. Then they'd met for a beer or two, went rafting. Then they'd kissed, and when they kissed she'd thought,

That was certainly nice. A few weeks later they'd tumbled into bed and it was likewise very satisfying. Iris was looking for the right man, but she wasn't a nun.

It took hardly any time at all to realize that she enjoyed spending time with Troy — rafting, snorkeling, hiking. And there was no question that she enjoyed sex. But what was *not* happening within her was longing. She'd just tried to ignore that little missing link, right up until Troy suggested they think about moving in together.

That's when she'd hit the brakes. The guidance counselor and the history teacher? Living together?

Thunder Point wasn't the most conservative town or high school on record. In fact, they were pretty easygoing about such things. Except when two teachers started dating or living together, it was *expected* that they were a serious couple, headed for at least a very long-term relationship if not marriage. There was spending the occasional night together, discreetly, and then there was sharing an address. The latter required intentions that wouldn't set a poor example for students. After all, part of her job was teaching them that sex between loving couples could be a positive thing, and sex for sport and kicks could be fraught with danger.

She knew instantly Troy was a relationship that for her was fun and for him was serious. That's when she'd told him the truth. "I'm sorry, Troy, but I think we have to cool this down."

Iris wanted to tell Troy about her and Seth before he heard it from anyone else. She had one of the student office workers take a note to him during second period.

Can we have lunch together in my office either today or tomorrow?

There was no reply. Then, just before the lunch hour he popped his head in the door. He wore that handsome, playful grin, hands plunged in his pockets. There stood the reason every high school junior and senior girl wanted his class. They sat through every lesson gazing stupidly at his pretty face, dreaming that he was just waiting for them to hit eighteen so he could marry them. She didn't ask herself, *Oh, why can't I be in love with him?* She knew why.

"Don't worry about it, Iris. I know. You don't have to break it to me gently."

"What do you know?"

"That you're hooked up with Seth. That

it's where you want to be and you're very happy. Good for you."

"Grace? Did she tell you?"

"I think I first heard it at Lucky's when I stopped there to get gas. Then at the diner. Then out at Cooper's. Then I asked Grace and she confirmed it. I hope you're serious because you've been outed."

"Will you come in, please?" she asked him.

He looked at his watch. "I'm going out to lunch. You don't have to explain anything. You were clear before. And I'm not surprised."

"But what if I want to explain?"

"Could we skip it? You needing to explain makes me feel like an idiot and I don't need that."

"Troy, you should understand about us, about Seth. We have a very long and complicated history, a good history with some enormous hurdles. But —"

"Look, I get it. You were always honest. Well, except about Seth, but that's okay. I think I understand that, too."

"Troy, I didn't think I'd ever work things out with Seth. I didn't talk to anyone about my feelings for him. I never thought we'd be able to sort it all out. It's really important to me that you and I are still friends. Good friends."

"Don't worry about that for a second, Iris. We're friends. We laugh at the same things, work well together, have the same work priorities, see each other all the time — we'll be perfectly friendly. I'll see you later."

And he was gone. Iris recognized his words. She'd used them on Seth. *Fine, we're friends, don't push it.*

It was really unfair, she thought. She hadn't led him on. In fact, when she'd realized she was less than sincere, less involved than he was, she'd tried to end the romance without sacrificing the friendship. So much for that idea. Adult relationships were such a minefield. She hated that a good man like Troy would feel hurt. Besides, she needed him in her life.

She talked to Seth about her feelings that night and realized she had never really had this before, this steady man who was interested in everything that went on in her life, even if it had to do with another man! He was so supportive and understanding. Not toward Troy, however. "He'll be fine, Iris. Everyone gets rejected and moves on. Don't torture him."

"But I didn't want to reject him," she said.

"That's the torture I'm talking about. Let him be."

"But I need him in my professional life!"

"Then make sure your contact is professional," he said.

"Simple as that sounds, it isn't that simple," she informed him.

"Don't I know it. I've had professional reasons to reach out to Sassy and Robbie. Not simple. Not at all."

In the end, it became very easy. And very frightening. It was later that same week, when Iris was again saying good-morning to the students arriving at school. She stood outside her office door for at least twenty minutes, through first bell. The stream of kids thinned as the hour for first period got closer and closer. Her eye caught a couple of stragglers behind the crowd, late for class, hurrying along and oblivious to her.

Rachel Delaney and Brett Davis were rushing down the corridor from the parking lot entrance. He was gripping her upper arm, dragging her along, leaning down and speaking heatedly, angrily, into her ear. He had a snarl on his face. He stopped in the hall right after passing Iris. He grabbed Rachel's other arm and gave her a shake, growling into her face with an angry shine in his eyes. He thrust her away and stalked off.

Rachel said nothing. Did nothing. She watched him go. She slumped along to her class, going in a different direction than Brett. Her head was down.

It's him! Iris thought.

Of course it was him! The most popular boy in school. Maybe the best-looking boy, a powerful football player. Rachel was about five-two to his six feet, one hundred and ten pounds to his one-ninety.

She could feel the blood drain from her face and her heart hammered in her chest. Why had she not thought of the boyfriend? It's so often the boyfriend, but she hadn't even suspected. Every time she saw them together, he seemed to be fawning over her protectively, romantically.

Besides, this was a school district very sensitive to bullying issues, especially since they'd had a bully a couple of years ago. That bully was so well-known and vicious he'd not only picked on every boy younger and smaller, but at the end of the day it had become obvious the kid had abused his parents and had even been accused of killing a man he'd been in conflict with. He'd been charged with manslaughter rather than murder, but it all stemmed from the same issues of dominance and abuse.

Iris worked closely with Coach Lawson and he had a sharp eye turned toward his football players and their behavior, on and off the field. Brett Davis had a sterling reputation as a leader, a good kid.

But, of course, boys could be charming and lovable boyfriends, until angry about some perceived infraction on the girl's part and then turn livid and brutal. And the frightened girl didn't want to do or say anything to piss him off. This behavior was common among young men who grew up watching their fathers abuse their mothers while managing to maintain solid relationships with other men.

There had been so many other logical suspects around her — a part-time father, a big and combative younger brother, a single mother no doubt stressed by everything, an aunt and an uncle who were giving shelter to an entire family.

An abusive boyfriend. How had she ignored that possibility — it was so often the case. High school boys were generally immature, possessive, egotistical, had short fuses and felt so bulletproof.

She didn't know what to do even though she knew what she had to do. She was obligated to report her suspicions. But she'd never been down this road before. She locked her office door and walked quickly to the other side of the building, rapping impatiently on Troy's first-period classroom door. When he opened the door he was obviously stricken by the look on her face because he quickly asked, "What, Iris?" in a panicked whisper.

"It's him," she whispered back. "It's her boyfriend! Brett Davis! The big man on campus."

"You're sure?" Troy asked.

"I saw him grab her and shake her. He was furious about something and she was completely passive. How could I miss that? How could we all miss it?"

Troy pulled the door to his class closed behind him. "Damn it," he said. "This is going to be ugly. I'll back you up. Do what you have to do."

She shook her head. "Whatever I do, I better be right. This can be a deadly game. That poor girl, she must be so confused. She must be terrified of him."

"Aw, Jesus," he said. "You should talk to Seth, too. Make sure he knows what's going on. The girl has already had a concussion."

"Oh, Troy," she said, almost in tears. "How did no one know?"

He frowned. "I bet a lot of people know. I bet the kids know. Cammie knows. You know how these kids can close ranks. He has a lot of popular power." He put a hand on her shoulder. "Go do it, report it. You can explain I brought the suspicion to you and you looked into it. You're not completely alone in this."

"Thanks, but I can't be worried about that. I'm a big girl. It's Rachel who's in trouble."

Before making the call she had to make, she went to Phil Sanderson's office. In the chain of command, he was next. She could have gone straight to the principal, it would have been appropriate, but Phil, as vice principal, handled most of the student behavior problems.

And of course Phil was busy. Too busy. A million things on his desk, every last one of them urgent. "Well, I'm going to have to place a call to DHS to report suspected abuse, so when do you think you can fit me in?" she asked.

"Now," he said. He ejected a couple of supervisors from his office and got behind his desk. "I hope to God this is a waste of time," he said.

"I'm afraid not. Believe me, I'd like that as much as you, but I was not looking for a reason to call DHS. In fact, I feel forced into it."

"Give it to me straight."

So she did. She didn't name Troy, even

317

though he had invited her to do so. "A teacher brought the suspicions to my attention and I took the appropriate action — I looked into it and sought the assistance of the girl's athletic director. She's in a position to see the girls when they're dressed out for gym or for practice. She not only sees more skin when they're wearing their PE uniforms, she also sees them in comparison to each other and whether one of them seems to have an unusually large number of visible injuries."

Iris described the suspicious injuries, her conversations with Cammie and Rachel and, finally, the hostility between Brett and Rachel. Phil listened, occasionally shaking his head.

When she was finished he said, "Fuck."

She cleared her throat. "That's four hours of detention, Phil."

"Right now I'd like to take it right up to twelve. So, you report. What next?"

"I don't know what they'll decide. If they think I'm on to something, they'll investigate. They'll interview, require medical evaluations, who knows? But I'm a mandatory reporter. If I fail to report this, not only could I lose my credentials, but the school could be in trouble. But please understand this, Phil. Reporting gives us an opportunity to keep the girl safe and that's the priority. I want her safe. I think she's in trouble."

"Then you have no choice," Phil told her. "This is what we do. It's called intervention."

"Why didn't I address this problem? It's not uncommon! We put together special programs for driving safely, for identifying diseases, the dangers of drugs, educating them about safe sex, for identifying and reporting bullying, for taking tests fairly, for the love of God! There are even survival courses — what to do if you're caught drifting out to sea or lost in the woods! Why didn't we address unsafe dating? What's the number-one concern of every young girl and boy in this school, huh, Phil? It's who they can date and whether they can get that date!"

"We do a good job, Iris. If we can't think of everything under the sun, I'll take the blame."

"Crap, it's not about blame. It's about being *awake*. I'm sorry, Phil — I should have been more aware."

He smiled at her gently. "I'm proud of what you do, Iris. Now go make your call and let me know what the follow-up will be. Let's just be grateful we've come this far without a need for this before. At least while you and I have had the watch."

"That we know of," she said. "I'll let you know."

"Oh, Iris, who was the teacher?"

She hesitated. "He said I could use his name, but I'd prefer to shoulder responsibility for this for now. If we need him to back up the complaint . . ."

"Ah, Troy," Phil said. "You know, I almost didn't hire him? His résumé was spotty — a vet who did an Iraq tour, taught a couple of years in a private school where they're not all that fussy about credentials, and a desire to live up here where the air is clean and the rafting and skiing plentiful. A kid." He laughed and shook his head. "I didn't think he was all that serious about teaching. He's one of the best teachers I've got. In spite of all his talk about his off-campus adventures, he's one of the most dedicated teachers here."

That made Iris smile. "I know. He's priceless. I want him to get his counseling credentials and work in my office."

Phil chuckled. "Good luck with that. I think he'll be on the slopes, not going back to school in his free time. What's his game? Snowboarding or skiing?"

"I don't really know," she said.

"Well, it was a lucky day I was so short-staffed he got the job before I even had a chance to take a closer look at him. So go — make your call. I'll be anxious to hear what comes next."

Iris was somewhat disappointed but not entirely surprised by the response. She spoke to a case worker who specialized in dating abuse. First, the woman gave Iris the statistics, which were awful. Then she outlined the procedure — the investigation and interviews of those involved, including the families of the teenagers. She listed several academic articles on the subject, many of which Iris remembered reading in her own case studies in postgrad counseling. And finally, she gave her the bad news.

"It's a busy time and I'm only one person," Connie Franklin said. "I'll certainly follow up at my earliest available time, bearing in mind we're coming into the holidays. Holidays for some families are harder than for others and I'm in demand. But I will follow up and I'll keep your name out of it while I can."

"They're going to know at once," Iris said. "As I said, I interviewed the girl and her best friend. They'll know it was me."

"The risk of our jobs, I'm afraid," Connie said.

"Listen, make your life simple — call Dr. Scott Grant. The girl had a concussion that was supposed to have been caused by slipping on an icy step. I don't remember any ice-over in Thunder Point. That doesn't mean her front step wasn't icy, but it bears looking at. Dr. Grant admitted her to the hospital. I assume emergency workers and hospital employees are also mandatory reporters and should have investigated the possibility of abuse."

"I'll do that. In the meantime, if anything more comes up, do call me. When things like this escalate from reporting to emergency, this agency can move mountains."

"I don't know if I want that or not," Iris said.

"I understand completely."

"How do you do it? Take complaints like this daily and pursue them?"

"The same way you do, Iris. One minute at a time."

Iris was nestled into Seth's arms late at night when she told him about the day.

"I've never had this before," she said. "I've never had a lover who cared about my boring high school life."

"I'm a little glad about that," he said.

"Something has really bothered me all

322

day. Girls aren't the only ones who get abused. Boys get emotionally abused by girls all the time, and usually they don't know it. Sometimes women are physically abusive."

He chuckled. "You're talking about me," he said.

"Seth, I hit you! I knocked you down! You could have filed charges, taken me to jail. I hit you!"

"How many men have you hit, Iris?"

"I think only you. I can't remember another one. Since I was ten, anyway. But it's so wrong. I was complaining to Phil that I hadn't put together a program about abuse and what to do about it and it came to me that I was an awful kid."

"I don't know about that. You thought you were a boy for a long time. Listen, kids get into it, strike out. Then they get disciplined and taught that you can't solve problems by hitting and hopefully through that, along with good examples, they learn that isn't the answer. That it's wrong."

"But I hit you a couple of months ago."

"Got off a good one, too," he said, laughing. "I'm not letting you do that again, by the way."

"I could've hurt you."

"No offense, Iris, but you hit like a girl."

"We should do better. Of all people, I should know better than to lash out like that."

He nuzzled her neck. "I admit, I'm completely surprised to find out you're human. Welcome to the club."

"Do you have anyone to talk to, Seth? To tell your feelings to? To complain to, to get sympathy from?"

"Huh?" he asked.

She took a breath. "Boys can be so much more alone than girls. Girls dump on their girlfriends, their mothers, sometimes teachers. But it takes a lot for a boy to do that, to admit he's worried or afraid or anything."

"It doesn't seem to be part of our training. We're trained from an early age to be tough and stoic."

"When I was in my postgrad program, part of the training was a volunteer assignment in one of the help centers. I worked on a crisis line. We had a guy call in. He said he was leaving the next morning for the trip of a lifetime, a vacation he'd looked forward to all his life. He said he was so excited he couldn't sleep. It was after midnight. The supervisor was listening in and we were all sure there must be something more to this call. We kept him on the phone for over two hours, asking him key questions, pretty convinced he must be suicidal or something. Who calls a crisis line in the middle of the night to talk about his trip? Well, it turned out he was just a guy taking the trip of a lifetime, something he'd saved for and planned for years. And he called the crisis line because he didn't have anyone else to talk to. He didn't have anyone he could tell."

Seth rose up on an elbow and looked down at her. "Thursday is Thanksgiving. I'm taking part of the day off — first time I've had Thanksgiving with my whole family in years. I look forward to it because you're going to be there. We're dividing up the schedule on Thursday and Friday — I'll work till about four, spell the guys for long meal breaks so they can be with their families. But after that, I'm taking the weekend off. I want to take you somewhere. I have someone I want you to meet."

"Who?" she asked.

"Someone I talk to. Now let it go. Be surprised."

Iris couldn't remember when she'd last been so nervous and excited about Thanksgiving. She'd had many a holiday meal with the Sileskis, Seth being away or working for the larger share of them over the past sixteen years or so. She knew everyone in the family. But this time she was a guest with a new status. This time she was Seth's significant other.

She worked it out with Gwen what she could contribute and had been assigned sweet potato pie, which turned out to be a challenge. Gwen's daughter-in-law, Sandy, was bringing the green bean casserole, some kind of mushroom dish that she said everyone hated but Sandy couldn't live without and a cranberry-and-orange mold filled with nuts and marshmallows. Gwen was taking on the turkey, potatoes and trimmings.

Iris went next door early, hoping she could help with other chores like setting the table, washing up serving dishes that were rarely used, anything. Of course, Seth was not there yet. He was watching the town. But Gwen was in a dither, waddling around the house like Edith Bunker. She wanted everything to be perfect.

"It looks like it is perfect, Gwen. What can I do to help?" Iris asked.

"There's nothing. I haven't been this worked up over Thanksgiving since Boomer brought Sandy to meet us! And that was at least fifteen years ago." She twisted her hands a little bit. "I want it to be perfect."

"Go put the final touches on your hair,"

Iris said. "I'll guard the food. It's always perfect."

Twenty minutes later they descended, almost all at once. Iris heard voices outside and opened the front door. Boomer's SUV was parked in front and his wife and kids got out, all carrying something for dinner. Nick had pulled up right behind them as if he'd followed them to Thunder Point. Norm was just parking in the drive, still wearing his blue jacket with his name on it as if he'd had to work right up to the last second before sitting down to his meal. And then she saw Seth. He was walking across the yard from her house. Could he be more obvious? His deputy vehicle was parked in her drive and he was coming over in a change of clothes.

Norm shook hands with Boomer, kissed Sandy, ruffled the hair of his grandchildren, shook hands with Nick, shook hands with Seth, and then they all walked to the front door en masse.

"Iris," Norm said with a nod.

"It was only a matter of time," Boomer said, giving her a kiss on the cheek.

"He finally woke up," Nick said, grinning broadly and giving her a big bear hug.

"Iris, I'm so happy," Sandy said, her hands full with a casserole dish.

"Hey, Iris," twelve-year-old Sonny said, passing her and walking into the house.

"Hi, Iris," nine-year-old Sylvie said, grinning, heading for her grandmother's kitchen.

Seth was last. He smiled and looked into her eyes. "How's your day, sweetheart?" he said, bending to put a gentle kiss on her lips.

"I think it might be okay now," she said.

"It's going to be okay from now on," he said. "Can I help with anything?"

"Keep your brothers from teasing me," she said.

"Baby, I can't do anything about them. I've tried."

This was the Sileski clan. They sat down to dinner within thirty minutes. Despite some wifely badgering, Norm didn't change clothes. He washed up a little, but he wore his blue gas station shirt with his name sewn over the pocket. The kids wouldn't wait for grace to be said, they were diving into the food even though their mother warned them they'd live to regret it. It took a long time for Gwen to sit — she was circling and hovering over the table, ready to provide anything that might be missing. Norm carved, Boomer passed heavy platters, Sandy fussed at the kids about manners,

Nick grinned his handsome bad-boy grin and Gwen didn't sit until Norm said, "Woman, you're making me dizzy."

"If there's going to be a wedding, we'll need some notice," Boomer said to Iris. "I have to get my suit let out and Sandy has to lose ten pounds."

"Boomer!" Sandy scolded.

"What, honey? I keep getting fatter and you always want to lose ten pounds. I'm just saying . . ."

It was perfect.

Late that night, finally in the comfort of her bedroom, Seth pronounced the day a success. Even Norm had been reasonably docile.

"I think it took ten years off your poor mother's life," Iris said. "I know why I was nervous — being presented as a girlfriend for the first time. I don't know why she was nervous."

"My mother has wanted the perfect family for as long as I can remember. What she got was a cranky husband and three scrappy boys. She deserves better."

"You have a nice family," she said. "And I saw Norm smile twice."

"It was probably just gas."

On Friday morning Seth went in to work

329

first thing, but Iris had the day off. It was hard to leave the bed. Waking up with Seth was still a miracle to her and it was tempting to just lie there and daydream about him. Almost every day she had to ask herself, is this really happening to me? Is the one man I've always loved really mine?

She could not indulge in the warm sheets long — it was a busy day in town, a day she used to look forward to when her mother was alive. It was the day that everyone, particularly the business district, joined forces to decorate the town. And it looked like they had a beautiful day for it. For once the sun was shining.

It was still early by the time she walked into town, but she was far from the first to arrive. There were dozens of people on the street and most of the decorations had already been pulled out of attics, storage sheds, garages and basements. Mac was standing in front of the diner with Seth, both of them enjoying a cup of coffee on the street while Gina was sorting through decorations. A cherry picker stood at the ready in the street, garland, wreaths and red plastic candles organized to put up on the lampposts.

To her surprise, Grace was pulling her shop decorations through the front door.

Iris said good morning to Mac and Gina, accepted a little shoulder squeeze from Seth and then made her way down the block to the flower shop. "What are you doing here?" she asked Grace. "I thought you were skiing!"

"I decided to pass on that. I hate missing decoration day."

"But what did you do? Where did you have Thanksgiving dinner? Why didn't you join me at the Sileskis?"

"Oh, that was a family day and you were breaking the ice with them — appearing in your new role as Seth's sex slave. . . ."

"Shh!" Iris said, looking around to see if they'd been overheard.

Grace laughed. "I had a very indulgent day planned for myself, but in fact I was kidnapped. I went by Carrie's late Wednesday to see if she had any holiday dishes for takeout, particularly dressing and gravy, and she interrogated me. When I told her I wanted to stay in my pajamas all day, eating and watching chick flicks, she wouldn't have it. She demanded that I join her at the McCains'. In fact, she picked me up to be sure I'd be there. She had Rawley with her. She seems to always have Rawley with her. We took most of the side dishes to the McCains'. She had gone out there early to put the turkey in and she served a feast so incredible I almost had to be carried out. There were sixteen for dinner! Al from the gas station, Ray Anne and the three boys were there as well as Mac's aunt Lou and her husband, Joe. It was quite a party. In fact, Lou and Joe escaped before charades began and gave me a lift home. Thank God. I managed to get in two chick flicks."

"What about Troy?"

"I guess he went skiing. When I told him I just couldn't make it he said it was my loss and I'd be lucky if he asked me again. But he said it nicely."

"Well, if you get another chance, let me know. I have stuff you can borrow." Then a thought struck her. "You know, you and Troy look good together."

"Iris," Grace said. "If I want your help, I'll ask for it."

"Well, do you want help with the shop decorations?"

"I could do with some help on that."

Sixteen

"You're a good sport," Seth told Iris as they were climbing into the car at five in the morning to head for Seattle. "It'll probably be seven hours. You can sleep. I like this drive."

"You do it often?" she asked.

"Every month or two. I use the drive for all those deep thoughts I have to mull and never have time for. I find it relaxing."

"This must be some friend," she said.

"Let me get us out of town and on the freeway and I'll tell you about him."

Once they were underway, Seth told her the story. "Oscar was the other driver in that accident when I was twenty. That accident changed both our lives, his more dramatically than mine. He's been in a wheelchair ever since. When I first went to see him, he was not happy to see me. There's no logical explanation for why I went back. A real glutton for punishment, I guess. Over time, we found we had more in common than you would think possible. More than our injuries. Of course, I didn't head for his house until I was up and walking. I still used a cane and wore the big shoe with the built-up sole. When we plowed into each other, he was forty-five years old and had a couple of kids. And we were both a little angry." He chuckled. "He was angrier, and understandably so — he was worse off. I might've lost a football career but he lost much more than that. And it turned out, over time, that we had things to talk about."

"The accident? Your injuries and disabilities?"

"Not so much," Seth said. "We talked more about life, philosophy, faith, death. Chess."

"Chess?"

"Well, once we started to communicate, we could only talk if we had something else going on. First it was checkers, but we graduated to chess. I don't know how it is with women, but men don't sit in two chairs and stare at each other and just . . . converse."

"Women can do that," she said. "Most women quilt or knit or drink coffee or wine, though. But women who have someone they trust can just go to them to talk. Just to talk.

If they need to."

"Who is that person to you?"

"Grace," she said. "I've known her since she bought the flower shop, but it's been the past year that we've gotten close."

"Did you tell Grace about me?" he asked.

"Uh-huh. In pieces. First I told her about the prom, then I told her about the prom and teenage sex, then I told her I couldn't get over you, then I told her those calla lilies did the trick."

He grinned. "I'm going to fill your bedroom with calla lilies."

"You don't have to do that. Now, about Oscar — you went to see him because he was injured?"

"We were both injured. He was worse. And he had a family to worry about. I felt so bad about that."

"The accident was your fault?" she asked.

He shook his head. "The cause of the accident was his — technically he was impaired. He fell asleep at the wheel. But I was also cited — I'd been speeding. Not speeding a little bit. I spent my first contract money on a hot car and I was a rocket. If I hadn't been going so fast I might've been able to avoid him. Or he might've cleared the intersection before I got there. Of course, no one knows what might've happened to him next. Maybe if I hadn't been there and if he'd cleared the intersection, he could've hit a tree or another vehicle or any number of possibilities. Or, he might've been jolted awake by my horn! But the fact is, the speed of my car and the impact was probably responsible for the level of injuries. There was no criminal trial but his family sued me for speeding."

"Oh, my gosh. And you're friends?"

"It didn't come fast," he said. "Not only was Oscar pretty grumpy, but he had a wife and kids who blamed me."

"And you went to him because you were sorry about the accident? The injuries?"

"I was definitely sorry," he said. "I don't know why I went. I wanted to see how he was getting along. I wanted someone to talk to about it even though I had a physical therapist and a counselor. I wanted to know how he was coping with his disabilities because I wasn't coping that well with mine." He shrugged. "I didn't have an agenda. I kept going back and I'm not sure why. But first only Oscar accepted my visits. Then his wife did. Eventually his kids did. Just so you won't be broadsided, Oscar is one of the people I talked to about you. About how it was important to have you in my life again. That was before I dared hope we'd be a couple."

"I'm almost afraid to ask, but how much have you told him about us since we've become, you know —"

He chuckled. "I haven't told him anything. But it will only take you five minutes with Oscar to understand there are a lot of things he doesn't need to be told. A few years ago when I was struggling to finish my degree, trying to get into the Sheriff's Department and failing time after time, having Oscar to talk to made a difference. We don't call each other on the phone and even though he has a bunch of online friends he keeps up with, we don't exchange many emails. I just like to spend a day at his house sometimes."

"It's a very long drive to do that," she pointed out.

"It always feels like it's worthwhile. I get the quiet and alone time of a long drive, a few hours with Oscar and Flora, time to think. I'd say it's been one of the highlights of my life since I was twenty years old."

For the rest of the drive, they talked about a hundred things, from careers to families to the town they were both so attached to. They stopped a couple of times for food and drinks but didn't waste a lot of time. Seth promised he'd take her to a nice hotel for the night and they could sleep in on

Sunday morning. They'd been on the road almost exactly seven hours when they pulled up to an ordinary small brick home. The ramp to the front door and the van with the handicap sticker were dead giveaways — this was Oscar Spellman's house.

Flora let them in and seemed so pleased to see them. Rather than shaking Iris's hand, she embraced her. "I'm so happy Seth brought you," she said. "He's talked about you a little bit."

"I'm glad to be here. I didn't know until just recently that you've been Seth's good friends for years."

"Yes, it's been a lot of years now," Flora said. "I did a little cooking. Sometimes one of the kids or grandkids comes by. Did you eat along the way? Do you need a snack? Coffee or tea?"

"I'd love a cup of coffee," Iris said.

Then the *whirring* sound of Oscar's chair announced his arrival in the room. Iris had been unprepared for the fact that he was a quadriplegic. When Seth said Oscar was in a wheelchair she assumed he had lost the use of his legs, but this was more dramatic, more difficult for the family.

And yet this sixty-year-old man had a grin as big as the sky. They all sat around the kitchen table for a little while, getting to know one another, having coffee. It took a very short time for Iris to learn that Oscar had partial use of one arm and hand but needed twenty-four-hour care, most of which Flora handled. They did have a physical therapist and a visiting nurse to help with those chores that were difficult for Flora, but the responsibility was on her for the most part. Now that their children were grown, there was a little help from that quarter, but Oscar and Flora didn't want to burden the kids with his full-time care.

"The worst part about all of this is being dependent," Oscar said. "Sometimes it puts me in a real mood. That aside, we get along pretty well."

"Speaking of getting along, is there anything I can help with while I'm here?" Seth asked. "Anything heavy or difficult that you'd like me to do?"

"There is something," Flora said. Then she looked at Iris. "I hate to give Seth chores. Usually when he comes, I leave him with Oscar and get out of the house for a while. They can be alone, I can take a break." She looked back at Seth. "Mark nearly finished putting up the storm windows and there are just a couple left and they're on the ground floor — no ladder involved. It shouldn't take long. Iris can visit with Oscar and I'll help you."

"I don't need your help, Flora," he said, standing. "If there's anything else you'd like to do."

"I'd like to come outside with you and breathe the outside air. I can take the screen off your hands and lift the storm window to you, but fastening it in is beyond me. Winter's coming fast and the insulation on this house just isn't good enough without those windows. Oscar, do you need anything before I go with Seth to do those last windows?"

"I don't need nothing," he said. "Turn off the stove or ask Iris if she can mind it."

"I can make sure things don't burn," Iris said. "What do you have going on over here?"

"Oscar's favorite that I don't make too often — greens and corn bread, pork loin, potatoes and cobbler. If you'll just make sure that pork doesn't flame up or the greens dry out, I'd be grateful."

"I can do that," she said.

Once Flora and Seth went outside, Oscar started the conversation. "Seth is mighty proud of you, Iris. He's mentioned you several times."

"Has he?" she asked, grinning.

"Oh, yes. Before he went back to Thunder

Point to work, he was talking about you. He said you were a team, growing up. I wonder what he was like as a boy."

"He was hyperactive, I think. He had white-blond hair when he was really young and I don't know why, but it was too long and cut real choppy and floppy. He reminded me of an unkempt Peter Pan."

"Was he always good at sports?"

"Always, I think. But no one made a real big deal over him until high school, then he owned the place."

Oscar laughed deep in his throat. "I can almost picture it."

"Do you want me to get out the checker board or something?" she asked.

"Nah. But maybe you can warm up that coffee some," he said, using his eyes to indicate the cup he kept in his cup holder. "I need as much milk as coffee so I don't scorch my gullet."

She jumped up and Oscar stopped her. "No need to be rushing around, girl. I'm not going anywhere. Say, Iris, did *you* want to play checkers or something?"

She brought him back his coffee and shook her head. "I'm fine. But Seth said men can't talk unless they're doing something else."

"Seth can't." Oscar laughed. "Some of us

have learned to sit still. That boy, he might never be still. I hope you're prepared for that."

"To tell you the truth, Oscar, I'm not real sure what to be prepared for. He's the same guy I knew growing up and yet, he's brand-new."

"How's he different? Tell me."

"He's a little more serious," she said. "And he's a lot more patient. He takes some things in stride that a younger Seth would've been all worked up about. Like his father. You know about his father?"

Oscar nodded. "Cranky, I'm told."

"I guess that's accurate. I don't know exactly why. I know he's disappointed that Seth isn't a football star, but you'd think he'd be over that by now."

"You know, Iris, some folks are just that way no matter what. I think they dislike the good turns in their life as much as the bad. I was a little bit that way when I was younger."

"Really?"

He nodded and bent his head to sip some coffee through the straw. "I was always worrying about things I couldn't do anything about. Always working too hard, sleeping too little, my brain whirring around all the time. That can get to be a habit, I think. In fact, right after the accident I was like that because I couldn't figure out any other way but being mad all the time."

"I guess you figured it out," she said.

"I did. Flora was a big help."

"She was?"

"Oh, yes, ma'am," he said with a big laugh. "Flora is a gentle woman. She hardly ever has a gruff word for anyone. It used to drive me crazy that she was too soft on the kids when they could've used a stronger hand. But after putting up with me and my temper while I was stuck in this chair she told me in her nicest possible way that from that moment on she was all done doing for me if I couldn't be civil and pleasant and most of all grateful. She said, 'I'm done with your bullshit, Oscar Spellman, and you can either be sweet as an angel or you'll get none of me. And none of me is gonna leave you real damn hungry!' " He laughed. "I think I always knew she had it in her."

Iris smiled. "Did you straighten right up?"

"Oh, yes, ma'am, I did. I didn't doubt her a second. Still, it took a while for me to slow down my mind and listen for a while. I move a lot slower, but I have some things now that I was moving too fast to notice before. I have a better relationship with my wife and kids. I taught my grandson to play chess. My grandson thinks I'm a lot smarter than I am." He laughed at himself again.

"You almost seem grateful for some of the changes in your life."

"Let's don't go that far," he said, but he smiled. "That young man of yours, I don't know where he got it, but if I'd been in his shoes I never would've visited me even once, much less all the time."

"I got the impression he felt really bad about the accident," Iris said.

"I reckon. But he could've come one time, said he was sorry it all happened and never come again. He's a strong boy, but he's got a very kind heart. He kept coming back even though Flora and the kids didn't make him welcome. Now, what makes a man do that?"

"I don't know. But I admire it."

"He's a generous man. We'd've been lost without his help."

"I thought he only visited every month or two?"

Oscar nodded. "True. And it was a good year before I'd even have a conversation with him. I made that boy work real hard. Even after the way everything turned out — the court battle and all. All the money that he gave us."

"He must have felt some deep responsibility after losing the suit," she said.

"Losing? Girl, he won. We lost that suit! Seth wasn't driving safely, but no jury would agree it was his fault we were hurt. Mighta been, no one will know."

Iris frowned. "He won? What money?"

"You don't know?"

She shook her head.

"Girl, he set up a trust for our family. Gave us every penny he had."

Iris scooted forward in her chair. "What money?"

"Well, all the way through his surgeries and rehab, he was pretty well taken care of — he had insurance, disability, plenty of support — he was a pro ball player. He also had some money set aside — a large sum he'd gotten for signing his contract. I imagine he could've used that to live on, to pay for college, that sort of thing. Maybe his father is mad about that — that the money didn't stay in the family. I told Seth we didn't want his charity and he just said it wasn't charity. That I'd have to earn it every day. It beats me just how he thought I'd do that. He set up the trust so that when some of my benefits ran out, there would still be help. He told me, 'Take care of this here, Oscar, because that's all I got and there ain't no more.' "

Iris was speechless.

"He didn't tell you?" Oscar asked.

She shook her head. "I bet he didn't tell anyone."

"He's got a big heart, that boy. And you remember, he was a kid then. Not a wise older man, but a kid whose dreams were destroyed. A kid who was gonna have a lot of work ahead just to get by." He shook his head. "He's going to make a good father."

"Has he talked about that? About wanting to be a father?"

"Here and there," Oscar said. "He mentioned that a couple of kids with the right woman would make everything he's done in his life more meaningful."

Iris felt her eyes well with tears. "What a coincidence. I feel the same way."

It didn't take Seth long to get those storm windows up and then he and Oscar got to that ongoing game of chess. Flora tended her dinner and then took Iris upstairs to show her some of her quilts and petit point — she loved needlework. And while Oscar and homemaking might be a lot of work, there was lots of time she could lose herself in sewing. Since Oscar couldn't get upstairs, one of those bedrooms was dedicated to her quilting. When she watched TV with Oscar in the evenings, she liked to stitch. "Now that the kids are grown I have lots of quiet time and, don't tell anyone, I enjoy it. The kids worry that I'm overworked and lonely and I think I'll just let 'em think so. Keeps them on their toes. Keeps 'em coming around to help their father."

They had a wonderful dinner together, though Oscar complained that he had to succumb to being fed, which he disliked in front of company. But Flora hushed him and had a very organized way of parceling out a bite for him, a bite for herself. They shared a plate, Oscar and Flora. And when the meal was done, she held his hand and they talked and laughed.

It was nine before Iris and Seth said goodbye and headed for a hotel.

"You did pick a nice hotel," she said.

"I looked for one with the best breakfast," he said. "We can relax in the morning before tackling that big drive. Thanks for coming with me, honey."

"I love Oscar," she said. "And I love Flora."

Seth nodded. "Kind of an inconvenient way to find new friends, wouldn't you agree?"

"They're very grateful to you."

"Not as grateful as I am to them. What

happened to us changed everything. You never really know how much one small single act can change things. At the end of the day, I think I'm better off where I am today than I could've been. I think this is where I'm meant to be." He smiled. "And when we get into bed, I'll be in an even better place."

"Seth, Oscar told me about the money. The trust you set up for them."

"He has such a big mouth. That's probably why I haven't ever brought anyone with me to meet Oscar before."

"Do your parents know what you did?"

He shrugged. "I didn't tell them. I don't know who the Spellmans told. It doesn't matter, Iris. No matter what any accident report or jury says, Oscar and I were in it together. It was our accident. I tried to help because I could, that's all."

When Iris got to school on Monday morning she saw what she expected. Many of the teachers had been in the building over the weekend to get a good start on their personal holiday decorating. There were wreaths and garlands, Santas and elves, images of gift-wrapped boxes on doors and Christmas trees on windows.

She brought her two boxes of decorations

from home and, for lack of a better idea, put them in the cubicle her student assistants used. The corridor that the school nurse, counselor, assistant principal and office staff shared looked like it could really use some cheering. But she had too much to do and it would have to wait until after school. She had phone calls to make, meetings to attend, paperwork to process and a couple of teachers to talk to about special presentations for students.

When she got back to her office after grabbing a quick lunch, the girls were giggling. She poked her head into the cubicle. "Someone making milk come out of his nose again?" she asked.

Krista lifted up a gnarled pile of twinkle lights from one of Iris's boxes. "No, not that. This year can I please help you put these decorations away so that next year Misty doesn't have to deal with this disaster?"

"By all means, you're hired. But I want you to know something. I put them away neatly and very well organized. In the eleven months I wasn't looking at them, they did this to themselves. I think they get bored and unhappy. . . ."

"Right," Krista said. "We're going to stay after school and help you put them up.

There's no way you could organize this wreck and still decorate. Really, Ms. McKinley."

"I told you, not my fault! I'm very tidy."

"Right," they both said.

A little while later Krista left for her next class and Misty stayed on for her hour in the counselor's office. Iris looked in on her later and saw that she seemed to have that tangle of lights pretty well organized. "Wow. Thanks, Misty."

"You're welcome," she said brightly. "They were a wreck."

"I know. Sorry. But in other areas of my life I'm neat as a pin. If you want some very bad news, I have lights for the house, too. I'm afraid to look at them."

"I'm not signing on for that," she said.

"Things seem to be going okay for you these days," Iris said.

"I think working in this office helped a lot," she said. "I like Krista. Hey, you didn't tell her to be my friend, did you?"

"Of course not! I asked her to help you if you needed any orientation in this office — she's been an assistant for a couple of years. She's a nice person but I think she picks her own friends."

"She is nice. And she has some good friends — they're nice, too. I've been having lunch with them sometimes. Three of them are going to the university together. They'll be roommates."

"You're going to miss her next year."

"We're going to chat on Skype," Misty said with a smile. "Stephanie asked to have lunch with us one day and I wanted to tell her to get lost, but Krista said it was fine. I asked where her new best friend was. . . . Okay, I didn't say it like that. I asked her where Tiffany was and she said, Algebra. But Tiffany used to have the same lunch, the one I wasn't invited to join. Something's up there."

"Friendships change a lot," Iris said.

"Krista told me no matter what, try to be nice, even if it's hard. Then she said that doesn't mean you have to be best friends again. Can you believe the same thing happened to Krista? A while ago, but the same thing! Krista — the cheerleader and who was in the homecoming court? Isn't that unbelievable?"

"I told you, Misty. It happens to absolutely everyone." She smiled.

"Well, somehow it helped to know Stephanie was getting a little of her own medicine. I apologize for that, but it's true."

"We're only human," Iris said. "Um, don't feel obligated to stay late."

"Oh, I'm looking forward to it. Krista has the car today and is going to give me a ride home. My brother will take the bus from middle school. And, hey — it's a long time before I get any kind of class schedule for next year, but can I work in this office again? As long as my grades are good?"

"I'd be honored. And I won't hold you to it if it turns out there's something else you need to do with that time."

"The connections in this office are pretty amazing," Misty said. "It even gets points with the teachers."

Iris raised an eyebrow, curious. "Good to know I have power."

It had only been a couple of months and Misty appeared to be finished grieving over being dumped by a best friend. Iris found herself thinking she wished she had been that strong at that age. Seth wasn't the only best friend she'd lost along the way. There had been girlfriends here and there, as well. It was never easy, letting them go, carrying on alone. And she had been telling the truth — absolutely everyone goes through it and it's heart-wrenching.

She was patting herself on the back for having done something right even though it had been such a shot in the dark. Decorating with the girls and a couple of their friends who didn't work in the office turned out to be a major undertaking and Iris was running late. She'd had two calls from Seth and they'd settled on him cooking dinner at her house. She knew he wouldn't go to too much trouble but was happy it was off her schedule.

She was finally cleaning up her desk at almost six o'clock. The school was quiet and dark except for the basketball practice coming to an end just down the hall.

"How *dare* you," a voice said from the door. "How dare you accuse anyone of doing anything *wrong!*"

She recognized the voice immediately even though she'd never before heard Rachel speak so angrily. She stood slowly. "Rachel, what's wrong?"

"We're being investigated! My family, Brett's family, even some of my friends. All this about someone's hitting me? We talked about this. You're crazy. No one is hitting me. No one is hurting me!"

"I'm not sure I'm clear on what's happening, but if there's nothing wrong, then nothing more will come of it."

"But it was you! Don't deny it!"

"There might be more than one person concerned that you're safe," Iris said calmly.

"No, there's not more than one — it's

you. Why don't you just mind your own business! I'm fine, I'm happy, I want to be left alone."

"Rachel, if someone has raised a question, just go through the steps. Tell the truth and move on. Who's investigating your family?"

"I don't know — some stupid child welfare person. And I am not a child! I'm sixteen. I'm old enough to get married if I want to. You're ruining my life! Now everyone is upset. My family is upset. Brett's parents are furious. It's just a mess."

"Rachel, sit down a minute. Let's talk about this."

She laughed meanly. "The last thing I'm going to do is sit and talk to you again!"

"Look, stay calm. You know I was concerned about your injuries, but are you so sure I'm the only one?"

"Yes, I'm sure! It's you!"

And with that she turned and left. Iris could hear her running down the hall.

Wow, Iris thought. The day after Thanksgiving break? After she'd talked to Connie at the DHS office, knowing how busy everyone was, she had not expected this case to be handled so quickly. In fact, Connie had predicted that it could be months if anything at all happened.

Unless there had been more than one

report, more than one complaint. Troy would have told her and she knew of no one else. She looked at her watch. It was too late in the day to catch Connie at the DHS office.

SEVENTEEN

The nice thing about the two weeks after Thanksgiving was that Grace wasn't worked to death. Aside from a couple of funeral bouquets and a centerpiece, there wasn't a huge demand on her time. There were very few weddings in December and this year she hadn't contracted any of them. Of course, the two weeks before Christmas would be frantic preparing wreaths, centerpieces, festive bouquets and orders of all kinds from out of town.

She closed the shop a little early and drove out to Cooper's. She thought about walking there, but after a day on her feet, designing and selling, enough was enough and she drove instead. She walked in the back door from the parking lot and jumped up on a bar stool.

Troy smiled at her. "What's up?"

"Just checking in. I hope your Thanksgiving was good."

"As a matter of fact, it was great."

"How was skiing?"

"I didn't go. The forecast wasn't that great and I had a couple of friends in a little town in the mountains in California. I went down there and did a little hunting. Then drove back."

"Aw, you missed Thanksgiving dinner?"

"No, I had a great Thanksgiving dinner. There's a little bar in that town — I'm friendly with the owner and my friend works there part-time. They put out a big spread. I had a good time. How about you?"

"Well, I was planning to lie around in my pajamas all day but Carrie found out. I ended up at the McCains' with their entire extended family."

"I thought you were going to the Sileski family gathering."

"I was invited," she said. "So were you. But in the end the only people I really knew were Seth and Iris and I decided I'd really earned a long day of movies. Well, and the parade. I always watch the parade."

He gave the bar a wipe. "Drink?"

"A merlot?" she asked.

He poured the wine and put it in front of her. "What will you do for Christmas?"

"I'm not sure," she said. "I have friends in Portland and a standing invitation, but I don't mind if I'm on my own. I kind of like it. What about you?"

"I'm committed to family. My mom and dad are in San Diego but my sister, her husband and three rug rats are in Morro Bay on the California coast. We'll all go there."

"That sounds fun. Big family?"

"A younger brother and sister. She's married, he's in college. How about you? Big family?"

"No, not really. I lost my parents and I have aunts, uncles and cousins scattered around the country. No sibs, but cousins who are like sibs. I've been so bad about keeping in touch since I bought the shop. My fault. I could make time. I should make time."

"I know," he said. "I'm not good at that, either. I get a lot of complaints."

"I just wanted to say, I'd like to go skiing some time. I'm not very good. You might want to rethink that invitation. I used to be athletic, but it's been a long time since I've been on skis."

"Then we'll snowboard," he said, grinning. "It's harder."

"I have exceptional balance," she said. "And Iris said she'd loan me some gear. I'd still have to rent a snowboard or skis or whatever the torture of the day is. And you can renege if you want because I'm sure I'd be a real load. Inexperienced skier, virgin snowboarder, it might get in the way of your ride. But things are slow over Christmas. There are weekends and you have time off. . . ."

"Let's think about that," he said.

If she wasn't completely mistaken, he didn't look unhappy about it. "How long have you been snowboarding?"

"Since I was about eight, I guess. Growing up in San Diego, we had access to everything. We could surf and ski and dive and climb. I learned to sail and parasail. The only thing that's a lot better up here is the river rafting." He whistled. "There are some rivers in this state that'll make your life flash before your eyes."

"And you like that?"

"I like that."

"Did you ever skate? Hockey or figure skating?" she asked.

"Never had an interest, but I love to watch hockey."

"Good. After you humiliate me on the slopes I'm going to cream you on the ice."

"You're a skater?"

"I was," she said. "When I was younger. I even took lessons. The past few years I'm only an expert at one thing — flowers." She lifted her glass. "But I'm thinking of taking up wine tasting."

It took two days for Connie to return Iris's call. Yes, she had scheduled meetings with the Delaneys and the Davises for later in the week. "There was an unexpected break in my schedule and I thought it was best to get this case cleared if possible. And no, I didn't mention your name to anyone, but if there's an issue here I might have to. You understand."

"I understand," Iris said. "And I can live with that. I was just doing my job and that's part of my job."

"And we thank you," Connie said.

Iris took a deep breath and didn't obsess about it. She hadn't had too many situations as delicate as this in her short history as a counselor, but it came with the territory.

Her office was relatively quiet and she paged through the newsletter from the state department of education, scanning. There was a section that listed suggested printouts, video aids, special programs, guest speakers and computer course assistance for both teachers and students. She'd begun looking for any kind of program that would address dating violence. She thought it might be something to take to the health ed classes. She'd already found a couple of online lectures and dramatizations, but they seemed dated to her so she kept looking for something better.

Then, she suddenly saw a driving safety video on the list of recommendations with the name Sileski attached. There were only so many Sileskis. The video was called *The Cop's Ticket Quota.* It was a YouTube video. She typed it into her computer, did a search and brought it up. And there he was. Well, he said he'd done a couple of programs for high school students.

It appeared to be an assembly. Seth stood on a stage behind a podium with a large screen behind him. He introduced himself as Officer Seth Sileski and offered the three best ways to get out of a ticket.

"But first, let me introduce you to me a few years ago, when I was eighteen," he said. Up on the screen appeared a picture of a handsome young football player in a Ducks uniform, posing like a Heisman trophy winner. "And nineteen." There he was in a Seahawks uniform. "At nineteen I pretty much had it all. My family was so proud of me. Especially my dad. He was the only dad in town who had a pro ball player for a son." There was a picture of him in civilian clothes, leaning against a silver Ferrari. "I loved that car. I didn't think I'd ever have a car like that," he said to laughter from the audience. "Most of the guys in this room would give their left . . . ah, ear? For a car like that." More laughter followed.

Then he walked out from behind the podium and crossed the stage about halfway and Iris noticed at once that he limped a little more than usual.

"And this is my best friend, Oscar. We shared some mighty important memories and are still close."

A picture of Oscar appeared on the screen. He was smiling his award-winning smile, but he was in the neck brace that held up his head, something he must have graduated out of in the years since the picture was taken. He looked happy enough. Anyone in that student audience who'd seen Seth in his football uniforms might have taken Oscar for a player who'd been injured playing ball. In fact, since these were not Thunder Point kids and Seth's days as a wunderkind were many years past, they might've thought his limp had something to do with football.

"But I'm not here to bore you with the

details of my exciting youth — I'm a cop now and we hate cops, right?" There was more laughter. "Cops just want to spoil our fun, right? And because I have the inside track, I can tell you how to get around 'em. They're not as smart as they think they are. So let's cut right to the chase. They're only looking for one kind of driver — the driver that looks dangerous. Frankly, we don't care that you're ten miles over the limit if there's no potential conflict involved. If you're tearing down the highway at sixty-five in a fifty-five and there aren't any other cars in sight, your cop probably has better things to do than go after you. But, if you're weaving down the road at two in the morning, unable to stay in a lane, and your cop is on his way home, he's going to say *damn it,* or worse, because he's now forced to pull you over and check your sobriety before you kill yourself.

"Cops don't really have quotas. Well, some do. We do get bonuses at Christmas for making quotas, but that's supposed to be a secret so don't tell anyone." He grinned, then grew very serious. "What we do have is a responsibility to prevent accidents. So there are three major reasons people have accidents. One — they're impaired. Now, that could be drugs or alcohol, but it might also be they're falling asleep. Or there's even the possibility of a medical event — a heart attack or stroke or seizure. We can tell if someone's impaired — they're all over the road. Sometimes we can't tell in time, so when we see it, we're right on it. That's gonna get attention — watch for that.

"Reason number two — they're distracted. Talking or texting on the cell phone will get you in trouble. We're looking for that and we're not waiting to see if that talking or texting is going to make you swerve — we're going to stop you before you swerve into another vehicle. In fact, there are all kinds of distractions — too many passengers in the car, fussy baby in the backseat, big bunch of balloons for the girlfriend, hyperactive dog bouncing all over the place . . . So what do you do if you're distracted and you know it? Before one of those self-serving, quota-making cops spoils your fun, just pull over and handle the distraction. I hate to tell you that because I'm thinking about my Christmas bonus here and I hate to give up a penny of it." He paused so the kids could laugh at the image he was presenting.

"Reason number three — excessive speed. Now, I know it's hard to trust the government. Hell, I don't trust the government, so why should you? But here's what I know from traffic school — the speed limits are established based on population, road conditions, usage, equipment, weather equations and a bunch of other silly little things. They take all kinds of possibilities into account, things like — you have this quiet suburban street that very few cars travel, hardly any parking on the street, no school in the neighborhood, road is smooth and wide, kind of a ghost town street, and the limit is set at twenty-five. And who are we kidding? Twenty-five?"

A new picture came up on the screen — a diagram. The road, a few nicely spaced houses, some trees and driveways and a red arrow aiming for a stick man and a trash can. "At twenty-five miles an hour on this street you can put on the brakes and stop before running into Mr. Miller, who is just putting out his trash." A new diagram came up. There were two red arrows. One went right over Mr. Miller and the other went right into a tree. "At forty miles an hour, if you apply your brakes the second you see Mr. Miller, you will not stop in time. If you swerve to avoid him, you'll hit the tree head-on. Someone is going to die."

The audience was silent. A third diagram came up — it showed all the same things, but a police car was added, and that car was on the far left of the screen at the very beginning of the arrow. "This guy is going to stop you if you're doing forty. He's a cop. He'll save your life, Mr. Miller's life *and* get his Christmas bonus.

"I could show you a diagram for every road and vehicle possibility — like the empty freeway, the deserted street or the mountain or desert road that is completely vacant, where there's no Mr. Miller or no Preacher Smith in his wobbly old pickup and there would appear to be no reason on earth for that speed limit."

He limped across the stage again. "Sometimes it might seem there is no logical reason for a speed limit of any kind. Except that at certain speeds the average person stands a better-than-average chance of losing control of the vehicle and having an accident. Now, where's a guy, or girl, with a really great car going to find out what it can do? I mean, if you can't even pick a safe, deserted road to have a little fun, then where can you give it a good test? The speedway. Every big city has one. If you can't locate one, call the police department and ask. They'll direct you to a safe speedway where you can work it out.

"And there you have it, plain and simple.

The three things that will get me my Christmas bonus — you're speeding, or distracted or impaired and I see it. I get to pull you over and make my quota." He was quiet for a meaningful moment. "You get to live."

And then Oscar was on the screen again.

"I told you Oscar is my best friend. I'm almost thirty-five and he's sixty now. Fifteen years ago when I was a Seahawks tight end at the age of twenty and he was a factory worker, we were on the road at the same time. I was testing how fast that Ferrari could get around the mountain curves and he was going home after work. I was on a good road and had a clear path. I was going pretty fast but that car was hugging the road like magic. It was an unpopulated area — hardly anyone on the road and no houses in sight. And then Oscar drove through a stop sign because he'd fallen asleep. He'd worked a double shift and he was toast. He was doing about twenty-five and I was doing about eighty — but I was in total control. Except for one small thing — by the time I saw his car and slammed on the brakes and skidded and lost control, I T-boned him.

"Here's the irony. I got a speeding ticket. I didn't cause the accident — I had the right of way. But my excessive speed combined with his impaired driving put him in a wheelchair and cost me my football career and an inch or so off one leg."

A new picture came up on the screen. It was a shot of Seth and Oscar separated by a chess board. "I really grieved the football. I wasn't happy about how many rods and pins were put in my leg. It hurt to even look at Oscar — he was a family man and he wasn't ever going to get better. But I think the hardest part was my own family and what it did to them. They were so supportive while I worked my way through several surgeries and years of physical therapy. But we were all changed — me and Oscar and all our families and friends. And I think that's when my father stopped being proud of me." He gave the kids a moment to absorb his message.

"Now I have one question for you. And be as honest as you can. Am I gonna get my Christmas bonus this year?"

"No!" they yelled.

"Well, damn. I knew it was a mistake to give you the inside tips. Thanks for letting me have the stage for a little while. Drive your best!"

Iris had to wipe the tears from her eyes. What a showman Seth was. He had obviously taken the lift out of his shoe so that his limp was more pronounced. He was magnificent and how she loved him.

She looked at her watch. It wasn't yet four and last bell had sounded. There were still some athletic practices and after-school clubs going on, but the school had quieted down quite a bit. She tidied up her desk, locked things up and left for the day.

She parked in her carport and walked across the yard. Gwen was busy in her kitchen as always but invited Iris in anyway, offering her a cup of coffee. "I'm going to pass. I discovered something at work today that I wanted to tell you about. Did you know that Seth has done some high school assemblies in the past few years?"

"He mentioned something about drivers' education or something of the sort. . . ."

"Has he told you about it?" Iris asked.

"No details. But I didn't ask. I thought it must just be the usual thing."

"He's extraordinary," Iris said. "I guess if he really wanted you to know about this he would've told you himself."

"But he told you?" Gwen asked.

"Yes and no. He told me as soon as he got to town that he wanted to help with programs directed at teens and asked if we could work together on some stuff, assemblies and that sort of thing. We weren't

369

seeing each other yet and I told him to put together a proposal for me. Today I was looking through a list of recommended videos and there was one of Seth at one of the high schools. Not in Thunder Point, but having seen the video, I have to convince him to appear for our student body. He's wonderful. And I know his story will be meaningful to the kids. The video is public, but I suspect he didn't think anyone would point it out to you. Certainly not me. But, Gwen, you should see it. It's short. Fifteen or twenty minutes. And so moving."

"Then yes, I want to see it. Can you help me find it?"

"Sure. Where's your computer?"

"In my sewing room. I only use it to look up recipes, patterns, pay the bills, that sort of thing. I don't have fun on it like some of my friends."

"Come on. I'll find it for you."

They went together to Gwen's sewing room. Iris sat down at the old computer and, of course, had to update some of the software to show the video. "I'll leave you to it, Gwen. I'm going to go home."

"Are you going to tell Seth what you did, showing me the movie?"

"Of course," she said. "I'm not going to start keeping things from him now. I don't

370

know how he'll react. In fact, I never expected something like this. I think it's important." She gave Gwen a kiss on the cheek. "I'll talk to you later."

Norm shuffled in the door a little earlier than usual, a little grouchier than usual.

"Oh, good, you're home before dinner. There's something I have to show you. It's about Seth and it's important."

"After dinner, Gwen," he said. "I got some mean heartburn today."

"When did that come on? What did you eat?"

"It was a couple hours after lunch. I didn't eat bad. I just had Stu's pulled-pork sandwich, which wasn't as bad as usual. And I felt fine."

"Is it food poisoning?"

"I don't feel that kind of sick. It's just heartburn."

"I'll get you an antacid."

"I hate that shit," he grumbled, sitting in his favorite chair.

"Do you like heartburn?" she asked, skittering off to the kitchen. She brought back the pink jar and a spoon, poured it, aimed it at his mouth.

"No," he said, shaking his head.

"Yes," she said, the spoon steady and

371

unrelenting. "Do as I say. I have to show you a video on the computer. Seth is in it."

He opened his mouth, swallowed and made a great many shudders and melodramatic faces. Gwen ignored him. When she returned after putting away the medicine Norm was even grumpier. "Put it on the TV," he said.

"I can't. It's on the YouTube. Iris showed it to me and now I have to show it to you. Right now."

"Jesus," he grumbled, holding his belly as he got to his feet. "You just live to make my life difficult."

"You live to make your own life difficult. If you'd ever go to the doctor you might find out how to stop having heartburn and headaches and all your other twitches and complaints."

"I went to the doctor for that insurance."

"Nineteen years ago!" she said.

"It wasn't that long."

"Sit down. I'm putting it on for you. Just make no more noise or complaints and watch this because this is our youngest son and it's important."

"He get an award or something?" Norm asked.

"Not that I know of," Gwen said. "Surely not from you! Just watch."

"I mean to tell you, that medicine shit does not work a bit!" he griped.

"I'll go make you something to drink. You watch."

He groaned, but he watched. Gwen went to the kitchen and made him a very watered-down brandy to settle his stomach, but she didn't hurry back with it. In fact, she checked her watch and crept close to the door to her sewing room and listened to Seth's voice on the computer. She could hear Norm make the occasional sound — murmur, grunt, groan. Only Norm would expect a spoonful of medicine to work in sixty seconds.

By the sound on the computer, the video was almost over. She wondered if it would reach Norm the way it had her. She'd had tears on her cheeks. She'd told Norm years ago that if he didn't talk to his sons, let them know how much he treasured them, he'd live to regret it. But Norm didn't listen to his wife.

Well, to be fair, he had listened to her a few times and actually surprised her. She got breast cancer and was pretty sick from the chemo and was frankly astonished at how concerned and doting Norm was. It wasn't as though he did all that much talking, especially never betraying how he felt, but he was there. Every time she rolled over in bed he was awake asking her if she needed the bathroom, a drink of water, a painkiller, anything. That was one of those times she knew how much he really loved her. But when she passed the crisis he stopped being so attentive. Which was all right, she supposed. He'd given himself away.

She'd long ago accepted that they were never going to be the romantic couple they'd been so many years ago. She could live with that. He still kissed her good-night, turned over his paycheck, thanked her for breakfast and told her if dinner was good. That should probably be enough at their ages. But she hoped she died first. She thought Norm was going to be a pain in the ass to take care of and thought it unlikely he'd be able take real good care of her when she became a withering old woman.

"Gwen," he said from the sewing room. She thought his voice sounded strangled with tears.

She rushed back to the kitchen, grabbed the diluted brandy and rushed back to the sewing room.

Norm was bent over in his chair, his hands on his chest, his face completely white. "Gwen, I can't stand up," he said in a strained whisper. "Call Seth."

She bent over him for a closer look. "Norm! What is it?"

"It's in my gut, my chest, my back — I can't sit up. I gotta . . . I gotta see Seth before . . . I have to talk to Seth."

He'd broken out in a sweat, his forehead completely damp. His hands were shaking. He pinched his eyes closed. "Oh, Norm! Are you having a heart attack?"

It took him a second to respond because his breath was short. "I might be," he finally growled out.

Gwen ran to the kitchen and dialed 911. Then she ran back to the sewing room to be with her husband while he died.

EIGHTEEN

Seth was standing outside the deputy's office, talking with Steve Pritkus. Steve had just arrived for the night shift. Both their radios started chattering at the same time. Paramedics were en route to an address for a possible coronary.

Seth and Pritkus looked at each other suddenly. They both knew it was the Sileski address.

"Go, go, go," Pritkus said. "I'll see if Doc Grant is still in the office and bring him!"

Seth jumped in his squad car and ran the lights and siren the short drive to his parents'house. He pulled in their drive, all the way up and onto the grass so he wouldn't be blocking paramedics, and ran into the house.

"Mom? Dad?"

"In here, Seth," Gwen called.

He followed her voice into the sewing room, finding Norm bent over in the chair, shaking, weak, white-faced, sweating. He got down on one knee. "Paramedics on the way, Dad, and we're looking for Doc Grant. Don't panic."

"I ain't," Norm said weakly. "If I don't make it, send your mother on a cruise."

"You can send her on a cruise. Don't talk now." Seth held his father's hand.

The next sound he heard was Iris, running into the house. "Oh, my God, Gwen, what is it? What's wrong?"

"He's having a heart attack," she said.

"We don't know that yet," Seth said. "But we need medical."

Right after that, Scott Grant showed up, a little less panicked but none the less moving at a pretty fast clip. He shooed Seth out of the way, got on one knee, immediately gave Norm an aspirin and took his blood pressure. He fished a small tablet out of a vial and instructed Norm to hold it under his tongue. He asked questions about the pain, looked in his eyes, ears, nose, taking his pulse and temperature, checking the blood pressure again, asked about the pain again.

"I did this," Iris said, tears streaming. "This is my fault!"

"What are you talking about?" Seth asked.

"No, it wasn't your fault," Gwen said. "He came home from work with the pains and I gave him an antacid before he watched the movie."

"What movie?" Seth asked.

"I found your assembly presentation online and I showed your mother," Iris said.

"And I showed your father," Gwen said.

"And he had a heart attack," Iris cried. "Oh, Seth, will you ever forgive me? I do things like that — just make decisions and then . . . God, I'm so sorry!"

"You found that video and showed my parents?"

"I know, I'm a very bad person. I should have asked you! And now look what I've done!"

"No, darling," Gwen said again. "He came home with the heart attack."

"Why did you do that?" Seth asked Iris.

"Because you were so brilliant. Because it was important for your parents to see. Because they'd be so proud of you and all you've done with your life!"

"Iris, what if you find something online that's embarrassing and humiliating and gives *me* a heart attack?" Seth asked.

Scott got to his feet, stethoscope around his neck. "I don't think there's any heart attack. I'm not real sure of the condition of his heart since he hasn't been a regular patient. His blood pressure is high at the moment, no doubt due to severe gastric distress and the pain. But I think what you gave him is a giant gallbladder attack. He says he's had indigestion before and had a big, fatty pork sandwich for lunch. And the whites of his eyes are taking on a jaundiced hue."

"Iris, you gave my father a gallbladder attack," Seth said.

"Oh, Seth, do you hate me?" she asked, tears running down her cheeks.

He just laughed. "I love you, Iris. But you're a runaway train."

The paramedics arrived, talked to Dr. Grant and they unanimously decided on transport to Pacific Hospital. Scott called the E.R. An IV was started. Norm quietly asked Scott if Seth could ride in the ambulance.

"Don't you want your wife to ride with you?" Scott asked.

"I'll take her and follow," Iris said. "Seth, go with your dad."

"I'll go," he said. Then he looked at his mother. "Mom, make sure you turn off the stove."

It was a pretty tight fit in the back of that ambulance but before they were out of town, Norm was much more comfortable thanks to a little pain medication. With Seth on one side of him and a young paramedic on the other side monitoring his blood pressure, Norm closed his eyes and his breathing relaxed.

Norm opened his eyes and looked at Seth. "If I die I want you to sue Stu for that sandwich."

"It's pretty unlikely you're going to die, Dad," Seth said. "I think animal fat is pretty famous for causing gallbladder attacks."

"He doesn't have any warnings posted," Norm said. "Sue him!"

"We'll talk about that when you're feeling better."

"I could die, you know. It's one thing to get a gallbladder attack when you're thirty but at my age . . ."

"You're going to pull through, I think."

"I watched that movie. I thought I was having a heart attack but I watched. Your mother told me it was a heart attack, otherwise I'd have been fine."

"You should always get a second opinion when Mom is diagnosing," Seth said.

"I watched it. Iris brought it over, I think."

"Iris has been a troublemaker since I was about four," Seth said. "You don't have to do everything she says, you know."

"I bet you do," Norm said.

"That's different."

The paramedic laughed discreetly.

"I gotta say something because I don't think these youngsters know squat shit about gallbladders and heart attacks and I think there's still a chance I could die. I don't talk much anymore. I lost the will. Your mother does all my talking for me and I got arthritis in all my joints. But I wasn't mad at you about that car accident."

Seth's eyes widened.

"Okay, for a little while maybe I was, but not that long. I figured you were mad at me since it was my fault."

"Your fault? How was it your fault?"

"I was the one pushing you the whole time, telling you you'd never get a chance like that again — going pro. I didn't think you'd turn your fast buck into a fast car. So for a while it just turned me sour, but I got over that. You never came around. I figured you blamed me for it."

"I never came around because I seemed to make you miserable."

"Shit, son, breathing makes me miserable! You should'a finished college before taking a pro contract. But hell, how'm I to know? Everything ever went right in my life was on account of taking the opportunity, hear me? I wasn't that smart — I was just lucky. You were lucky and smart. I pushed on you and you were just a kid and I guess not smart enough to know better."

"Dad, you're the smartest man I know," he said. "You turned a one-pump gas station into a success and sold it at a profit."

"Lucky," he insisted. "Before I die . . ." He cringed and made a face. "I want you to know, I was proud of you. No need for me to say so. Your mother never stopped talking long enough for me to get a word in anyways. When I die, tell your brothers. They mighta never got a pro contract but I was proud of them, too. They did all right."

Seth smiled. "You're not going to die. But on the off chance you do, anything you want me to tell Mom?"

"Yeah." He cringed again. "Tell her have a good time on her cruise. And, Seth? If you're going to stick with Iris, you might want to see if you can rein her in a little."

"I'll keep that in mind. Thanks, Dad."

"And you sue the diner, you hear me?"

"Sure, Dad."

Norm didn't die. Instead he had his gallbladder removed about twenty-four hours later, as soon as it settled down and his stomach was empty. It was a simple and pretty uneventful procedure . . . unless you asked Norm.

"Horrible thing," he told Seth. "I nearly died of it. So, when are you filing the suit against the diner?"

"We're not suing the diner for a pulled-pork sandwich," Seth said.

"Then how about a citation of some kind? Isn't there some law he broke by not warning people they could end up in surgery from eating his food? Maybe he could just pay a fine or something?"

"I think you should stop blaming him for your gallbladder before he sues you," Seth advised.

"What's he gonna sue me for?" Norm demanded.

"I don't know — defamation of character? Slander? Giving him a headache?"

A couple of days later when Norm was home and possibly permanently embedded in his easy chair, Stu came to visit. He was still wearing his apron and bearing gifts. A pulled-pork sandwich, still warm. "I heard you were suing me," Stu said. "I thought I'd bring you this, see if you think it's any better."

"You think I want another ambulance ride?" Norm shouted.

"It's not like you still got a gallbladder," Stu said. "And I checked with Doc Grant to see if there were any diet restrictions. Go ahead, give it a try. I pulled out all the stops on this one. It's perfect."

With a scowl, Norm reluctantly bit into the sandwich. He chewed thoughtfully. "I think you're getting a little better," he said. "You want half?"

"Naw, I'm good. I gotta get back. Glad you're feeling better. When you back to work?"

"Ten more days or so. Not that I have any problems."

"Of course not," Stu said. "Take care."

Iris was very relieved to be forgiven and even teased about her drama. She did agree to run things by Seth in the future on the off chance she discovered something that could mortify him. "It's a little dicey, knowing all the rules when I'm living in sin with you right next door to your parents."

"I like the sin part," he said. "Just check everything else with me."

A couple of months earlier Iris had not thought it possible that they'd overcome their conflicts and wind up in each other's arms. It was fair to say that never before had she enjoyed this kind of confidence and satisfaction with Seth. They weren't kids anymore and it was such a relief to be able to approach everything they shared from the perspective of adults who knew what they wanted from life. It gave Iris a peace of mind and spirit she had never anticipated.

But relationships were not without challenges, of course.

A text came in from Seth while she was working.

Call please. When you have a minute.

She called him straight away. She half expected him to ask her what she'd like for dinner and that's where her head was when he said, "Do you have an hour today or tomorrow that you can come to my office? Robbie Delaney is concerned about Rachel, about his family, about the interview they had with DHS and he'd like to talk to you, but he can't come to the high school or invite you to Sue Marie's house. He seems to need some advice."

Her mind shifted back to that problem. It hadn't preoccupied her lately, not with Norm's surgery and other things going on. But it was back. It was here. It was now.

"I have two meetings tomorrow, one at eleven and one at three. I can sneak away any other time."

"Good. Let me get back to him and call you right back. Thanks, baby. This is good of you. He's pretty confused and worried."

Since Rachel's outburst, Iris had steered clear of Rachel and Brett. She'd handed the case over to the authorities. She hadn't been the object of anyone's anger over it lately, hadn't had any calls from Connie and DHS, had been blissfully ignorant of any details.

Three hours later she was walking into Seth's office. Robbie Delaney was sitting on the corner of Seth's desk. Iris had seen him occasionally over the years, here and there. The past year since Rachel had been one of the football cheerleaders she'd seen him more often. She had never given him much thought; they exchanged greetings and moved on. Now, here was a man who clearly had burdens. He looked into his coffee cup and when he looked up his expression nearly shouted fear and shame.

Robbie's hair was thinning. He was a little heavier, the lines around his eyes a little deeper. And now that winning smile was more hesitant.

"Hi, Iris," he said.

"Robbie. How are you?" She pulled up a chair. Seth was behind his desk, with Robbie perched on the corner and Iris sitting more or less between them.

"I'm not great right now. I hope you can help. Rachel says it was you who alerted the social workers. That right?"

"Would that upset you? If you found out I was concerned?"

"No! I'd thank you! We got a mess right now."

She took a deep breath. "I had a talk with Rachel about all the bruises that were showing up. She had a reason for every one. But then I saw what appeared as suspicious behavior — Brett was a little rough with her and clearly very angry. Very angry! I just couldn't let it go. Robbie, it's my job. I have to notice things like that. Did Rachel deny it?"

"To the social workers, she totally denied it. She kept that up for a couple of hours after, too. Look at this," he said, withdrawing a cell phone from his pocket. It was pink. He clicked on the text messages and handed it to Iris.

Parking lot. 3:15

I can't. I have cheer practice.

B late. 3:15. Come on baby.

I can't! I've been late 3 times!

U gonna give me trouble?

Please!

3:15. I mean it.

Sorry, babe. Does it hurt? U no I love U. Y do U push me?

Rache? Rache? U gonna be mad now? U better answer me or I'm gonna be mad!

Brett, I was at practice! Give me a break!

Don't I come before practice?

I met you didn't I?

U were late to me! But on time to cheer?

OMG, I do the best I can! Call me later!

A flood of texts calling out to her followed, texts she couldn't answer because her father now had her phone.

Iris lowered the phone and looked at Robbie. Her mouth was open in question.

"That was yesterday before the social workers got to the house. Rachel was furious about the accusations. After the women left, I dumped her purse and grabbed her phone. I pay for that phone. I saw the texts and read them out loud and she went berserk. She pitched a holy fit, but I hung on to the phone and demanded the truth and she went to pieces. 'It's not fair,' she said. He doesn't *really* hurt her, just a couple of accidents. When I asked her what had to happen in the parking lot at three-fifteen she fell apart and started to sob. She never would say what he wanted but my stomach is sick. Maybe because I was once a teenage boy in that same parking lot. I can't let this happen, Iris. Tell me what to do."

She took a deep breath. "I brought you some names of counseling groups for teen-age girls in crisis and the name of a counselor you can talk to."

"What about you?"

She shook her head. She passed the phone to Seth so he could see the messages. "Unfortunately, I can't reach Rachel. I tried. She's very angry with me for questioning her about her injuries. Listen, here's what you have to know about battered girlfriends. It's right here in the texts. He loves her. He wants her and can't live without her. If he strikes out at her, it's her fault, but he's sorry and he won't do it again. He promises. He loves her. He needs her. He strikes out again and she made him do it again but he's sorry and loves her. Again. It's the worst roller coaster. She'll protect him and won't give him up easily. And, Robbie, it's not just physical abuse. Sometimes it's emotional. It's complicated and so challenging. Not only does the abuser learn that behavior from parents or other family members, so does the abused. It takes intervention and therapy to break the cycle."

Robbie stared at her for a long, quiet moment. He let his eyes close for a moment. "I have to do something about this," he finally said.

Iris wondered if Robbie, always so physical and aggressive as a boy, had ever been an abuser. *"This?"* she asked.

"This cycle of abuse. I have to get Rachel out of here. I have to take her home with me. She just can't stay here anymore. I can't help her change this if she lives in Thunder Point and goes to school with him every day. How'm I gonna keep her safe?"

"Is that an option for you, Robbie? Can you take her out of Thunder Point? Would it be possible?"

"I have my own business. I make my own hours. I work all the time anyway. If I need to leave a little later in the morning or run home in the afternoon to make sure everyone is all right, I can do that. We don't have any custody agreement, me and Sue Marie. I just have to get her to go along with it."

"Do you think she would?"

He shook his head, looking dismayed. "I don't know. She should. I mean, she's got a job working evenings at the casino — she can't keep an eye on the kids. And she likes to go out when she's not working. Kids can be a drag. But I like having the kids. I haven't had Rachel too much this year because she's busy with school and sports and a boyfriend. I didn't know . . . I didn't know. . . ."

He shook his head again. "Can you help me with this?" he asked Iris. "Can you come with me to talk to Sue Marie?"

"I'm afraid that probably wouldn't work," Iris said. "It's one of those things, Robbie. Sue Marie and I haven't really been rivals, never out in the open at least. But the unspoken fact is we've often been interested in the same man." She shrugged. "She's been a little flirtatious with Seth. . . ."

"I never responded," Seth said, weighing in for the first time and holding up his hands, palms toward both Iris and Robbie. "Well, I did turn down her offer of getting together sometime to catch up. There's nothing to catch up on. From the time we broke up in high school, she hasn't been on my radar. At all."

"But *you* could help," Iris said. "You could help Robbie talk to his wife about where the kids live. I don't think Sue Marie likes me much and I know Rachel is angry with me, but she respects Seth."

"Aw, Iris," Seth said in a low moan.

"Well, it's a thought," she said. "You've been trained in domestic violence. You answer domestic disturbance calls. You know a lot about this stuff. And hey, there was that night in the bar — I saw you in action."

"She might listen to you," Robbie said. "Not for the right reasons, but she might listen."

"Iris," Seth said in a warning tone.

"Well, you can always just say no, Seth," she replied.

"I don't care what I have to do," Robbie said. "I just have to get my kids in a safe place where I can watch them. Iris, I can't watch them when they're at school."

"I know. As long as Rachel is at the high school, we have to be diligent. I wasn't the only one concerned about her. I'll remind her gym teacher to watch closely and I'll be very observant. I have their class schedules. I can post myself nearby when the bell rings.

I'll do my best."

"Seth, you'll come talk to Sue Marie, right?" Robbie asked.

"I shouldn't . . ."

"Just be a witness while I talk," Robbie suggested.

Seth mulled it over for a moment. "Okay. I'll meet you at Sue Marie's at five-thirty. She's gonna be there, right? And Rachel?"

"Sue Marie goes to work a little later. I told her I was coming over again. She knows I want to take the boys back with me but Rachel has refused. I told Rachel I'd be at school today to pick her up and bring her home. Maybe she'll listen."

"Well, good luck," Iris said.

"Thanks," he said, heading for the office door, hat in hand. He turned back and looked at her. "You know, I think maybe we have one of those abusive relationships. No hitting," Robbie said. "But there was yelling and cheating and breaking up and getting back together and more fighting and yelling and cheating."

"Oh, Robbie," Iris said.

"Not me," he said. "All I ever wanted to do was make Sue Marie happy, but I never could, at least not for long. We had more fresh starts than any two people I ever knew. I'm not the best catch in the world, but I was willing to do about anything. In fact, if she wanted to try again right now, it'd be damn hard to say no."

Iris went back to school. There was still a little time before the final bell. She found Spencer Lawson in his office in the boy's locker room and had to make it fast before classes let out and his teams converged on that space and started stripping to get into their sporting gear.

"Got a minute?" she asked him.

"You bet." He looked at his watch. "You either get ten minutes or we should step into the hall."

"Let's see where we are in nine minutes," she said. "You know how the students tighten up when they're being sneaky? Closing ranks against us?"

"Only too well," he said with a smile.

"We have a very delicate, potentially volatile situation. I had to call DHS to report suspected abuse between our most popular couple — Brett and Rachel. Social workers are investigating the situation. I don't know what their findings will be, but I can say without a shred of doubt that the relationship is abusive."

He frowned. "Seriously? Who's abusing who?"

"Brett seems to be the one with the slippery punch. The girl has been wearing a lot of bruises that I questioned. She had some very creative excuses. She finally admitted to her father that Brett's very rough with her, that he hurts her sometimes, but of course he doesn't mean to."

Spencer shook his head. "I've seen this before," he said.

"It's a first for me. When have you seen this?"

"We tread a very fine line in this department. We want our men to be killers on the field and pussycats everywhere else. We have some good role models for that and I watch for those pro ball players who can hit real hard and treat everyone off the field with great care and respect. I use them for examples every chance I get. But just like in the outside world, we have those who only know one way, to control everything, no matter what. I've dealt with my share of bullies and bad boyfriends. I keep an eye on that, a very serious eye. Brett's one kid I never would have guessed for a brute. He's polite, keeps good grades, works hard." He shook his head. "Shows you just never know. Want me to talk to him?"

"He's been talked to. He was interviewed with his family, though I don't know the outcome and I may not be told. For now, can you just watch? I have their schedules if you need them. I'm going to become quite a hall monitor for the next few days. I'm afraid that's all I can do. Back me up?"

"Absolutely. And if I see an opportunity to say something, I will." He shook his head. "Brett's got most of the faculty eating out of his hands. He's one of those soft-spoken, well-mannered kids. His mom and dad seem to be strict but quiet and polite. Can't remember what his dad does, but he does it in a shirt and tie. See, you can never tell, can you?"

"Please, let me know if anything comes up. My priority right now is to do what I can to keep Rachel safe, whether she cooperates or not."

"What? Whether she cooperates?"

"She loves him," Iris said. "And of course he didn't *mean* to hurt her."

NINETEEN

Iris owes me, Seth thought as he left Sue Marie's house. They'd experienced some success or at least a difficult compromise, but it was awkward. She'd flirted with him, placing a hand on his forearm and turning her big blue eyes up at him to make comments or ask questions. Rachel was silent but oozed hostility.

Robbie wanted to pack up the kids, move them to North Bend where he still occupied the little house they'd all lived in before Sue Marie left a couple of years ago. He wanted to become their primary guardian and have them change schools. He thought he could manage.

Sue Marie had a lot of arguments against it, but probably the biggest one was alimony and child support. They didn't even have a divorce decree and there was no legal separation agreement, but Robbie was paying all the bills. How he managed on his sketchy income was beyond Seth.

"Now, there are safety issues, Sassy," Seth said, forgetting to use her preferred name. He went on as rapidly as he could, before she could correct him. "Rachel needs serious supervision and counseling and since Robbie makes his own hours, being self-employed, that's a little easier for him to do."

In fact, there were too many issues to count. There were eight people in a small four-bedroom house, for one thing. And that was just one thing.

Sassy finally agreed. The kids were going to go to Robbie's, at least for the time being, and Robbie would drive them to Thunder Point for school and pick them up afterward. It occurred to Seth that Sue Marie, who had a car, could offer to help with some of the transportation, but he held his tongue. They would revisit changing schools over the Christmas holidays.

Rachel had only one comment. "I want my phone."

"We're going to talk about that tonight. When we get home," Robbie told her.

That's when Seth ran for his life. He texted Iris that he was finished at Sassy's but had a couple of things to do before he could get home. Home now meant her house. She texted back that she was throwing together dinner and would see him when he was done.

Seth drove to Brett's house. It was after six. He had done a little check on the family. Sid Davis was an office manager who worked with lawyers in North Bend. Mrs. Davis didn't work outside the home. They had moved to Thunder Point two years before, possibly for the football opportunities for Brett. There were four children, Brett being the oldest.

Sid Davis answered the front door. He held the glasses he had just pulled off in one hand and wore a pleasant and welcoming smile. "Hello. How can I help you, Deputy?"

"If you have a minute, I'd just like to talk to you."

"About?"

"Well, about a situation with your son and another student. I believe it's his girlfriend. . . ."

"Ah," he said, shaking his head somewhat sadly and opening the door wider. "Of course. A surprising and confusing turn of events. Come in, come in. I'll get Brett."

"Only if you want to. I really wanted to have a word with you, but —"

But Sid walked away.

Seth looked around. It was a very nicely decorated house for Thunder Point. Like so many others, it wasn't large, but it was homey and roomy. There wasn't a sound in the house, not even the distant sound of a television. The house was very tidy; there were no toys or gadgets scattered around. The enticing aroma of dinner filled the air. Seth could see that Sid Davis had been sitting in a chair in the living room, his laptop on the coffee table.

Where are the kids? he wondered.

Sid returned with his son. They were equal in height though Brett was a little broader in the shoulders. They didn't resemble each other too strongly — Sid had a long, pointy nose — but they both seemed to have generous smiles and a nice crop of hair. Brett had a nasty bruise on one cheek — a little puffy and red, giving way to purple.

"Deputy," Brett said politely.

"Hi, Brett."

"We know why you're here, Deputy," Sid said, still smiling that welcoming smile. "We were visited yesterday afternoon by a couple of child welfare workers from the county. We have all the details. Shocking. I had to come home from work early to meet with them. They insisted it be my wife, myself and Brett. Apparently they have rules about that and the penalty for not following the rules, even if your job is important, is a court order to immediately remove your children."

"Seriously?" Seth asked. Seth doubted that was true. He would expect DHS to try to schedule a meeting that accommodated all involved. "Wow, that's very rigid. I had no idea. Hopefully, they also provide an excuse from the court or something so your boss doesn't get his knickers in a knot."

"I wouldn't know," Sid said.

"I'm sorry? You have me at a loss. What do you do?"

"I'm in charge of a legal aid office for the county. Public defenders."

"Ah. I didn't realize you were a lawyer," Seth said. Sid didn't clarify. *Interesting,* Seth thought.

"Now what was it you wanted?"

"Oh, I just wanted to find out where we all stand on this investigation the county is doing for their case. Suspected dating abuse, right? Something like that?"

"Tell the deputy what you told the women who were here, Brett."

Brett's eyes narrowed slightly. "She made it up, I guess. We were dating, but I never once did anything to hurt her. I don't know why she said that."

Seth reached his hand toward Brett's face and the kid backed away instinctively. "What happened here, son?" Seth asked. "You walk into a wall?"

"I wrestle," he said. "I don't know exactly what happened, but I think it was a foot."

"You don't wear helmets? I thought the team wore helmets. I love wrestling. Look forward to taking in a few matches this winter."

"Look, seriously, I don't have any idea what's up with Rachel. I don't know why she'd make me look bad like that. It makes no sense. I'm real good to her. I'm —"

"Well, sometimes you're pretty demanding," Seth said, cutting him off. "I had a look at just a few of your texts to her from . . . Gee, was it yesterday?" Seth asked, rubbing the back of his neck. "Her dad confiscated her phone and showed me. You were telling her to get to the parking lot by three-fifteen and when she said she couldn't, you threatened her, told her she was pushing you, warned her you might get mad. It was very demanding, very angry and insistent. That didn't seem like her making you look bad. That seems like —"

"She had notes for me! I needed them! It was from a class I missed and she said she'd get 'em to me by three-fifteen! It's all out of context, it's —"

"She had to get those notes to the parking lot?" Seth asked. "I'm sorry, I'm a little confused. Why couldn't you meet at her locker to get those notes? I mean, there were a lot of texts back and forth about you insisting she get to the parking lot and I just wonder why that was so important."

"Exactly what's the question, Deputy?" Sid asked.

"There's no question, Mr. Davis," Seth said. "It sounded threatening to me and I'm very concerned about the possible violent nature of the relationship between Brett and Rachel. I want them safe, after all. So I thought I'd come by, put in my two cents and see where we stand." He looked at Brett. "I take it you and Rachel have decided to cool things? As Rachel's parents requested?"

"*Rachel's parents* have no need to request anything of us," Sid said. "Brett, of his own accord, broke it off with her immediately. Obviously she's a little off balance. We don't need this kind of aggravation. Brett certainly doesn't. He's a gentleman, athlete, straight-A student and life is too short to put up with this kind of defamation."

Seth smiled. "Good decision. Sorry that romance didn't work out, but really, staying away from the girl right now is an excellent decision." He sniffed the air. "My God, that smells good! What's cooking tonight, Mr. Davis?"

Sid smirked. "I believe that's chicken and rice. Nothing special."

"But you got the table all set there. You having company tonight?"

"I have four children, Deputy. Anything else?"

"Nothing from me. I think everyone is on the same page right now. The kids are better off putting a little distance between themselves. Doesn't that sound like a good solution, Brett?"

"She's crazy. I don't know why she'd do that to me. She's just screwed up, that's all."

"Sure," Seth said. "Then give her a lot of space. Right?"

"No kidding," Brett said sullenly.

"Good night, then. Enjoy your dinner," Seth said.

He stepped outside and took three long steps down the walk, then three long steps back to the front door where he stood, quietly listening.

"Didn't I tell you to keep your mouth shut? When I say keep your mouth shut, that's what I mean. You sound like a fool, a pussy! Some little girl picking on you?"

404

"He asked! I just answered!"

"I said keep your stupid mouth shut!"

"Ow. I told you, I didn't do nothing! She's out to get me! Ow."

Seth opened the door. Sid was gripping his son by the arm, his face pressed close to Brett's. "Problem, gentlemen?" he asked.

Sid didn't let go. He glared at Seth. "What do you want now?" Sid asked.

"I want to know if everything is all right," Seth said.

"You have no right to walk into my house!"

"Oh, you're completely wrong, Mr. Davis. I heard shouting and noises that indicated imminent danger which, in fact, it appears there is. Now, it's really my responsibility to read you your rights, cuff you and take you to my office to process you for battery. You appear to be battering your son. But seeing as how I heard it happening and didn't witness it happen, I only have my suspicions. Which, by the way, appear to be on target. So, I'm going to leave you with a warning. Lay one hand on any member of your family and it will be my pleasure to take you for a little ride. Brett, you ever get knocked around or see the rest of the family being abused, you have only to make a call. Understand?"

"This is none of your business. Get out," Sid said.

"I can't wait to leave, as a matter of fact."

"Don't even think of making a big deal out of this," Sid warned.

"Sorry, pal. Making a big deal of it is at the top of my list. I'd recommend you calm down and get under control before you make things worse." He stepped out and started to pull the door closed. "Oh, by the way. You're not a lawyer. You might've corrected me."

"It's none of your goddamn business!"

Seth traded glare for glare with Sid. "Yes, it is," he said.

Seth let himself into the kitchen of Iris's house, holding his hat in his hand, and just took in the scene. There was a nice smell of food cooking and Iris was sitting at the small kitchen table with her laptop open, making notes on a legal pad.

He'd never had this before. There had never been a woman to come home to, a warm, good-smelling kitchen welcoming him, this promise of contentment to ease him.

She looked up. "Hi."

He tossed his hat on the table and went around to her side. He pulled a chair close

406

to her and sat down. She turned in her chair so her knees were inside his. He leaned toward her for a kiss and she put her arms around his neck and met his lips.

And he felt brand-new.

"Something smells good," he said.

"Some chicken thing . . ."

He laughed against her lips. Iris, he'd learned, didn't do a lot of cooking and certainly nothing fancy. But then, neither did he. "What kind of chicken thing?"

"Sort of an enchilada thing, but not really."

"Iris, you going to make me guess?"

"Well, it's a couple of cans of cream soup, a can of tomatoes, some chicken breasts, sour cream, taco seasoning . . ."

His lips went to her neck and he sighed, resting them there. "Sounds delicious."

"We used to make it in college a lot. It takes no skill, no brains."

"Is it ready?"

"A little longer," she said. "Want to tell me what's wrong, Seth?"

"I don't want to move," he said. "Are you going to get mad if I say I need you? Because I need you, Iris. Like I need air."

"I need you, too."

"Can we stay like this forever?"

She laughed and ran her fingers through

the hair at his temples. "With food and bathroom breaks?"

"Together," he said. "I just meant can we stay together forever?"

"I'm hoping so. I've loved you forever. Except when I hated you . . ."

"Good, then." He kissed her neck and pulled her closer. "Forever, then. We should get married before I do something stupid again. Maybe the second school is out? Whenever you can be ready."

"Do you want to talk about what's bothering you?" she asked him.

"No," he said. "I don't want to talk about anything sad or mean or wrong right now. You make me feel like everything is good. When I'm holding you, everything is sweet and clean and kind." He pulled away a little and smiled. "And aroused."

"I like that, too."

"I should get a shower before that chicken thing is done."

"I should, too," she said.

"We should save water," he told her.

"We should. I think I'll just go ahead and turn off the oven so we don't have to rush too much while we're saving water."

"Good idea. I'm not that hungry. For food, that is. Baby, I love you so much. You make my world right."

■ ■ ■ ■

Late that night, after lovemaking and chicken casserole that vaguely resembled an enchilada pie, Iris snuggled in Seth's arms and listened to him talk about his day. He groaned about Sassy wearing eau de vineyard, flirting with him a little sloppily while Robbie was trying to negotiate some kind of custody shift to try to protect Rachel. Rachel, who didn't seem to want too much protection. Then on to visiting with one of the biggest assholes in town, the guy who had probably personally taught Brett Davis how to pummel a woman.

"I wake up in the morning thinking how lucky I am to live in a sweet little town where the people are nice and generous and care about each other. And then I'm reminded that all people have problems, sometimes of their own making, and that it's my job to recognize them and do what I can to protect the innocent," he said.

"If the town and people were as perfect as we like to sometimes believe, we wouldn't need a deputy, Seth. We're humans. We stumble all the time. And now, from what you tell me, even Brett is innocent, in a way," Iris said.

"In a way that bears watching very closely. The fact that maybe he can't really help it is no excuse to let him run wild. Watch, Iris. And be careful. Apparently he has a real short fuse, even if he doesn't let it show often."

"But his own father! Even though I know that's pretty typical, that very often the abused grow up to become abusers, it still throws me."

"One of these days, Brett is going to realize he's bigger and stronger than that jerk and there could be a dangerous power shift. I'm not supposed to ever say things like this, but I hope I see it."

"Seth!"

"I know. That's no solution. . . ."

When Iris was back at school the next morning and took her post outside her office door, it felt like the sweet little town again. The next few days were happy with the student body anticipating the holiday break coming soon. The kids smiled and waved, stopped to chat, held hands with their boyfriends or girlfriends, laughed and carried on. Sometimes they could make her feel so old, like when a couple of rowdy boys rushed up to a girl in the hall and tried to make a sandwich out of her, putting her in the middle to the hysterical giggles of the girl and everyone around them. Then they'd see Iris standing there and it would be *Oh, no! Ms. McKinley! Oh, sorry, Ms. McKinley!* And she'd give them a stern look and waggle her finger at them and they'd run off, laughing at their close call.

There was invariably some kind of game of catch taking place in the hall — baseball, basketball, football or personal items like a phone, book or purse. She would yell at the kids. *Give it back or get detention!* Or a great big guy would pick up a smaller boy and carry him over his shoulder, a classic fireman's carry, until Iris told him to put the kid down. The response was always the same. *Yes, Ms. McKinley.*

Some of the kids clutched their books seriously, some moved in packs down the hall, laughing and gossiping as they went, some clung close to the walls while others strutted proudly.

So often she would think, wasn't it just a few months ago I was that age? Then the town deputy would come down the hall and she'd have a serious time warp. When they had been students here, they'd spent so much time together. She'd adored him then almost as much as now.

"Good morning, Ms. McKinley," Seth

said, smiling at her.

"Deputy," she acknowledged.

"Everything calm this morning?" he asked her.

"In fact, it's almost hopeful-looking," she reported. "I saw Rachel with her girlfriends and they were whispering and laughing, headed for their lockers. They're some of the prettiest girls and have been to hair-flipping school." She demonstrated the movement of flipping hair over a shoulder. "Brett passed by with one of his friends and he said good morning to me with a smile. Robbie has called me twice to say that he thinks the worst of it is past — Rachel agrees it's not a good idea to date Brett and claims they're broken up for good. She wants to stay at Thunder Point but live with Robbie if that can be arranged. And Robbie, bless his little heart, said anything can be arranged as long as it doesn't involved her getting treated badly by some guy. She's going to cheer practice again and Robbie's coming inside to pick her up at the locker room door. There hasn't been a single issue, he says. Not even phone calls or texts. Things have been peaceful. Maybe this is going to be okay."

"Don't count on it," Seth said. "I want it to be, but don't relax your watch."

"I won't. I never do. At least Brett's graduating and going to college," she said.

"You know there will be challenges after this," he said.

"I know better than anyone," she said. "Are you hanging around awhile?"

"I kind of like walking these halls now," he said. He looked both ways and when the coast was clear, he gave her a little kiss. Then he moved down the hall.

There was a lot of hall walking. Seth dropped by the high school three or four times a day, had friendly little chats with teachers, visited with some of the students.

A week went by peacefully and the second uneventful week was coming to a close. School would be dismissed for the Christmas break and Iris felt as though a weight had been lifted from her shoulders. All the kids would go, enjoy their holidays; the school would be closed and, most importantly, they'd all be off her watch.

Then came the late hour of the day that Iris loved. She packed up her briefcase, locked her desk and went into the hall. There was the sound of basketball practice coming from the gym, but the lights were dimmed and the halls darkened. Very few students remained, just the teams confined to the gym and locker rooms. Given it was the last day before vacation, practices would be shortened. There were probably a few teachers finishing up paperwork or meetings before going home for the holiday. The principal's office was open but was quiet. She poked her head in and wished the office staff happy holidays. She waved to the school nurse, who was leaving the building carrying a large tote filled with little gifts given to her by students.

Iris decided to make one last lap around the building and see who was still there. Troy was just closing his classroom door. "Hey," she said to him. "When are you leaving town?"

"Not for a couple of days. What are you doing for Christmas?" he asked.

"Nothing very exciting. I'll spend some time with Seth's family."

"Ah, yes, the new boyfriend," Troy said.

She tilted her head. "Please tell me you're not being snide."

"Nah," he said. "I probably should've known there was someone else on your mind. I just want you to be happy."

"I am happy, Troy. I wish you could be happy, too. And not upset with me."

"I'm working on that. The happy part, that is. I'm not mad at you, Iris. You can't really help who rings your bells."

"No hard feelings, then?" she asked.

"Of course not. The hell of it is, I could never be mad at you. I'm going to go to Morro Bay, spend some time with the family and go to many bars to pick up chicks. I'll take my younger brother — he's a chick magnet."

She laughed. "Best of luck. And be careful!"

He gave her a brief hug. "Merry Christmas, Iris. I hope next year is your best year ever."

"Thanks, I wish the same for you."

She continued down the hall and turned left. The building was a big square. She passed Louie, the janitor, wished him well. She turned down another hall, dimly lit, all the teachers apparently gone for the two-week break.

As she walked, she heard a noise. It sounded like cats. She kept walking, listening carefully. She realized it was talking and sighing and mewling. *Oh, crap! I'm going to catch teenagers doing it! And then my eyes are going to hurt forever!* she thought. But she couldn't just ignore it — students were supposed to be out of the building unless they were in supervised clubs or practices or meetings.

There were so many classrooms along the

corridor and she stopped at each one, trying the doors. They were all locked. If she couldn't find the source of the noises, she'd go back to the office and summon some security or the janitor with a set of master keys. It was entirely possible a couple of young lovebirds had snuck into an unlocked classroom, locked themselves in and were making out. At the very least. She hoped it wasn't worse.

Iris caught kids skipping classes, smoking, talking on cell phones they weren't supposed to have at school. All the staff did. She had caught them making out in dark corners, causing them to blush and run. High school kids had been doing that since long before she was a student herself.

She heard the chime of her cell phone — a text was coming in. She pulled it out of her skirt pocket and stood under a light to see what it said. It was from Seth and that made her smile.

I'm going to leave a little early tonight. Want me to take you out to dinner?

I'd love it.

When are you done?

Just making a final sweep of the halls.
Everyone should be gone but I hear suspicious sounds.

Go get some backup!

It's probably someone smoking or making
out.

Iris! Backup!

Relax. I'll be done in five min.

She put the phone in her pocket and kept
walking. Every door was locked and the
mewling sound came and went. Seth was
going to have his way — she was going to
end up in the office looking for someone to
help her search because she couldn't find
the little culprits.

Then she heard a loud thump and a yelp.
It was followed by a girl's cry. *Where are
they?* she wondered. *Where?* And then she
heard another sound, a louder moan, that
made her sure these kids would be naked
when she found them. The thought made
her shudder.

But she *had* found them. She pressed her
ear against the door to the boy's bathroom
and heard soft talking and murmuring.

417

There were a couple of thumps. And then, indisputably, a *slap.*

She texted Seth — Help! NE BR. Call school security! 911

She pushed the door open and saw her worst nightmare. Brett Davis was holding Rachel up against the cold, green ceramic tiles on the back wall and he was choking her. Rachel appeared limp against the wall, her arms hanging loosely at her sides. Brett was banging her head as well as choking her. Iris was too shocked to speak for a moment. "Stop!" she finally shouted.

Brett turned to look at her. His eyes were narrowed. "Get out," he said. "Just *get out.*"

"Let her go," Iris said, approaching them. "Let her go now!"

"Get out," he said again. "This is between us."

"I called the police," she said. "They're coming. Let go of her."

He gave her one last angry glare, then looked back at Rachel. He talked to her with his hands still around her throat. "Tell her, Rache. Tell her, we're together."

Iris didn't feel she had any options, he was going to kill the girl. She rushed him, grabbed his arm and pulled, screaming, "Let her go! Let her go!" Then she bellowed as loudly as she could. *"Help!"* Again, she

418

demanded that Brett let the girl go.

Iris was pulling on him. She even stuck her hand under his belt and pulled, to no avail. Rachel tried to lift her arms and push at him weakly. He seemed bigger than Iris had ever seen him and given his position, pressing the girl against the wall, Iris couldn't do anything. She tried pounding on his back, and she tried choking him as he was doing to the girl; she tried pinching him and pulling his hair. Finally, desperate, she bit the back of his arm. She bit him *hard.*

He yelled, and his elbow came back and up, hitting her under the chin.

Iris reeled back and landed against a sink, dazed. She slid to the floor between two sinks, holding her jaw. Brett let go of Rachel and turned toward Iris with fury in his eyes. The girl slithered weakly to the floor. He approached Iris, fists clenched.

"I'm not afraid of you!" she screamed. "You're a bully and a wimp! You hit *girls!*"

For just a second, he stopped. It was like he was thinking about that. Then he growled and grabbed Iris around the throat, pulling her upright from the floor, shaking her. She got a knee to his crotch, but it wasn't hard enough to stop him.

Suddenly the intercom came to life.

"Lockdown! Lockdown! Teachers, students, staff, emergency lockdown!"

Brett raised his head like a deer smelling a hunter in the woods. He dropped Iris and looked around as though he was just recognizing his surroundings. He even looked at his hands.

And then he bolted, crashing out the door at a dead run.

Iris sank again to the cold floor. She pulled her cell phone out of her skirt pocket, but she was shaking too hard to use it. Rachel, crying, began to crawl to her. Iris reached out a hand to her. Rachel had a small trickle of blood running from the corner of her mouth; her cheek and neck were red but there were no visible bruises yet. In twenty-four hours, she might look frightening. "Come," Iris said, enfolding the girl in her arms, still holding the phone.

"I'm sorry, I'm sorry. He wanted to talk," Rachel said. "Just talk, that's all. He begged for just a few minutes to talk because he didn't want us to be enemies. I'm so dumb. I knew better, but I believed him. . . ."

"I know," Iris said, a little hoarse and breathless. She stroked Rachel's hair while she cradled the girl against her. Rachel sobbed. Iris knew the story. He called, she went, danger followed. And they were just kids.

■ ■ ■ ■

Troy went back to his classroom for a book he wanted to read over the break. He was just closing his door, keys in one hand and book in the other, when the announcement came over the PA system. "Lockdown! Lockdown!"

When you heard that, you had no way of knowing if it was a gunman, a terrorist, a naked lunatic or invasion by alien beings. All that was clear was that there was potential danger to teachers and students and the procedure was to lock everyone in the room and barricade the door with desks if possible.

He had no students to protect, but there were still people in the building. He had just seen Iris making a hall walk. He dropped the book to the floor, pocketed his keys and listened. Within seconds he heard feet running, the hard pounding of heavy footfalls. Brett Davis careened around the corner and skidded to a stop when he saw Troy.

The kid was rumpled, flushed, had a look of panic on his face. "Come here, Brett," Troy said.

Brett hesitated for a second before he

turned and ran like the wind. Troy went after him without hesitation. And the kid was *fast*! Troy closed within six feet of Brett and lunged, hitting him around the waist and tackling him to the floor. He pinned him facedown, captured his hands, pushed his cheek to the floor and wouldn't let him move. All the while Brett was yelling that he hadn't done anything, which made it even more obvious he'd done something.

Troy heard running and prayed Brett didn't have any accomplices in whatever it was he was up to. Then Seth came around the corner, pulling handcuffs off his belt as he approached.

"What are you doing?" he asked Troy.

"Tell me this kid has nothing to do with the lockdown."

"He could've been armed," Seth said. Once Brett was cuffed Seth looked at Troy. "Where are we?"

"West hall. Math and science. Hey, I saw Iris right before the lockdown."

"I know," Seth said. He keyed his mike. "One in custody, west hall, math and science area." Seth proceeded to pat Brett down to make sure there were no weapons, not even so much as a pen. "Can you handle him for a minute? Pritkus is right behind me."

"Believe me, he's not going anyplace," Troy said.

"I gotta get Iris," Seth said, jogging off.

TWENTY

Just because Thunder Point was a little town on the coast and there was rarely any excitement didn't mean they ignored threats or potential danger. When Seth got Iris's text for help, he did what he was trained to do — take every precaution. He didn't know exactly what Iris was up against. The Sheriff's Department, State Police, Coast Guard and all area first responders were well trained and took zero chances. It's not as though school shootings and other such tragedies were unheard of. In fact, they happened in the most unexpected places. He called the school and said, "Lock it down! I'm calling backup and medical."

Within minutes the building was surrounded by local and semi-local police. SWAT arrived soon after and the USCG landed in a safe but close parking lot. Paramedics waited on the scene for possible injured. Teachers still inside were locked in their classrooms, secretaries were under their desks, athletes had exited the building through the locker room's back door. SWAT and the police cleared the building.

The threat was one unarmed sixteen-year-old boy. *Thank God.*

By the time Seth walked out of the school with Iris and Rachel, most of the town had gathered there. The women were taken straight to the paramedics where Rachel agreed to go to the hospital to be checked, mostly because she'd had so many recent injuries including a concussion. Iris, on the other hand, decided on a visit with Scott Grant; she was a little bruised but didn't think she was seriously hurt.

SWAT brought Brett out of the building. Troy walked behind them. One of the things that had been overlooked around Thunder Point was that the thirty-year-old history teacher was a marine who had served in Iraq. He was a very capable assistant to dealing with the emergency and he could be credited with stopping the suspect before he got away.

Seth looked at the scene surrounding the high school. He was grateful it hadn't been a full-scale war, but even that didn't lessen the impact.

Mac McCain walked toward him. Mac

was still in civilian clothes, but Seth noticed his department car was parked at the back of a long line of emergency vehicles. "So it was a kid," he said. "Lucky."

Seth shook his head. "Lucky. Mac, I don't want to ever see my school surrounded like this again. Never again."

"I hear that. On the other hand, it was a damn good drill. Excellent response, outstanding performance. It's always good to know we're ready for anything."

Seth looked over at Brett, who was being loaded into the back of Pritkus's car. He was going to the headquarters in Coquille where he would be booked on every charge Seth could think of.

Robbie Delaney was a smart guy, Seth decided. He'd gotten himself derailed when Sue Marie got pregnant in their first semester of college. He wanted to marry her, make a family with her; he loved her. He *still* loved her, but he realized there were issues. In fact, he told Seth, Rachel might have come by some of her problems through her parents' dysfunctional relationship.

"Rachel sees the light where Brett's concerned, but that doesn't mean she's a hundred percent ready to have a healthy relationship — she needs some help with that. We all need a little help with that. Rachel's going to start in a teen group in the new year, and the boys and I will get a little family counseling. Sue Marie can join us if she wants to, but if she has better things to do, we're pressing on. We're celebrating Christmas here at our house. We're putting up the tree, laying in the Christmas ham and we'll invite Sue to be here. We're going easy on presents this year — everyone gets forty dollars to spend. But you know what? It might be our best Christmas yet."

"It sounds like you're making progress."

"I think the kids are changing schools," Robbie said. "Rachel was the last holdout, but she doesn't think she can be in the same school with Brett. And if she changes right after Christmas, she can try out for cheerleading in the spring."

Seth laughed. "Sounds like the timing is on your side."

"We have to get it together by spring," Robbie said. "When the weather lightens up and spring hits, I do a real good business — painting lines and trimming trees. Running back and forth to Thunder Point really cuts into my time. There are more things like a computer and some cheap cell phones when Papa makes money!"

Papa. Seth smiled to himself. Robbie

might have some serious problems to re-
solve, but he was devoted to his kids and
did the best he could. A lot of guys just succumbed when the problems looked bigger
than they were. Robbie, he realized, had
always been focused. Nobody's perfect, but
he was a loving dad.

Brett Davis faced a number of charges, all
misdemeanors. He served thirty days in
county and, thanks to the committed case-
workers in DHS, they were working on an
intervention to get him into a program of
some kind, which was required during his
probation. Whether it was anger management or domestic battery intervention, Seth
had no idea. But there was still hope for
Brett. How much hope would depend on a
lot of things, mostly his desire to change.

The Davis family, allegedly headed by an
abuser, was not so lucky. There were no
charges and no probation of any kind. Mrs.
Davis was encouraged to phone for help if
she needed assistance, but that was all
anyone could do. Right before Christmas,
the house was vacated and listed for sale.
As Seth well knew, getting people in situations like this to reach out was difficult.
Brett's advantage had been a judge.

All was peaceful once again. Families were
ready to celebrate Christmas in their indi-

vidual ways. Carrie James did all the cooking at the McCain household for the usual large crowd. Rawley spent part of his day there and the later part with Cooper and Sarah, Spencer and Devon and all the kids — two families bonded by the children they shared. Lucky's, the gas station, was open but for a shorter day because Al Michel, his three foster boys, his girlfriend, Ray Anne, Lucky's owner, Eric, and his fiancée, Laine, were all at the McCains' for Christmas Eve and at Ray Anne's small house for Christmas day. Al cooked a magnificent meal. Peyton Lacoumette, Dr. Scott Grant and Scott's kids were up north — he'd invited the two grandmothers to join them with about a million other people at the Lacoumette family farm. It was so crowded they had to sleep in shifts, but there were many contributors to the planning of a spring wedding.

For Seth and Iris, the events of the previous week were transforming. It was *their* town that had the traumatic experience, even though it had all played out fine. Seth had always thought of himself as just a working man and Iris admitted she thought of her life as pretty ordinary, even if the implications of her work with kids could have a huge impact. Now they were changed.

On Christmas morning, while they were still in bed, he nuzzled her awake and gave her a small box to open.

"Well, I never expected this," she said, ripping into it. "I thought we decided we'd be each other's presents this year."

"Just a detail that really couldn't be ignored," he said.

Inside was a diamond ring and band, a beautiful platinum-and-diamond wedding set. "Oh, my God, how could you pick something this perfect without even asking me what I like?" she asked.

"I don't really know how," he said. "Everything about you seems completely right and easy to me."

"We've come a long way, then," she said. She handed him the box. "Put it on me? Say the words again?"

He slid the engagement ring on her finger. "Please, Iris, be my forever wife. Let me be your forever husband."

"Okay," she said. "If you're sure."

"I'm going to be in love with you until I die. I think at least ninety years. And then some."

"Are you ready for today?"

"Oh, yeah. And I want you to know, it's hard to get Christmas off when you're the

430

new guy."

"You probably had to have a really good excuse, huh?"

"I had to scramble, that's for sure."

They had decided that Friday night, after the school emergency, they didn't want to go forward separately. They couldn't wait any longer.

Grace was in charge of flowers, not only for the house but for Iris and Grace to hold. She put together some fantastic arrangements that showcased the red-and-green of Christmas along with wedding-white flowers. Carrie provided a small but elegant cake. Seth had an acquaintance, a semi-retired judge who had lost his wife a couple of years back and who was alone for Christmas. He'd eagerly accepted the invitation. Seth's parents approved and agreed to hold Christmas dinner a little later than usual, although Norm was concerned. "How late, exactly?" Now gallbladderless, he had quite the appetite. Seth's two brothers and Boomer's family would come to Thunder Point. Pulling everything together was actually quite easy.

So, that Christmas morning, they showered and dressed for an important day. Iris's house was in perfect order when Grace arrived with the flowers. The women got ready

431

together while Seth drove to Coquille to pick up Joe Falsbrook, a seventy-five-year-old circuit court judge who didn't drive in sloppy weather. Gwen's dining room was set up to serve Christmas dinner to a large group while Iris's house was decorated for the ceremony. At exactly two o'clock, everyone was assembled in Iris's living room. Everyone except the best man.

"What do we do?" Norm asked. "Just stand here?"

"We wait," Seth said.

"I could go get some snacks," Gwen said.

"I'll open the champagne," Boomer said. "Ain't like it's bad luck or anything. . . ."

The champagne was barely poured when there was the toot of a horn. "A little help, Boomer?" Seth said.

Together they lifted Oscar, chair and all, into the house. Oscar made his presence felt immediately. "You better not'a done this without me!" There would be plenty of lifting today since the houses were not equipped with ramps. Introductions were quickly made, Iris hugged Flora and kissed Oscar's cheek. Then Seth and Iris put down their champagne flutes and stood in front of Judge Falsbrook, holding hands and looking into each other's eyes. Oscar was on Seth's right, Grace beside Iris.

"It took me a long time to find my way home to you, Iris."

"You took your time," she said. "I was right here."

"I love you, honey. I'd be so lost without you."

"You won't be without me again," she said. "This time, if you start to wander off, I'm going to put my foot down."

"I'm home for good," he said.

The judge cleared his throat. "We just about ready here?" he asked.

Iris and Seth had nearly forgotten about him. They both laughed and nodded.

"We're gathered here today to unite this man and woman in marriage. . . ."

ABOUT THE AUTHOR

Robyn Carr is a RITA® Award-winning, # 1 *New York Times* bestselling author of more than forty novels, including the critically acclaimed Virgin River series. Robyn and her husband live in Las Vegas, Nevada. You can visit Robyn Carr's website at www .RobynCarr.com.